Success

Martin Amis

Success

HARMONY BOOKS / *New York*

Published in the United States of America in 1987 by Harmony
Books, a division of Crown Publishers, Inc., 225 Park Avenue South,
New York, New York 10003

Originally published in Great Britain in 1978 by Jonathan Cape
Ltd., 32 Bedford Square, London WC1B 3EL

HARMONY and colophon are trademarks of Crown Publishers, Inc.

Manufactured in the United States of America

Library of Congress Cataloging-in-Publication Data

Amis, Martin.
  Success.
  I. Title.
PR6051.M5S8   1987   823′.914   87-7564

ISBN 0-517-56649-4
10 9 8 7 6 5 4 3 2 1
First American Edition

TO PHILIP

1: January

(i) It seems that I've lost all
   the things that used to be
   nice about me — TERRY

'Terry speaking,' I said.

The receiver cleared its throat.

'Oh hello, Miranda,' I went on. 'How are you? No, Gregory isn't here at the moment. Ring a bit later. Okay. Bye.'

Gregory was in fact sitting next door at the kitchen table, his hands palm-upwards on its grained surface. 'Success?' he asked. I nodded and he sighed.

'She's started sending me obscene poems now,' he said.

There seemed no point in not humouring him. 'Really? What sort of obscene poems?'

'Has a girl ever sent you an obscene poem?'

'I don't think so.'

'I can't cope with this. Things to do with my "proud beam". And stuff about her "amber jewel". Or perhaps it's *my* amber jewel — I'm not sure.'

'Sounds as though it's her amber jewel. I mean, she wouldn't have a proud beam, would she?'

'*She* might. I wouldn't put anything past her. She might have *two*.'

'What has she got to say about your proud beam? In this obscene poem.'

'She just goes on and on about it. I could hardly bear to read the thing. I can't cope with it. I don't need this.'

'How disgusting,' I said with enthusiasm. 'Well, what are you going to do about it, Greg?'

'That's just it. What *can* I do? Say, "Look, let's have no more obscene poems, okay? Cut out the obscene poems"? Scarcely. I could always call the police, I suppose ... let the police clear up the matter. And the horrible things she makes me do in bed ... '

'Why don't you just tell her to go away?'

Gregory looked up at me with puppyish awe. 'Can one do that sort of thing? Is that − is that what you'd do?'

'Christ, no. I'd make her make me do horrible things in bed. I'd even let her write me obscene poems. I'd even write her obscene poems back.'

'Would you really?'

'You bet. I'm desperate. I'm tortured by need. Hardly anybody seems to want to fuck me any more. I don't know why. Gita won't fuck me any more.'

'The tiny one with huge ears? Why won't she?'

'How the hell should I know? She says she doesn't want to. She doesn't know why she doesn't want to. But she knows she doesn't want to.'

Gregory perked up at this. 'Curious,' he said, leaning back. 'In my experience it's the other way round. People always want to fuck me far more than I want to fuck them.'

'Ah, but you're *queer*, aren't you. Practically, anyway. *Anyone* can get fucked if they're queer. That's the whole point of being queer, surely − no one minds what anyone does to anyone else.'

'Nothing in that line at the moment, actually,' he said, his shapely neck stiffening. 'It's this bloody Miranda.'

'Ah, yes.'

'Miranda and her demands.' Gregory's face disappeared into his hands. 'I can't cope with another night like the last. I just can't.' He looked up. 'She's absolutely voracious. Shall I tell you one of the things she does? Shall I? *She goes down on you after you've fucked her*. After. She does. Bitch. What about that?'

'Sounds unimprovable to me.'

'It's total agony, let me assure you. *And* she fiddles with your prick all night when you're pretending to sleep. *And* she sticks her ... you know.'

'What, up your bum?'

'Precisely.'

'What's the problem there?' I asked with some petulance. 'You must be used to that by now.'

'But she's got these huge tart's fingernails.'

'Can't you just — Christ, you know — just have a word with her about it all? Just tackle her on these points?'

'Of course I can't. What a revolting thought. And do you know how many people she's slept with? Guess. Go on. Guess. Over a hundred in two years!'

'Balls.'

'She *has*. She admits it. It's only one a week, after all, when you work it out. Everyone at Kane's has fucked her. Everyone at Torka's has fucked her. Everyone everywhere has fucked her. Everywhere we go people have fucked her. Just walking down the street — everyone has fucked her! I've never met anyone who hasn't fucked her. The porter's probably fucked her. The liftman's definitely fucked her. The — '

'I haven't fucked her,' I stated, deciding to bring this harrowing exchange to a crux.

And so:

'You could, Terry. Honestly. No problem at all. She's said more than once she likes you. And *she* fucks people she loathes. I tell you, she'll put you through your paces all right. Oh yes. Look, I'll tell you the first thing she'll do. The minute you go to kiss her she'll put *both hands* on your ... '

Will she? She doesn't look as though she would. (No one else does.)

The girl I'm currently supposed to be peeling off Gregory's back is called Miranda. She is nineteen. She

9

has coarse blonde hair, a friendly figure, ever-moist blue eyes and a wide square mouth. She is pretty — some way out of my league, I should think. But she is quite posh and probably very neurotic (perhaps she does do all those things he said, for anyone who asks her right). Apart from the consideration that I happen to be very deeply in love with Miranda, I have three excellent reasons for agreeing to the transfer.

One. I quite like her. In contrast to Gregory's standard female consorts (they're all haughty sirens with convex faces, collar-stud bums and names like Anastasia and Tap. They're sheeny, expensive and almost invariably twice my height. I practically call them *sir*), Miranda contrives to give the impression that she is a member of the human race — having met her, you could quite easily run away with the idea that you both belonged to the same planet. Instead of the torpid distaste — or, more often, trendy indifference — with which Greg's girls habitually salute my comings and goings, I get from Miranda hellos, goodbyes, recognition, stuff like that. And I've only really run into her twice: once when the funny little thing was puffing up the stairs to the flat (she said she'd 'forgotten about' the lift), and once when the stupid little slag was getting dressed in the morning (after Gregory had fled to work. No, I didn't see her tits). She chatted to me sympathetically on both occasions.

Two. I'm very keen indeed, as a matter of general principle, on picking up intimate details about Gregory. I want details, I want details, actual details, and I want them to be hurtful, damaging and grotesque. I nurse dreams of impotence, monorchism and premature ejaculation. I lust for his repressions and blocks; I ache for his traumata. (Why can't he just kick the girls and be a proper queer? It would make things much simpler for me.) And above all, of course, I long for Gregory to be dismally endowed. I pine for it. All my life I've wanted his cock to be small. Even before I met him the meagreness of his member was paramount to my well-being.

Three. Not since eleven o'clock on the night of July 25th last year (and even then it wasn't easy. She was an ex-girlfriend. I got us both drunk. I cried when she said she wouldn't: she was so appalled by this that she said she would) have I managed to get anyone to go to bed with me.

That was six months ago.

What is it with you fucking girls all of a sudden?

Or what is it with me?

I've never minded much about the way I look (Gregory, I know, is unprepared to think about anything else). I look ordinary. Apart from my rather gingery hair — I was in fact called 'Ginge' for a short time at school — I look ordinary, I look like educated lower-class middle-management, the sort of person you walk past in the street every day and never glance at or notice or recognize again. (You don't gaze my way. But who cares?) I've always perfunctorily assumed that I looked, well, not bad — not actually *bad*. In my life I've had an average amount of girls with an average amount of anxiety, embarrassment and gratitude.

Now it's changed. Why and how is that? They'll talk to me, they'll agree to go out with me, they'll eat with me, they'll drink with me, they'll neck with me, they'll even get into the same bed with me. But will they fuck me? Oh no, not them. Not them — *oh* no. (Who the fuck are they, anyway, that they won't do that?) This would merely gall and confuse me if I'd ever thought of myself as *attractive*. But I've never thought of myself as that. What made them fuck me then? Charm I once had, kinder girls, cleverer ploys, good nature, luck. It seems that I've lost all the things that used to be nice about me.

I'm still trying to laugh it off, really (I think), which is probably why I sound this way ... It's got so bad now that I've more or less exhausted my stock of old girl-friends, taken them all out again — all the ones that weren't married or pregnant or dead — and tried to make them fuck me. None of them wanted to. I've rung up girls I haven't seen for three or four years. I take trains all over England to visit girls who can't remember a single thing about me. I stop neurotic and disadvantaged girls in the street. I court especially plain secretaries at work. I proposition the old and the ailing. I try to get them to fuck me. They don't want to.

Won't someone tell me what's going *on*? What's the gimmick? What's the angle? My breath's okay, I think — or at any rate it hasn't radically deteriorated (if my ceaseless reinhalation tests are anything to go by). Nothing recent has gone wrong with my face. My nasty hair falls out no faster than it did before. (Mark you, I'm going to have a problem with my ass in later life. But they're not to know that, are they?) I take a bath every thirty-six hours, except in winter, and groom alertly for these horrific dates I sometimes have. I'm putting on a bit of weight, yes, but that's only because I'm drinking a lot these days. Wouldn't you be?

(I think I'm losing my bottle. I think I'm going *tonto*.)

Gregory must never find me out. He doesn't suspect the truth, for all my plebeian banter. I've told him I've got someone in Islington. I sit in pubs and coffee-bars pretending I'm there. I stumble in late and tell him lies. Gregory must never know. He must never know that I sit up in bed at night in my room like a fiend, hating everything there is. (The daytime is different, of course. With its tramp-dread and street-sadness, the day has special terrors.)

What am I doing here? My job, I think, is to make *you* hate him also. It shouldn't be difficult. All I've got to do is keep my eyes open. So long as you keep yours open too.

Will she?

'Will she?' I asked him. 'How do we swing it? When's she coming, for instance?'

'Any minute. Are you ready?'

Gregory stood by the window; he twirled a silver-topped cane. I'm not sure I can bear to describe what he was wearing: that vampiric crimson-lined black opera cape, a waistcoat of his father's, harem trousers — were they? — apparently clasped at the ankles by costly bicycle clips. His almost sickly good looks were, as always, very much in evidence; he looked clever, delicate and incredibly queer.

'How are we going to do it?'

Gregory gestured wristlessly. He stood by the window; he twirled his cane.

'You told me it was going to be easy,' I said, quite startled by the note of crude complaint that had entered my voice. (Sometimes I say things which sound like insults from other people. They leave me wounded and speechless.)

'Well it will be, Terry. Let's just think what's best to do.'

After a few minutes we had mounted a plan, and a fairly rudimentary one. Greg was to be appreciably crappier to Miranda than he was currently in the habit of being, reduce her to tears, then flounce out, at which point I was supposed to cruise on in — having alerted her to my gingery presence in the flat by answering the door when she arrived.

'Are you sure you can manage that?' I asked lightly, not wishing to spook him.

'Oh yes,' he said. 'Nothing simpler. She cries almost all the time now anyway, as far as I can see.'

'Why's that?' Sounds good, I thought. She really might do all those things if she's fucked up too, like me. (I'd do them, to anyone.)

'I don't know,' said Gregory, 'I'm always too embarrassed to ask. She's just mad, I expect. Most girls are these days.'

'Where are you going? That queer's place?'

'It's not a queer's place. There are lots of girls there too.'

'That bisexual's place then.'

'Yes. Now look here — how are you off for wine and so forth? You might as well get her drunk.'

'I've got lots.'

He looked me up and down with plummy distaste. 'She goes totally to pieces when she's drunk. She'll do anything.'

'Honestly?'

'Honestly. There really isn't anything she won't do.'

'Well, I'll give it a go.'

'Give it a go? Listen, I bet she'll hardly have her foot through the door before she does something quite revolting to you. I bet she'll get her — '

The bell rang.

'Let's go,' said Gregory.

Having opened the door to the girl — white jumper and jeans, shy eyes I didn't dare meet, the taste of milk in my mouth — and directed her up the stairs, I swam back to my dark room. I took whisky until I heard Greg's imperious footsteps.

'Go on then,' he whispered to me in the hall. 'Go *on* then.'

I was hoping that Miranda would be in tears or hysterical or — best of all — unconscious by the time I ascended the stairs. But she stood small and calm by the high window. And a bit fat and very pretty, I thought. I saw with pain that her denim satchel still hung on her poor shoulders.

'Has he gone?' she asked, without turning round.

Turn round when you talk to me. 'I'm afraid he has,' I said.

She turned now.

'I'm sorry,' I said, feeling the air buzz. 'I'm sorry if you're upset.'

'I don't know what to do,' she said without emphasis. 'He's like that.'

'Has he always been?'

'No, he hasn't. Come downstairs. He was nice once. Do you want to take a drink down? When he was young. Go on, I'm having one. He's changed more than most people change. There you go, girl. I don't know why. Come downstairs and talk. About things, about Gregory and me.'

(ii) Funnily enough, it gets quite
boring being chased and squabbled
over the entire time — GREGORY

'Gregory speaking,' I said with a voice that rustled.
'Oh,' said the telephone. 'Gregory, it's me. Miranda.'
'Well?'
' ... How are you then?'
I examined my fingernails against the light — shiny almonds.
' ... Gregory?'
'Speaking.'
'Why are you being like this to me?' she asked. 'What's gone wrong? Is it something I've done?'
'Must I listen to sentences such as those?'
In expectation of hearing the usual wet sob or fat gulp, I pressed my ear so much the closer to the telephone. It came — a warm swallowing sound.
'We've got to meet,' she said.
'Absolutely.'
'You've got to see me.'
'I certainly shall.'
' ... Can I come round then?'
'Do,' I said, replacing the receiver, my long fingers lingering on the dial.
And so I considered how to invest this cool deliverance of an evening, this sudden cargo of hours, standing at my penthouse window, gazing at a winter roofscape that seemed once more to be crowded with secrets and friends.
All day at work the anxiety had been quite frightful. Home to another evening à la Miranda — why do we put up with it? — another evening of my epic coldness

and her clumsy awe, of my nauseous small talk and her snatched panicky kisses, another night of sculptured sleep, her large lips hot with tears at my side. Why do we let them put us through these ordeals? Why are we so tender with them? Why? Well — that's your lot, bitch: you get no more of me.

In fact, of course, there hadn't been much difficulty. That fool Terence was in the kitchen when I got home from work. He isn't really allowed in this part of my flat — hence his furtive air, his look of hunted gratitude when I asked him to stay upstairs and talk.

'Gita won't fuck me any more,' he explained.

I asked, with real interest, why he thought this to be the case.

'I don't know. Gita doesn't know either.'

I straightened a finger at him. 'Which one is Gita?'

'The small one who wears those ear-rings.'

'Ah.' *All* Terence's girls are, perforce, tiny, and their ears are among the things I try very hard not to think about. 'Didn't she spend Tuesday night here?'

'Yes.'

'And?'

'I tried to fuck her.'

'And?'

'She didn't want me to.'

I thought this extremely odd, Gita being the sort of girl — surely — that you can do whatever the hell you like to. What would be the point of her otherwise? But I said, out of politeness, 'Curious — in my experience it's usually the other way round.'

A fatuous digression ensued, during which Terence made great play with his sexual insecurities at the imagined expense of my own. Gauche stuff — this dread he has of his own homosexuality can get quite alarming when so candidly displayed. 'Nothing in that line, as it happens,' I said coolly: 'It's this Miranda.'

'Oh?' he said with attention.

'Miranda, and her demands.'

Miranda's robust physical appetites, my own sloth and lassitude, Terence's more stolid gifts in this department, the ease with which the delegation could be made ...

The work of a moment. And now, tonight, while Terence gamely grunts, while Miranda cracks him in her dappled thighs: I'll be up here chuckling about the things I didn't tell him, about her raw-liver kisses and her sweet-sherry tongue, about the ghostly smells that issue from her pouches and vents, about the underworld effluvia she leaves glistening on your sheets.

What's happening to you girls these days? After spending the night with a neurotic girl — and so many of them *are* neurotic now — I feel more than my natural repugnance at the prospect of examining the bedclothes once I've shooed them from the flat. There will of course be the usual grim femininia — a dollop of make-up on the pillowslips, the school of pubic hairs on the sheets, that patch of hell somewhere further down: so much one expects. But these days I twitch back the blankets with a premonition of wonder, of dread; they're all in pieces, these girls — they could have left almost anything behind ... I can see it now: Gregory stands in the middle of the floor, the room still shimmering with the girl's demented exit; gingerly he approaches, face half-averted, gathers the heavy quilt in a muscular fist, breathes deeply, throws back the blankets — and finds an entire leg marooned on the sheets! I wouldn't put it past them.

Did you know, for instance, that girls now go to the lavatory? Shaking news, I agree, but they do. Oh yes. And not just to pee, either. I once nursed a fond dream — silly really — that they left all that sort of thing to the menfolk — except when they're in hospitals or other suitably equipped establishments. Indeed, whenever I heard an ambulance siren, or saw one of the white vats whizz past, I was always cheered to imagine that it contained a few fortunate females being rushed to the wards for just this purpose. What a romantic I was ... They do it all the time these days. They even talk about it. They even try to do it in front of you! But they're like chaps, these days, like fellas, like blokes.

It's their nerves which really drive me mad. When did they start thinking they had to be nervous all the time? Who told them? Why, fidgety fingers I find hardly less repulsive than warty knuckles and rank nails. Agitated gestures seem to me a negligible improvement on misshapen or ill-assorted limbs. I see little to choose between subsultory mastication (or twitchy mealtime banter) and rotten teeth (or scum-lined lips). Post-coital tears disgust me as thoroughly as do pre-menstrual pimples. And the dreadful things they *say*. They keep trying to understand you; they keep wanting to talk about proper things; they keep trying to be people. We take it, we talk to them back. We're not supposed to let on that, for all their many charms, they just aren't very interesting.

Has Terence said anything about my sexual dispositions? No doubt he has. Well, I won't deny it. If it's a 'sexual equal' I want — i.e. a boy, and a boy's unyielding musculature — then it's a sexual equal I go ahead and have, rather than a thing with breasts that happens to urinate sitting down. (Terence will stick up for them, of course. The pungent witches whom he tends to squire are, expectably, among the heroines of this unhappy genre.) What I like are moneyed chasubles of silence, soft topography of flesh, the trickle of retreating satin and the white avenues of underwear, the mute secrets of dew and down.

Imagine, then, my incredulous horror on discovering the true colours of this Miranda, this jumpy little idiot whose immediate transfer I have gulled Terence into accepting (a tedious mode of dismissal, you may think, but a relatively painless one. I detest scenes). It was at a noisy after-dinner party in the flat of my fashionable friend Torka that I incautiously made her acquaintance. Tired, stifled, and almost completely exasperated by

Adrian's vulgar rot, I was at first perfectly willing to give some of my time to a young, deferential and — I concede — reasonably pretty girl who seemed to be prepared to refill my glass and to take an intelligent interest in my work and opinions. She stood there; she listened; her teeth were clean. Only when I offered to drive her home in my powerful green car did the nightmare truly begin. She stuck with a kind of dumb immobility to my side throughout the entire course of the party — even when the famous Torka tried to pry me loose for a chat — kissed me with repulsive candour on the stairs, and then blandly announced, as my handsome sports car roared into life, that she had missed the last train back to the provinces and had nowhere in London to stay! I'm never, ever, going to fall for that one again.

I was putty in her hands. I always am. 'I don't want to hurt their feelings.' Why don't I? What feelings? I don't mind if they hurt *my* feelings. They've got no more feelings than I have. Miranda is just a bloke, anyway, like me, the mad bitch.

The physical aspect of what happened next — and went on happening practically every night for the following two weeks — has already been adequately delineated by me. I think that one is entitled — no? — to a reasonable helping of startled indignation when an eighteen-year-old girl has a dented backside, tropical armpits *and stringy white lines on the undercurves of her breasts.* That first morning she sprang out of bed — having had her noisome way with me — and knelt naked before the bookcase, rummaging in her bag for some item that her genes loved. I watched, dressing her with my eyes. Her bottom is quite out of control, I thought; and I can't take the smell she has down there. It's not her fault, I know. It's her nerves' fault.

An even stronger threat to my ease, however, was what one might call the girl's character. Not yet twenty, and each turn in her conversation opened up a chapter of wretchedness and squalor in her past — an infatuation unrequited, a pass snubbed, a pocket of pleasureless promiscuities (fifty men in two years, *and* she admitted it). Small wonder that I've seriously hated her ever since that first impact. I hate it when she comes near. When she touches me I close my eyes and pray for patience. When we make love my face lives on another planet. She doesn't mind. She wants lots more where that came from. Such people will take your money, take your body and take your time, but will they take your hint? Not them, *oh* no. I'm too tender-hearted. I just weather these hormonal storms. No wonder I get exploited.

I dialled seven digits. I spoke in whispers to Adrian — sulking, as usual — and established that whereas the wealthy Torka would not be home that evening, the redoubtable Susannah, a new discovery of ours, most assuredly would be. 'Perfect,' I murmured, dropping the receiver into place as I heard Terence clump up the stairs.

'What time's she coming?' he asked.

'Any minute. She just rang.'

'How did she sound?'

'As if she were having a nervous breakdown, naturally.'

'Excellent.'

'Uh, "Terry" ... ' I paused, frowning. 'Are you actually ready?'

I unconditionally promise you that Terence was wearing Sherwood-green velvet trousers, a flounced orange shirt, and a red corduroy jacket. He *was*. But then Terence's taste in clothes, as in most other things, has always been quite beyond the pale. He possesses, for instance, a leatherene belt with a silver buckle on it the size of a hearth-grate; because of his want of inches he is moreover obliged to wear stilt-like yob's boots — you can do that if, like me, you're already very tall, but not if, like him, you're actually very small (Terence, in fact, is, oh, 5′ 7″; I of course am six-foot-one-and-a-half); also he favours paint-by-numbers colour schemes — an absurd motley of nigger primaries and charwoman pastels — and is fond, too, of cute appurtenances (braces, scarves, lockets) which he tends to sport all at once, like a tinker. He is quite prepared, you know, to wear dark boots with light summer trousers. He'll put on V-neck jerseys over T-shirts and think nothing of it. He's perfectly capable of doing up the middle buttons of his —

'How do we swing it then, Greg?'

'Simple,' said I. 'A row will be precipitated. Miranda shall be rendered hysterical. I then stalk out. At this point you, "Terry", sweep in with tequila and sympathy. What could be more agreeable?'

'What, get her drunk, you think?'

'You might as well — it would put the matter beyond serious doubt. You've got masses, I expect?'

'You bet. Drink is one thing I've got plenty of. Drink I've got.'

'I recommend white wine. She'll drink herself sick on that purely out of natural greed. Also I've got some smoked salmon you can give her. She likes that too, because you can have bread with it.'

'Mm?'

The bell rang.

'Let's go,' said Terence.

'Ah. Come in,' I called.

I heard Miranda thank the lingering Terence in the hall below as she started to make her heavy way up the stairs. Me? I stood rocking on my heels by the window, the black cape already thrown over my broad shoulders, the keys of my custom-built car jinking in my hand, the pewter-tipped cane leaning ominously against my desk.

'Hello,' she said — obviously in particularly dazzling form.

'Well? And what do you imagine we're going to do now?'

Miranda's porcine good looks were minimally in evidence tonight: yellow scarf of hair, those fat lips of hers, scared eyes. She sat down with a grunt on the edge of my bed, her ridiculous denim knapsack tumbling to the floor.

'I don't mind,' she said. 'Whatever you want to do.'

'My God,' I began, 'that's just what I can't bear about you. Why must you be so hopelessly null?'

'I'm sorry. Why don't we have dinner somewhere? Or that film you wanted to see is on at the ABC. Or we could do something different — we could go bowling.'

I averted my appalled gaze. 'Oh, we could do that, could we?'

'Sorry. Or we could stay in. If you're tired, I'll just cook you something.'

'That sounds absolutely riveting, I must say. Just what I feel like after a — '

'Why don't we go to the little place round the corner? It's — '

'Don't you *dare* interrupt me like that again. It's bloody rude.'

'I'm sorry.'

'*Bloody* rude.'

— And with that of course I swept out of the room and clattered down the stairs. As I suavely paused to put on my gloves in the hall, Terence emerged from the shadows, breathing audibly.

'Success?' he said.

I pondered for a moment, then said, 'You'd better get in there, "Terry". I don't know what she might do to herself. She's quite distraught.' (Let's have a laugh at Terence's expense, I thought. That's what we're here for, after all — to have some fun with him.)

Rain had warmed the air. I stopped a passing taxi — my sleek car is sick again — and was incompetently driven in it to Howarth Gardens. I depressed the marble bell-push. Torka's houseboy giggled shyly as he took my cape.

It was two o'clock when I came out of Torka's house and stood impatiently fastening my cape on the steps. I had left with some precipitateness, certainly far too dramatically to telephone for a cab on my way out, and the chances of hailing one at this hour were dangerously slim. (There have been several incidents in the area recently. Not that this worries me in the slightest. Things simply don't happen to proper people, people of my height, bearing, etc.) I had no choice, then, but to walk, to walk back through the liquid sounds and quicksilver gloss of the night.

Adrian and Susannah had behaved intolerably. No sooner had we removed our clothes before Adrian went into a ridiculous huff about Susannah's scent; he complained that his back hurt — and actually accused me of not washing before I came out! We had to go through the most impossible contortions to distance these fancied danger-spots from his hideous, wide-pored nose, including some repellent new combinations he had learnt in New York. It was bloody uncomfortable and my elbow still hurts when I flex my arm. Oh, but that was nothing to the way *she* carried on. The very instant that Adrian turned his attention to me — which is all he's really interested in, Susannah, though of course you're too vain to see it — she claimed a headache and said she just wanted to watch. She isn't nearly as expert as people keep claiming, anyway, and her breasts are far too large.

Funnily enough, it gets quite boring being chased and squabbled over the entire time. Idiots, with their possessive feuds. Can't they see that I am there to be tasted, to be mulled over, to be adored, not to be fought over like a piece of meat?

I returned without incident — a bit puffed in fact, having elected to jog the final half-mile. The flat was dark: dust and silence in the air. I walked on down the passage, alert, springy. As a rule the location of the bathroom — through the hippie nightmare of Terence's quarters — is the theme of much annoyance to me when I get home late, but tonight I welcomed a chance to pass by his bed. Would Miranda be in it? I knocked on the door.

' "Terry"?' I whispered.

I turned the cold doorknob noiselessly and switched on the light.

I assume in retrospect that what surprised me was not Miranda's presence at the far side of Terence's large and unfastidious double bed so much as my own obscure irritation that this should be the case. Any token regret, any reflexive pity I might have felt for her was instantly chased away by the sight of that bulked behind swelling the blankets. To think that she would even go to *these* lengths to make me jealous, the hysterical bitch.

Confident that I would not rouse Terence — who surrenders consciousness with truly plebeian ease and snores like a motorbike the moment his crimson eyes are closed — I picked up a hairbrush from the table with my gloved hand and skilfully lobbed it at the tent-like convexity of Miranda's nethers; she twitched, half-turned, and looked up blinking; I offered her a classic, Parnassian sneer and cruised into the bathroom. (On the way back I looked straight ahead, pausing only to catch her muffled sobs as I threw off the light.)

Up in the kitchen were two half-finished glasses of hock, the remains of my expensive smoked salmon and a wedge of clawed-at French bread. I clicked my tongue, tasting this scene of snatched food and hurried lust. Oh well. I decanted the wine into a clean glass, drank it, folded the salmon into a section of crust, and then lay on my bed for a few minutes in thought, munching it all up with my superb teeth.

2: *February*

(i) It's easy enough to see what it was
that fucked me up — TERRY

Gregory Riding is my foster-brother. He is. I was adopted
by his parents when I was nine. That first bit of my life,
which was full of crappy things, took place at Dawkin
Street in the Scovill Road area of Cambridge, not quite a
slum but going that way (I haven't been back. It probably is one by now), clutches of post-war semi-detacheds
flanking thin yellow streets, sections of grass that they
considered you ought to have, old scooters in back
gardens. My mother died when I was six and for three
years my sister and I lived under the sole care of my
father, Ronald Service. Then my sister died on me too.
I don't know whether my father killed my mother; but I
bloody know he killed my sister, because I was there at
the time and watched him as he did so. (Suck on that.
It's easy enough to see what it was that fucked me up.
I go on about all this a lot. I make no apologies. It's just
too bad. I'm allowed to go on about it, on account of it
fucking me up.) Rosie Service was seven when Ronnie
Service killed her; she had fat freckly cheeks, pencil legs
and impossibly narrow shoulders that cause me to ache
with tenderness for her even now — even now, as I sit
here slumped in the middle of what appears to be my life,
with its days and days. That mad fuck (my language, like
everything else about me these days, gets worse and
worse), he probably didn't mean to do that to her. But
did he mean to do this to me?

Anyway, the murder claimed a fair amount of local attention at the time. Indeed if it hadn't been for a whopping lapse on the part of the authorities my case might never have come under the twinkly, philanthropic gaze of Greg's family. I stayed on alone at the scene, at 11 Dawkin Street, for over a week: people came to take my father away, people came to take my sister away (she went quietly — he didn't), but no one came to take me away (someone goofed. Someone fucked up. Take me where, anyhow?). And for a week I picked my terrified way through the dead rooms, through the rank scullery-world of thickened milk and glaring butter, through the nights on that nail-bed of nerves, and through the slow time of the pendulous afternoons. Can you imagine? I didn't go out and I stayed away from the windows. I was hiding. I was very, very ashamed of what those two had done.

An exultant newspaper reporter found me (he found me out: he knocked on the door and heard me running up the stairs; he quickly knelt and peered through the letter-box: he found me out). The reporter seemed delighted by everything to do with me. So did the journal for which he worked (they took me and they splashed me). It was their gloating feature on my plight which first captured the imagination of the Riding household — or at least that of its patriarch; I later gathered that Mr Riding would read out the daily reports, with morbid insistence, over the spanking family breakfast table, much to the boredom and exasperation of everyone else present. As I myself was soon to learn at first hand, Riding Sr was an insatiably compassionate man (i.e. off his chump in a posh kind of way. He still is, basically) and in a very real sense he could not allow himself to rest until I was taken care of to his satisfaction. Which, again, in his sleepy world of whimsical cause and effect, meant being taken care of by him. Evidently, too, he was intrigued in a quirky way by certain parallels between our families, parallels at once so fortuitous and insistent that for a while I longingly suspected that some Fieldingesque parentage mystery would one day resolve our destinies: Mr Riding and my father were the same age, and Greg's and my birthdays were only twenty-four hours apart; Ursula, Greg's sister, and mine were both seven at the time, and were alike the survivors of abbreviated twins — and so on ... As the scandal about my displacement grew, so did Mr Riding's wayward but intense anxiety. He let it obsess him, for all the irritated now-nowing of his wife and the confusion and unease of his children.

I was in some sort of custody by this stage. Leading a posse of plain-clothes detectives, a fat social worker came round to take me to a place from which I could more decorously be taken away again. Look at the state of me. For a fortnight I was regularly bathed and fed, and deposited nightly between rayon sheets which by morning had always formed a burning garrotte about my neck. I had no affection for the place, with its self-sufficient hysteria, nor gratitude for the people who worked there; I was at their mercy, or thought I was, so they all got to hate me a bit. On the last morning a special matron looked in to comb my hair and to piss on me mildly for my good fortune. 'Be polite, keep quiet, and think yourself lucky,' she counselled.

Well aware of the full corniness of my status (orphan of underprivilege, changeling of panic and disgust), my feelings about the proposed adoption could be fairly painlessly guessed. I stared at the formal family study displayed on the front page of the local paper (caption: *The Ridings — 'We Must Act'*) until — it's hard to describe my sense of it then ... I stared until the photograph's four edges unravelled diagonally away from me into an overlit, unknowable world of correctness and symmetry. A very old man called Henry Riding, chin up in a dark suit, beside his younger, formidably hatted wife: in the turret between their faces you saw the smart portal of Rivers Hall — the bent metal knocker, the two urns, the retreating steps. In front of them, on either side of the tall parents, are positioned, well, my new brother and sister (no, surely not. They can't want me to be that. I wouldn't want me): the daughter, a girl with a sharp, knowing face like someone in a half-sinister fairy-tale, and the boy, the son, Gregory, a serious Fauntleroy defined by his frill shirt and pageboy collar, with that same taut look of angled distaste; and beyond them, past their neat shoulders (on each of which nestles a protective palm), the long black windows, the vine-matted walls, the grand perpendiculars of the house. Something's coming. What would it be?

So the small black car edged up the pebbled drive, and through its rear-side window Rivers Hall was framed for me once again. A nylon drizzle hung from warlike clouds: the place looked all full up with autumn. We disembarked; I was led into a hall — everything bright and various suddenly — then guided into the kitchen by the housekeeper, Mrs Daltrey (these days referred to as 'the staff' by Gregory), who made some tea while Mr and Mrs Riding signed what was presumably a receipt and listened to the valedictions of the special matron and the fat social worker before seeing them out. They followed into the kitchen and introduced themselves anew as my foster-parents. I was in tears by this time, of course (tears of apology and remorse), and willingly agreed to Mrs Riding's suggestion that I felt tired and wanted to go straight to bed. Mrs Daltrey preceded me to a high damp room on the first floor, where she remained until I said I was all right. (I wasn't all right. I was all fucked up.)

During that first chapter of my time at Rivers Hall my face must have been perpetually florid with either embarrassment or shame, but I now tend to see my long-ago self there as a wan and wary child, subject to a smaller spatial scale than everything about me, a downy white cheek fronting the gloss of an opulent Brobdingnag. When I awoke on the first morning, a shrivelled grub in the corner of someone else's bed, I remember thrilling

as if for the first time to all the dazzled self-pity of childhood; I felt that the reduced outlines of my body (the
poor thighs, the poor arms, the poor shoulders) expressed
an almost abrasive pathos — much too much to bear
(I could bear it, just about; I had some bottle then. I
can't bear it now). My eyes stayed shut. I didn't dare
move — and sensed also that this was an intelligible
procedure. The contours of the blankets I lay in: that
was all there was of my space.

Mrs Daltrey entered the room with Dickensian bustle,
carrying the whole world in her wake, threw back the
curtains to a rush of sun, and told me to get dressed.
As I obeyed she limped round the room singing forcefully
and arranging my clothes in a vacated drawer. Groomed
to her satisfaction, I was taken out of the door, along a
passage, down a staircase much smaller than the one we
had come up by, through the kitchen, into a vivid
conservatory where four people sat round a crowded
tabletop.

'Now this is your sister, Miss Ursula,' said Mrs Daltrey,
gesturing towards the girl, soft and sleepier in white,
who smiled, 'and this is Mister Gregory' — that dark,
thin-faced boy who turned and gazed at me with stolen
eyes.

So this is how the days start.

My big cheap alarm clock, invariably set for 7.55, is
placed on the window-sill at the far end of my room.
When I sleep at all — as opposed to simply lying in bed
all night, gagging and flashing with booze and nerves — I
do so with a cloying, musty, vascular heaviness (I die a
little), and if the clock is positioned within my reach I'll
just lean over, slap off the alarm and burrow back into
unconsciousness. This used to happen so often, and used
to make me feel so incredibly insecure at work, that I
took to placing the tinny round bomb under the cocked
lid of my record-player (for extra resonance) with
nastily worded notes by it saying things like FUCKING

GET UP or GET UP, YOU FUCK, necessitating a hot-eyed stumble across the room; usually, though, I would merely stumble back to bed again, to rise clogged and guilty at 10. For an experimental period I fell into the habit of placing various obstacles in my path, obstacles intended to jolt and scare me awake with sudden noise and stubbed pain, only to weave obliviously through the tripwires, angled chairs and upended wastepaper-baskets, press the clock's quivering nipple, and weavingly return to the moist warmth of the sheets. I hate sleep, anyway (and wish to Christ I didn't dream so much). I don't know why I still bother with the stuff. Anything can happen when you're asleep. Sleep just pulls the wool over your eyes.

Now I get out of bed as if someone were trying to keep me there, and stand all shocked and *tonto* before the gingerly opened window. It takes cold air, will and time. It takes, for instance, at least a minute of gentle panting and gasped obscenities before I am able to storm the bathroom (via the little dressing-room in between, where Gregory's clothes hang on the walls like mosaics) and get to work on reclaiming my face. Before they are prepared to open, my eyes demand ninety seconds with a wet sponge, and a further gook-rinse with plain water until such time as they regain their rather suspect cheer (I get lots of sleepy, even when I don't sleep. To look at the basin, you'd think I had spent a day at the seaside). Then, too, my mouth will put up with no less than three minutes of brush and gargle if its dry paving of dust is ever to retreat, my nose a furlong of lavatory paper if the airways are ever to open. The corralling of my face lifts the seven veils of the daily hangover (why do I drink so much now? I never used to. I want to be drunk all the hours there are. I expect I drink so much simply because I'm losing my bottle. I used to smoke hash, too. I don't any more. It makes me feel *tonto*. Unless of course I'm drunk. I do then): in a heat haze of peeled and gonging crapulence I go back to my room and insert my body among items of bristly clothing.

On account of the perverse design of the flat we live in (it's meant for someone flash living alone, or someone flash plus his girl), the trip to the kitchen takes me through Gregory's room, within a couple of feet of his bed. Quite often, he brings it about that there is someone else in there with him (never a boy, though. Why not? I'm *glad*. I don't like queers. I don't like them, which I suppose means I'm queer). This morning, at the far side of Gregory's slender torso, there is a lot of brown hair and a light, intermittent truffling sound; and, as usual, maximum de-proximity between their bodies has been established, with Greg's narrow face bent to one side in that familiar expression, askance, unfriendly, replete and disgusted in sleep. I want to shout with pain and pull the world apart, but I just vaguely peek in the direction of the girl's breasts (I've seen a couple every now and then: it's the most sex I've had for months), then carefully turn the squeaky kitchen doorknob. I am sincerely terrified of waking Gregory, despite my intense envy and disapproval of his freedom to rise as late as 9 or 9.30. (He might chuck me out. Could he? Would they let him?) So I creep downstairs with a big mug of instant coffee and sit at my desk drinking it and smoking lots of cigarettes. I pour the dead ashtrays into the wastepaper basket. (The wastepaper basket is one of the Bad Things about my life at the moment. I haven't emptied it for several weeks. I daren't. I just compress the rubbish even further. One of these days it's going to get up and walk out of here all by itself.) I make a last visit to the bathroom to pee and adjust my hair, then it's the streets.

We live in Bayswater — district of the transients. Nearly everywhere is a hotel now; their porches teem like Foreign Legion garrisons; a fucked-up Arab comes here and is an automatic success. (The local boys are taking over, too. They work the streets, roping off the bits they want. They're winning. I feel that I could join them if I could just wire my nerves up tight.) But I can't. I try to like the way the world is changing, but there seems to be no extra room for me inside. I hate this daily ten-minute walk, along the outlines of the cold squares, past dark shopfronts where cats claw at the window panes, then into the tingling strip of Queensway, through shuddering traffic and the sweet smell of yesterday's trash. I look at girls, of course, watch aeroplanes (take me to America), buy a paper and lots more cigarettes on the way, but I don't think I'm convincing anyone by all this. No one senses my presence; they walk on by (you might pass me one of these days; you wouldn't know it. Why should you?). At kiosks and stalls of which I am an abjectly faithful patron I attract not the slightest notice — never mind my identical good mornings and well-enunciated demands for goods. The huge, exhausted newspaperman who sells me my *Guardian* (and who has a smile and a hello for virtually everyone else, I see) never returns my greeting when I give him the exact money and will stare at me with sick hatred should I offer him a trembling one-pound note. Underground officials throw me a knowing glance as they dispense a ticket or check it over at the entrance gate, but it isn't standard, all this. Sometimes I will turn, halfway along the stone corridor, to see that I am being followed by curious and unfriendly eyes. And once I'm down there, down in the streets of the earth, and the train bursts angrily out of its hole, and I try to join the people stacked inside — I keep expecting them to make some spontaneous gesture of protest, hardening their van to keep me out. (This can't be alienation, can it? I want to belong. I'm dying to belong.)

At the other end of my journey a relatively small-time ordeal awaits: I have to call in to buy my sealed carton of tea at Dino's, a little Italian-run café in the bowels of Holborn Viaduct. Dino himself, a foul-tempered ted with a great glistening quiff, is far too grand these days to prepare any dish less specialized than a Bovril-toast or a tomato-takeaway, so the quotidian hot-drink commerce falls to the old (British) dog and incompetent, Phyllis. Phyl, who is incredibly slow and bad at her job, goes on as if she's *fucking* most of the people she sells things to. 'Tea, Frank?' and 'That's Ron's orange' and 'Your coffee-no, Eddie' — even girls get a smile and a fruity good-morning, and complete strangers, people who have come into the café not to *buy* things, not to give her and Dino *money* in exchange for goods, but just to ask the bloody way, will frequently be blessed by a 'dear,' a 'love' or a 'darling'. *She has never spoken to me in my life* — and once, when the old cow was dithering with the plastic cups and I tentatively called her 'Phyl' (everyone else does), she gave me a look of such startling dislike that for a week I had to go all the way to the taxi-drivers' sandwich bar in King Street. (I say the words 'thank you' five times a morning in places like these. Thank you for letting me in, thank you for acknowledging my presence, thank you for taking my order, thank you for taking my money, thank you for giving me change. The other day, in London's Paddington station, I said the words 'thank you' to a hot-drinks machine. To a hot-drinks machine: it gave me a hot drink and I said, why 'thank you'. This constitutes another Bad Thing that has happened to me recently. I think I'm losing my bottle. I think I'm going *tonto*.) Approximately the same treatment is accorded me by the whiskered doorman of Masters House, by its normally talkative and vivacious liftman, and by the tarty chars who tense on all fours in the carbolic vestibules. Once inside, I begin to feel much, much better. Because nearly everyone here is as fucked up as I am.

I do a job. That's what I do. (Most people do them. Do you do one? It's what nearly everybody does.) For a while, after the school bit of my life was over, I bummed around (now where did I ever find the nerve to do *that*?), then I started to do this job. I was pleased when they gave it to me — I certainly didn't ever want to give it back. I still am pleased, more or less. At least I won't be a tramp, now that I've got it. I wonder why they let me take it away. (I think they think I'm posh.)

I don't really know what I do here. Sometimes I want to say, 'What do I do here — just in case people ask?' I don't know what I do here, but then no one really does. (This used to worry me, or surprise me anyway. No longer. When you're young you assume everybody old knows what they're doing. They don't. Hardly anyone does. Hardly anyone seems at all clear on that point.) I sell things — so much is obvious. I *think* I buy things too. It's all done by telephone; we talk about 'items'. I am required to say things and to listen to things. Some of these things often strike me as possibly evasive or misleading or not quite 100 per cent true. But I shall say whatever I have to say to sell whatever it is I sell. What *do* I sell? Whatever it is, they pay me £50 a week for it.

We're getting taken over — that's for sure, also. Everyone is a bit sweaty at my work these days. We're all having a bit of a bad time these days. It now looks as though we will be obliged (I expected this) to affiliate with the Union, regularizing staff rates of pay, holidays, office hours, luncheon vouchers, going to the lavatory, etc. In return, the office will enjoy considerable increases of salary and proportionate rationalizations of personnel.

It's a nervous time for all of us here. This is not a bad office, but at the moment it has a bad feel. Disgruntlement hangs in the air; it hangs in the air like migraine. These are not bad men: on the contrary, they are in some ways the last of a certain type of good man. They are gentlemanly in their dealings, and have read something (whereas the people we have to talk to all day are cocksuckers, who have never read shit). They just don't want to lose their jobs. The ones who aren't queer or whatever invariably have kids ('what for?' I think again and again, seeing the extra they suffer). Three of us would be tramps within a week, not including me. There are no new jobs and nobody wants to go looking for them. Nobody wants to go. (And it seems that we can't protect each other. If we were in the Union we would be able to, but you can't get organized until you get organized.)

Who will it be? There are five people in the department and we all think it will be us. Burns, the moustachioed ex-schoolteacher, thinks it will be him. He could be right — he doesn't seem to sell as much as I sell. I would quite like it to be Burns because he is going bald slightly slower than I am and because he eats fish at his desk during the afternoons (this can't be good for business, I feel). Herbert, the fat ex-beatnik, who is nearly as young as I am, seems pretty well convinced it will be him. I hope it is Herbert, and am always slyly goading him to resign anyway, because he is ponderous and slow-talking (though fairly diligent), goes on about mental instability and collapse much too much, and is nearly as young as I am. Lloyd-Jackson, the urbane, pooh-poohing ex-copy-writer, says he wouldn't be in the least surprised if it were to be he. He is senior to the rest of us (deputy-Controller, in fact), but claims that a Unionized department would be unable to accommodate his urbane, pooh-poohing ways. I'm reasonably keen on it being Lloyd-Jackson, because I feel some affection for him and he is the only person here who *might* be cleverer than me. Wark, the mad ex-Stalinist, says he doesn't give a shit whether it's him or not. That's all he'll say about it. I crave for it to be Wark because he is a mad cunt who has recently had all his teeth pulled and I can't bear his new mushy voice and the way his fag-ends sometimes go red and heavy in the slack corner of his mouth ... No. The only people here who really don't care about the coming rationalization are John Hain, the frightening new Controller (he came in after I was hired — not easy on the bottle either), who has fought brilliantly for Unioniza-tion all along, and Damon, the sickly office-boy, who already has a different Union to uphold his brooding, adenoidal needs.

It could be me, of course. Yes, it could be.

Now I nod in the direction of the ailing Damon (never known anyone so shockingly candid about his origins: he has 'working class' scribbled across his features like acne), who this morning sits with a mind as blank as writing-paper in his gloomy nook by the department door. Damon's crepuscular nook is in fact the envy of everybody in the department except – another affinity – its Controller. The office was completely open-plan when I moved in here and only with the arrival of John Hain did we succeed in forcing the management into giving us our own cubicles. (Everyone agreed that this was a necessity because everyone likes saying, on the telephone and to each other, unpleasant things about everyone else.) The result is depressing in the extreme – it's like a cramped honeycomb of round wooden telephone-booths (which I suppose is what they are), a toytown land of mazes and hidey-holes. The only quite good place, apart from Damon's dark nook, is the bit surrounding the broad table in the central office area, where the clerical girls sit (they're all pretty rough at the moment but turnover is high and you never know) and which I now skirt, getting a gap-toothed smile from the lame temp who does the proofs and whom I am seriously thinking of asking out.

In my capsule, to my potent gratification, I see that a card and two letters await me on the desk. I uncap my tea cup and thoughtfully light a cigarette, my ninth of the day, before inspecting them (I take a paper-clip and pry at it with my thumbnail; I break the match in half and rub the two sticks together; I get into gear). The card I read with only half-interest, as a run-in. It is from the hand of my foster-sister Ursula and so has no true bearing on my socio-sexual self-betterment. She is in town again, learning how to become a secretary (yes, you have to learn how to become one); she wants me to take her out to dinner – a flattering irritation. (Sometimes I think she's the best friend I have. At other times I can't imagine minding *that* much if she died.) The letters. The first is from a shop-assistant I talked to twice in Cambridge and have since tracked down to Cumbria;

her burden is that there's no point in me coming all the way up there just to see her (and Barry, her husband). The second is from a girl whose address I picked from the pen-pal section of a rock magazine; she turns out to be twelve, and an upholder of the view that there's no point in having a pen-pal who lives half-a-mile away. Fair enough, ladies, fair enough: this is, by current standards, a pretty sexy start to the morning (Miranda didn't, incidentally. Don't ask me why not. She kissed me, she let me smooth her breasts, she went to bed with me, she even slept with me. But she didn't. I wanted her to, I went on at her to. But she said she didn't want to. Don't ask me why.

Ah fuck it, my cock's conked out anyway. It doesn't work any more — it's downed tools. It can't even masturbate properly now. I keep on thinking it's going to retract into my body, or drop off, or just disappear — what is there to keep it here, after all? It just wants to pull the blankets over its head and forget. Sometimes I have trouble finding it in the bath. 'I know you're in there somewhere,' I say. 'I used you to pee with only half-an-hour ago.' Even when I'm allowed to kiss girls these days — even when, as with Miranda, I get to touch their breasts or sleep in the same bed as them — it doesn't stir. I try to have fun with it, to be nice; I tweak it, poke it, strangle it — I monkey with it every which way. But it's dead, dead. It wants reassignment. It wants out. And who on earth am I to tell it any different?); I am dreaming up something horrible to go and make Damon do when Wark, the mad ex-Stalinist, ducks hurriedly into my cubicle. He says,

'It's Herbert.'

'*Christ.* How do you know?'

'John Hain took him into his office. You could tell.'

'How?'

'You just could.'

At this point I turn towards the window. Before he had all his murky little teeth out, Wark's voice was rapid and distinct. Now it is slow, drunken and wet, and I can't cope with it for more than a few seconds at a time.

'Of course it's Herbert,' says Wark, with sudden wistfulness, like someone identifying a line of poetry.

'You really think so, Geoffrey?'

'It must be him.'

'Good. That's very heartening,' I say insincerely (insincerely not because it wouldn't be heartening if it were Herbert but because Wark is much too mad for his information to be reliable. Wark no longer appreciates the difference between what is and what is not; he no longer has any choice of what he wants to think about). 'Of course,' I add, 'it might be two of us. Not just one. Herbert and one other.'

'Of course it could be. It probably is.' Wark says this briskly, contemptuously. I can tell the thought has never occurred to him before. But Wark likes to behave as if everything has. (Wark is all fucked up, come to think of it: no mind, no teeth, no bottle — and no job? We have the equivalent of a mental sweepstake here on how soon it will be before Wark kills himself, or goes too *tonto* to continue.)

'Still, it'll be incredibly depressing for Herbert,' I say to cheer Wark up. 'I know he says it won't, but it will. He's too old to go back to being a down-and-out. Think of all the things he — '

'Terry?' says a new voice.

It is Burns — balding, moustachioed, carrying a faint tang of fish on marble. Burns and Wark dislike each other more than is customary even here, so I am rather taken aback to see the ex-schoolteacher enter my capsule and wedge the door shut behind him. This must be big.

'We think it's Herbert,' I tell him in pre-emptive alarm.

Burns swirls a flat hand in the air. 'It *is* Herbert. But not just Herbert. A Union chappie tells me John Hain is going to gut the entire staff.'

'Of course he will,' says Wark indignantly. 'Bound to. Nothing else he can do.'

'Jesus, no,' I begin (that fuckpig wouldn't dare), 'he can't, can he? Can he? How could he? He couldn't.'

'Terence,' says a new voice.

Lloyd-Jackson!

'The Controller seems to think he'd like a word with you.'

He can. Oh yes he can. John Hain has power over us, he owns us: he can do anything he likes to us (he can kill us if he likes). He's got the power and — rarer — he's got the bottle. He's got nothing else, though. And, as I walk through the office area to his room, the air misting over with danger and urgency, I see myself from behind, my craven tread, my hair, and beyond me, through the blue window, I glimpse that second figure up in the streets of the sky, that familiar, shuffling, grubby, mackintoshed caricature, Terry the Tramp. (Gregory, you heartless bastard, what did you ever do to be like you are?) I want this job. It's *mine*. They gave it to me and I'm *not* giving it back.

(God, the sort of things people can become, and so quickly. As a child, when I looked at shop-assistants or parkies or milkmen — or anyone else going about their business — I assumed they had always wanted to be the things they were, as if there'd never been any choice in the matter, as if none of it could ever have changed. These creatures seemed unvolatile; surely they did not harbour vitality and appetite. But now I see that practically no one wants to be what they are. They may not especially want to be anything else, but, boy, they don't want to be what they are.)

'Morning, Terry. Kathy, leave us alone for a moment, all right? Sit, sit. Now. Tell me what you think of the job you do here.'

Don't ask me. Tell me what to say. Tell me what to say and I'll say it.

(ii) In a saner world, of course, one
      would expect to be able to zoom
      off to work in one's expensive
      green car — GREGORY

And *my* day — how does it start?

Unpleasantly. Ill. The flat I live in is an eldest son's flat: it is designed for one person: it is designed for me. The spacious drawing-room, with its high knobbly cornice, serried bookcases, and white blaze of window, was, in days of yore, an ample stage upon which the blessed young Ridings could muse and wander, wander and muse — then saunter down the curved wooden steps to the stylish vestibule, along the cupboard-walk to what was once a perfectly good bedroom, and off it a dressing-room, where a man could dress, and off that a bathroom, where a man could bath. Now we share it. Oh well.

Due, then, to the perversely imperial design of my flat, the day begins with a quite traumatic glimpse of its second inhabitant, Terence Service. The blacking-factory he works for, do you see, requires him to be at its premises no later than 9 a.m., and Terry, a good simple lad, likes at least a quart of some cheap, piping beverage before trudging off. This brings him through my room and, invariably his cumbrous passage summons me from sleep. I don't need this. I find sleep an unkind mistress and am a diffident courtier in her ante-rooms. I don't need this: I need my sleep. *I* have to go out every night, so I never get to bed till late. Anyway, I'll part my heavy lashes to glimpse Terry's canted, theatrical tiptoe — thighs aloft — for the kitchen door, and then, a few noisy minutes later, his harrowing return, equipped with a mug and possibly some starchy little snack. I wish he wouldn't do it. It's so embarrassing if I have a friend here. What am I supposed to tell them? What am I supposed to say? I think it's only my enjoyment at watching him clockwork past, fancying himself so nimble, that stops my forbidding him ever to set a foot in here before lunch. Surely he could fix up some kind of device in his own room? I might well challenge him about it today.

I bask, at any rate, until I hear him leave my flat; I am planning outfits the meanwhile, and resolving in my mind the adventures of the night before. Either it will have been Torka's, or else an expensive romp with Kane and Skimmer, my two chums. They're marvellous fun — you'll like them. We always go to the grandest restaurants. We're always in those plush, undersea cocktail bars (we can't bear pubs). We always love spending lots of money. We rage on late into the night and always end up doing mad things. Often I'm musty in the morning; I feel fragile until I have my Buck's Fizz before lunch. It's not a hangover, of course: I don't have hangovers; only yobs have hangovers.

... I spring from my snowy double bed, and — silk-robed, in bikini pants, or quite possibly naked — saunter into the kitchen. Fresh orange juice, real coffee very black, a croissant, some rare honey. Then, as I draw my bath (you have to club your way through the miasma of Terry's room for this purpose), I'll brush my hard and brilliant teeth, poke fun at my gypsyish hair, trim my nails. In the hall — I am towelling myself with vigour — there will be a stack of letters, sifted through by Terence and placed intact on the windowsill; I select the most attractive of these, the missive most redolent of money and sex (which is what all letters try to be about), and peruse it while the sun dries the playful waves of my hair. Next I dress with the kind of to-hell-with-it abandon that only the naturally stylish ever dare attempt, salute my slanting demeanour in the vestibule looking-glass, tolerate the obsequious banter of liftman, doorman and porter, and sweep through the double glass doors. Then it's the streets.

In a saner world, of course, one would expect to be able to zoom off to work in one's expensive green car.

Wouldn't one. But some resentful, chippy, grimacing authority or other has now seen to it that parking is more or less stamped out in the bijou area of the West End where I happen to be employed. So I walk the streets, the same as everyone else, the same as you; I walk them gamely enough, head in air, ignoring alike the appreciative glances of the men, the wolf-whistles of the secretaries and shopgirls, the querulous cries of the newspaper vendors, ignoring too the great bus-borne ecologies of fat-faced identical Germans, check-trousered colonials and arachnoid Arabs. What *is* happening to the area — or to the city, or to the country, or to the planet? (I sometimes roar about at night terrorizing these monkeys in my virile green car: I adore their atavistic cowerings, at once submissive and panicky, as I bellow down on them, klaxons ablaze.) Get out, I think. Get out of my way. I'm trying to go to *work*.

Spryly I elude the wheeling, clueless hordes in the underground station. I select a no-smoking compartment and stand throughout the journey, whether 'seats' are available or not, usually with a cologned neckerchief cupped over my lips. Confidently I emerge to the February splendour of Green Park, pausing to buy a tulip from that delightful barrow-boy in Albemarle Street, and within seconds my keys are twinkling in the cold sunshine of Berkeley Square.

I work in an art gallery. Yes, the job *is* rather a grand one, as you'd expect. High salary, undemanding hours, opportunities for travel, lots of future. It's all very relaxed and genial. Everyone knows what's going to happen, short-term and long. I never have to do anything I don't want to do. It's hardly a 'job' at all really, in the sense of trading one's days for cash: I just turn up here in Mayfair pretty regularly, behave more or less as I wish in fairly acceptable surroundings (chat, read the paper, ring my innumerable friends) — and there is this vast, blush-making cheque on my table, every Friday.

The answer is, of course, that I am the chuckling puppeteer of the two simpletons who run the place. Everything they do is in response to a twitch from my strings. They are called Mr and Mrs Jason Styles − a couple of early-middle-aged roués who jewed their way up from a Camden Passage antique shop and are now trying *so* hard to be decadent. Under their auspices, I need hardly say, the gallery is little more than a rumpus-room of socio-sexual self-betterment: they deal in down-market investment Victoriana, hang the curiosities of the rich, lease out their walls to the doodlings of the famous. They will, in short, do anything to get along. For instance, there is little doubt that I was given the job here on account of my breeding and looks; when I arrived to be interviewed for the assistantship, the Styleses heaved a moan of longing in unison, thanked me for my attendance, and dreamily dismissed the hopefuls queueing without. They are both desperate for me in a playful, candid sort of way and I do try not to be too abrupt with them − though *Mrs* Styles, in particular, grows bolder by the hour. I expect, at any rate, to be in complete control here within the next six months or so; already I am nursing along a school of youngish talent, and I have tentatively scheduled the first of my one-man shows for December.

The glass door wafts shut behind me. I swoop for the mail, refasten the lock from inside, and stride on into the gallery, whose cork walls are at present defaced by the loud 'moodshapes' of some celebrated hysteric or other. I flick on the silver spotlights and remove from the paintings any deposits of dust which present themselves to my eye. Silly old Jason once joked that I should spend the first ten minutes of every day here 'cleaning the canvases' − going round the gallery with a handbrush and rag! Had a good laugh about *that*. In the Styleses' small and incredibly smelly office I remove my cape and curl up with the mail on their squat leather sofa. A postcard − she always writes to me at the gallery − from the exquisite Ursula, my sister, my love; she offers family news, endearments, and a delicious weekend tryst. She is coming down to London to be taught how to become a secretary. Ridiculous. She should come down to London to be taught how *not* to become a secretary. Still, it might amuse her for a while. Along with her note there are the usual eight or nine invitations — openings, launches, at homes; of these, perhaps three or four might get lucky. I glance at the arts pages of the dailies, synchronize my watch with the hideous fluted clock on the Styleses' filing-cabinet, and wander back through the gallery to my desk, lodged in a gloomy nook a few feet from the door — annoyingly, there 'isn't the space' for an office of my own: yet. Within two or three minutes Jason and Odette Styles — I wonder when it was that they made those names up — are shuffling and grunting in the porch, hugging themselves, stamping their feet. I glide up to let them in.

'Good morning, Gregory,' says Jason.

'Morning, Greg,' says Odette.

'Everything all right?'

'How are you today?'

'I'm fine. Everything is fine. How are you?' I say, in genial disbelief.

As a connoisseur of ennui, as satiety's scholar, I'm always rather taken aback to see them arrive here each day, still together, still arm in arm, still solicitously aware of one another as sexual beings. They are in their middle or late thirties; they have shared an office and a bed for ten years now, possibly even longer; they are both, by any reasonably humane standards, hell to look at. And yet — here they come again, and again, and again. They *leave* together too, which never fails to give me a special jolt. They leave together, they go home together; they drink and eat and drowse together; they turn in together; and they get up together again, and again. Phenomenal!

'Ooh, it's so *cold* today,' says the thick-hipped woman to the disgustingly fit little unit of a man under whose whippety pummellings she has staked herself out on the rack of bedroom boredom. 'Not much warmer in here. I'll check the Thermaco,' says the pepper-haired man to the faintly moustachioed, pungently menopausal hillock of a woman through whose doomed forestry he has cantered baying for a decade of neuter night-times. I look on appalled as, even now, they reach out to steady each other while rounding the unspeakable 3D abstract by the door. My God, no wonder they're *swingers*, no wonder they play pimp and whore, no wonder they're desperate, absolutely desperate, for a taste of me.

'I shall put out the OPEN sign,' I suggest.

The day starts with a vexing personal *fracas*. Corinthia Pope, an absurd girl whom I recently scorned after some vague fling we had — and who's been pestering me for weeks on the telephone — takes the unprecedented step of bursting in on me here at the gallery! I whisked the fool outside again and smartly sent her on her way with a definitive rebuke. Returning to my desk, I felt quite ill with rage, and had to shrug my helpless apologies at the two sets of eyes watching me from the glass slit of their office.

Talking of rejects, by the way, Terence is now claiming that he *didn't* enjoy that Miranda after all. Amusing, you think. Well, I thought it was funny myself at first. But now he's sticking to the story: he tried to, he says, and she wouldn't let him. Curious business, because little Terry does enjoy a fair degree of success with the bashful shopgirls and aromatic students he used to bring back to my flat; if I returned late at night, and the kitchen tasted of smoke and human sweat, I'd almost bank on seeing some frizzy mat on the pillow next to his as I popped through his room to wash. Perhaps Miranda really wasn't within his range. Perhaps, like so much else, it's all a question of class. Has he said anything to you about it?

The incident with the Pope girl is enough to trigger the usual morbid badinage. There's no one in the gallery anyway, of course, save for the odd taciturn alien moving from frame to frame like an inspector at an ID parade.

'I must say, Gregory,' Mrs Styles is compelled to remark as I emerge from the downstairs lavatory, the hearty ballcock flushing resplendently in my wake, 'I can see why all the girls are chasing you. You are a very elegant young man.'

'And I must say too,' I am obliged to reply, 'that *you* are a very elegant Older Woman.' In the nature of things there must be some who would think her handsome – sleek black hair, barmaid face, embarrassingly swelly breasts and behind (I don't know where to look – they're everywhere), decent though unacceptably flossy legs, tall.

'Come on ... have you ever known an Older Woman?' She moves closer – it is impossible for me to duck past. Breasts teem inside her manly shirt.

'No, I don't believe I have, funnily enough – not in that special sense.'

'They have so much to show one,' she goes ahead and says – the trite horror.

'Oh? For example?'

She moves closer; so do seven veils of old make-up. A gargoyle jeers behind my slow diamond smile.

'It would be simplest to show you,' she says with a brazen nod towards the bathroom door. 'There's one thing I'm really rather expert at.'

'Well?'

But the old trout is gone – *my*, how tantalizing – to service the stray scaffolding of her stays. Tubes rustle and gasp as I sprint upstairs.

Recuperating at my desk, I sense the compact Jason's diagonal approach. I look up.

'Of course, I don't go in for that much any more,' he says, looping his right arm in a bowler's swivel.

'In for what much?'

'Played tennis this weekend. Terrible mistake. I feel like I've been beaten up. Very rash. Never again.'

He plants his pert derrière on the edge of my desk

'Did you go in for all that, Greg? Games and so on?'

'I rowed and played squash for the school and was captain of the First Eleven,' I tell him, averting my gaze from the coarse lustre of his shantung suit.

He leans forward frowning to sample the muscularity of my thigh. 'Wouldn't have thought soccer was your game. Stronger than you look, though.'

'Not "soccer" — cricket. Football was forbidden at Peerforth.'

'Quite right too.'

His hand is still idling on my kneecap when busybody Odette shoots up the basement stairs.

'We've got work to do!' they say to each other in startled harmony, veering off like evasive aircraft to the shared shadows of their room.

Where, at about a quarter-past eleven, I am expected to join them as the three of us assemble for a morning drink variously described to me as 'coffee', 'tea' and 'chocolate' (the last one is, I think, rather sweeter than the first two, but that may be pure fancy). Now the mood changes — rivalries are forgotten, jealousies set at naught. We are warm in there, and after a few minutes I can even start breathing through my nose without undue discomfort. I let them gossip for a bit; I let them tell each other wistful lies about the viability of the gallery; I let them discuss important fixtures in their diary. Then, with hardly any direct prompting from me, it starts:

'In what terms, Greg, in what — how do you see your future here?'

'The boy we had before, you know, he wasn't very happy. He had too many interests, really.'

Boy? Boy? The pathos of it — these people wear their needs on their sleeves!

'In the end he left for a more ... a job that appealed to him more.'

'As you know, Greg, we're childless, but we've always thought of the gallery as a family affair. Silly really.'

'We've grown very fond of you, as you know, and we'd

feel a lot easier if we could feel that you were, well, sort of a permanent fixture here. Wouldn't we?'

'Because — let's face it — we've no one else we can leave it to. Have we?'

And so on. And so on.

God, the horror of being ordinary.

When I see them, other people — a woman who looks like a remedial art-therapist releases a soft gurgle of satisfaction as she and her colleague find seats at the wine-bar, a stroke of luck which considerably lightens her day; in the underground carriage a big man in a cheap grey mackintosh, breathing that bit too hard, is wrestling with a newspaper so explosively that he misses his stop, a reverse which causes him to rise and pace, and to stare suddenly at his watch as if it were a syphilitic boil; the porter at my flat stands becalmed on the stairs all day wondering how old he can be, as if the very air were full of strange equations that would somehow make his life add up — I think: you deserve to be what you are if you could bear to get that way. You must have seen it coming. And now there's nothing for you here. No one will protect you, and people won't see any reason not to do you harm. Your life will divide up between the fear of madness and the panic of self-preservation. That's it: feed up for going mad. I'm afraid that's all we have to offer you.

Well, well (I bet someone is asking), and what would happen to *me* if ...

If I weren't beautiful, talented, rich and well-born? I would beg, fight, travel, succeed, die.

Terence thinks — he doesn't actually dare say it — that my life is in some sense a gloating parody of the huff-and-puff of his own quotidian dreads, slumped where he is now in his days and days. All my gifts — social, monetary, physiognomic — take on monstrous shape, loom large like muscle-clouds, in his sallow mind. He sees me as somehow the active champion of the privilege which I merely passively embody. That sad bastard, he didn't do anything to end up like he is. Only he let what happened to him happen to him, and that's enough these days. The world is changing; the past has gone, and from now on it is all future tense. The yobs may be winning, but they've left no room for him inside.

Do I mind — do I mind the guaranteed dazzle of my days, the way I surge from one proud eminence to another, the way my life has always pounded through the unequal landscape about us on arrow-straight, slick silvery rails? I hold my eye in the glass — funny feeling: it's always nice; we have a good time together (it's like catching nature rhyming). I suppose it's a gift, like any other, and the inordinately gifted have always had a certain dread of their own genius. There's a pang in it somewhere ... lonely are the beautiful, like the brilliant, like the brave.

(Terence Service is my foster-brother, by the way. I know, but there it is. My parents went and adopted him when he was a lad of nine. The first chapter of his life was spent in some hired box in the Scovill Road area of Cambridge, the meandering slum that lies between the railway station and the cattle-market. His mother, a freelance charwoman, died when Terry was six or seven, and for a few years he and his little sister lived under the sole care of their father, a perfectly able carpenter by the name of Ronald. It was conjectured that Service Sr had an intimate say in the death of his wife, and, in due course, the view received pointed corroboration when the brute savagely murdered his own daughter. Terence was, as I say, nine years old, and there at the time, so you should indulge his going on about it. The melodrama won a fair amount of attention in Cambridge — not least because Terence lived on for a week in the deserted hovel before anyone realized he was there — and it was only through the local rag's shameless mawk-campaign that little Terry's tragedy came to the benign notice of my family, the Ridings. I remember my father, over the breakfast table, reading out the daily bulletins in that soppy old voice of his, while Mama and I exchanged wary yawns. He was going through one of his gluttonously humane phases — or, more accurately, he had recently read something somewhere about humanity, or had read something somewhere about someone being gluttonously humane — and 'literally' could not rest until Terence had been satisfactorily housed. What took my father's fancy, you see, was not the corny squalor of Terry's plight so much as certain imagined affinities between his family and our own (too boring to rehearse — get them from Terence). His concern for the waif grew; he longed for him to be taken into care. Mama and I did our best to reason with him — 'But the boy, the boy,' he would say, slowly shaking that big crazy head. Father's considerable influence was brought to bear: the plans were formed, the authorities notified ...

As the village princeling and household cosset, the toast of the family, the *mignon* of the minions, the darling of the staff, my feelings about the proposed adoption would not be hard to divine. I stared at the small visage splashed on the paper's dirty front page (caption: *Terry Service — Friday's Child*) until the grain of the print seemed to stir with a writhing furtive life: this, just this, was soon to push me to one side of my cloudless childhood days, an alien and frightened boy, a scurrying cur, no more corporeal to me, really, than a smudge of sooty newsprint, its uneven edges spanning away into another world, a world of degradation and hate, of panic and the smell of roused animals. I thought of the sparkling astronomy that *my* life had up until that moment formed: the scrubbed angularities of nursery and bedroom, the busy friendship I enjoyed with the garden's vast precincts, my fairy-tale sister, the congruent rake and perspective of every doorway and stair-well — only three places a certain toy might be if abducted from its rightful nook, the time the leather ball needed to jump back from the ribbed garage door, the creak of joists a hidden code of distance and identity: the thousand certainties on which childhood leans to catch its breath were all reshuffled in blurred travesty, as blurred as the picture of Terence's face on that smudged news-sheet now slipping from my father's thigh.

Terence arrived one brilliant autumn morning, while the Ridings were having one of their halcyon breakfasts in the raised East Wing conservatory. Imagine a circular white table on a checker-board stone floor, deep troughs of fabulous greenery, a receding backdrop of pink and purple blooms, and four decorative seated figures glimpsed through the echoic, yellow light: Henry Riding, a tall, shaggy, 'artistic' patriarch in white jacket and collarless shirt; his handsome wife Marigold, silver-haired, grey-suited; the delicious, vague, sleepy-eyed Ursula — still in her nightie, the minx: and Gregory, who, having recently celebrated his tenth birthday, is already a tall and athletic figure, with driven-back raven hair, a thin, perhaps rather brutal mouth, and a vivid, evaluating stare ... I remember I had just dispatched Cook with some rather sharp words about the consistency of my soft-boiled egg and, while waiting the required 285 seconds for its successor to be prepared, I leaned back on my chair, teasing my palate with a sliver of toast and Gentlemen's Relish. Then I heard a sudden flurry from the maids in the hall — and there was our housekeeper, good Mrs Daltrey, bustling into the light and guiding on an invisible leash a small wondering boy in grey shirt and khaki shorts, Terence, my foster-brother, who turned and gazed at me with stolen eyes.)

3: March

(i) I'm no good at all this any more. I've
got to lock myself away until I'm
fit to live — TERRY

You'll have to excuse me for a moment.

Mouth-fuck, bum-fuck, fist-fuck, prick-fuck. Ear-fuck, hair-fuck, nose-fuck, toe-fuck. It's all I think about when I'm in my room. Bed-fuck, floor-fuck, desk-fuck, sill-fuck, rug-fuck.

And in the streets. Tarmac-fuck, lamppost-fuck, shop-front-fuck. Bike-fuck, car-fuck, bus-fuck. Rampart-fuck, railing-fuck, rubbish-fuck.

Pen-fuck, clip-fuck, paper-fuck. (I'm at the office now.) Char-fuck, sec-fuck, temp-fuck. Salessheet-fuck, invoice-fuck, phone-fuck.

And everywhere else. Land-fuck, sea-fuck, air-fuck, cloud-fuck, sky-fuck. In all kinds of moods. Hate-fuck, rage-fuck, fun-fuck, sick-fuck, sad-fuck. In all kinds of contexts. Friend-fuck, kid-fuck, niece-fuck, aunt-fuck, gran-fuck, sis-fuck. Fuck-fuck. I want to *scream*, much of the time, or quiver like a damaged animal. I sit about the place here fizzing with rabies.

No, they still don't want to. I'm not at all certain *I* want to any more. I mean, what happens when they ... you know. I'm clear on the mechanical side of it (I hear about that in books, and I'm also buying quite a lot of those magazines, the ones in which girls show the insides of their vaginas and anuses to the world for money. Do the police know about those magazines, incidentally, the ones you can get anywhere? I don't think they can do), but it all must seem rather awkward and embarrassing. Do you do it much? How often? Less often than you want or more often than you want? I used to do it as much as I possibly could, and I liked it a lot. Then I stopped. No one would do it with me (and doing it with people is half the fun). Soon I'm going to stop trying — I can tell. I'm getting cordoned off. Barriers are slamming down all about me. Soon it will be too late ever to get out again.

Supplementary Bad Things continue to happen. Last week I bought a chalk-stripe suit from a second-hand shop in Notting Hill Gate. It was a ridiculous suit in all kinds of ways — obviously an incredibly old and fucked-up man had used it before me — but I knew of a good place that would taper and restyle it cheaply (that was the idea). They tapered and restyled it cheaply, I took it home and put it on, it fitted and it looked all right. Then I realized that it smelled, very very strongly, of the sweat of the dead man who had worn it all his life. Fair enough, I thought, as I soaked it in ammonia overnight, hung it out of my window ditto, buried it in the square double ditto, sprinkled it with ashtrays, steeped it with aftershave and whisky, and put it back on again. It smelled, very very strongly, of the sweat of the dead man who had worn it all his life. I threw the thing away in a dustbin. It wouldn't go in my wastepaper-basket, which still glowers rankly at me from the corner of my room, still looking for trouble, still wanting a fight.

Nothing happens at work. The rationalization hasn't taken place yet (we still think it's Wark, however. Even Wark thinks it's Wark by now). John Hain isn't letting on (the cunning fuck was just sounding me out that time); he will not be rushed; no one can make him do anything he isn't already very keen on doing. Work has dried up. We no longer get our sales-sheets and telephone lists in the mornings. We're not given anything to sell (though we still get paid for it. I hate getting my wages now. When the old woman runs her fingers over the envelopes under 'S', I _know_ mine won't be there). I sit at my desk all day as if I were Damon (God that boy's teeth are a mess — he admits they're all jangling in his head, like a pocketful of loose change), a split match in one hand, a paper-clip in the other, chewing chewing-gum and smoking fags. I can't even read right any more. That'll be the next thing to go. We wait and sigh and watch the rain (rain on windows always takes me back, or it tries. I'm not going back). We don't dare talk to each other much; we're frightened we might know something we don't. Yesterday, a man called Veale with an immensely calm and sinister voice rang me from the Union. He's coming to see me, he says. His voice held neither menace nor encouragement; it was just calm and sinister. I asked around a bit: he isn't coming to see anyone else, or so everyone says. Just me. I hope he doesn't think I'm posh.

I did ring Ursula eventually, in response to that card of hers. I'm not sure why I waited so long (she's a girl, isn't she?), but I did wait. I'm grateful to her, I hope, for her kindness in the past — or rather her complete lack of cruelty, which was better still under the circumstances — and I'll do what I can to make things all right for her. I love her. Yes, I do love her — thank God for that. It's hard to give you any sense of Ursula without making her sound a bit of a pain in the ass (which she is half the time anyway — and for Christ's sake don't listen to a word Greg says about her: he's totally unreliable on this point). She is nineteen and looks about half that. I have never in my life seen anyone so unvoluptuous — pencil legs, no bum, two backs. In repose her face has an odd neutral beauty, like an idealized court portrait of someone plain. As soon as her face becomes animated it loses that beauty, but at the same time it becomes, well, more animated. (You'd fancy her, I reckon. I'd fall in love with her instantly if she weren't my sister. But that's not saying

54

much.) See what you think. For the record, she is in my view a pure, kind, touching, innocent, quite funny, very posh, erratically perceptive and (between ourselves) slightly *tonto* girl.

I spoke to the matron at her secretarial lodgings and was serenely told by her that Ursula would ring me back at the number I left the moment her class was finished. I sat at my desk with some coffee that Damon had limped out to fetch, unable to do anything until she returned my call.

'Hello, Ginger. Are you happy?'

'Of course not. Have you gone out of your mind? How are you?'

'I think I'm all right. This place is jolly mad, though. How nervy are you?'

'Very, I think. I hope I am. I don't want to be any more nervous than I am now. How nervy are you?'

'Lots.'

'It's a thing, isn't it.'

'We'd better meet soon, don't you think?'

Yes, I do think. But I've got no advice for you. All I've got to tell you is: don't grow up, if you can possibly avoid it. Stay down there, because it's no fun up here.

Out of habit — and out of anxiety and shame and self-dislike — I asked my foster-sister to meet me at a bus-stop on the Fulham Road. I do this to girls (or to me) because if they fail to turn up you simply hop on a bus, as if that was what you were waiting for, as if that was all you had in mind, rather than standing on an exposed and lonely corner while the streets about you go soiled and ripped and dead. She came. She jumped off a 14 on the far pavement, and, her small body canted forward intently, like a well-trained child, ran across the road. We hugged awkwardly and separated to appraise each other in the streetlight. Half-fringe, large pale eyes, her incongruously strong nose reddened in the cold, a thin but open face, without much angularity; she looked pre-pubescent — non-pubescent; I felt that if I ever slept with her (these thoughts wriggle up) it would cause some lingering and poignant hurt that would take me my whole life to nurse. (Does she fuck? I wonder suddenly, with a nauseous lurch. Nah. She probably doesn't know about all that yet. And I hope no one ever tells her. Oh God I miss my sister. No one ever told her either. Well, that's something. She may have got fucked up but at least she never got fucked. I'm *glad*.)

'Come on, you look all right,' said Ursula. 'For a yob.'

We went to a noisy, conservatorial hamburger place I know some 200 yards further up the Fulham Road, a place where tall, handsome trend-setters go on as if they were your friends while they give you food and take your money. It's popular there. We joined a short queue consisting entirely of couples, denimmed men and their far more flamboyant and varied-looking women. I don't like couples, as you know (they're like a personal affront), but Ursula and I pretended to be one, and within five minutes we were inside and within ten had secured two seats at an unoccupied table for four. Immediately a rangy young man with toothbrush eyebrows pulled up a chair opposite. I turned to him resentfully and he met my gaze. This guy wants a fight, I thought, until he said, 'Hi. What would you like tonight?' and produced a yellow pad from his top pocket.

'Oh. Just some wine, while we think. Red. A bottle.'

'I won't be having any,' said Ursula.

'So what?' I said.

The waiter nodded grimly and sloped off.

'I wish they wouldn't do that,' I said.

'What did he do?'

'Sat down next to us like that. He's a waiter, isn't he? I don't want waiters sitting down next to me.'

'Come on, Ginger. He looked nice. He looked intelligent too.'

'Oh yeah? Then why's he dealing them off the arm in a dump like this?'

'Chippy chippy chippy,' said Ursula.

(Do you know what 'chippy' means, by the way? I think I do. It means minding being poor, ugly and common. That's what *chippy* means.)

'You bet,' I said.

Ursula chose this moment to take off her duffle-coat; this was a thick, studently item and I knew that its removal would diminish her personal presence by about two-thirds. From her dark flower-patterned dress (clean, unironed, shapeless, not a dress for winter) now protruded thin stockingless legs and thin forearms whose shade of fluff caught the light. When she strained to hook her coat on the stand's tall curlicue, the dress rode wispily up her Bambi thighs. See? She really is my sister and she really is about ten.

I opened my third packet of cigarettes that day and poured out the wine brought to us smartly enough by the uppity waiter. Round about us, sexy youngsters laughed and whispered.

'Whew, Terry!' said Ursula. 'You *are* nervy tonight.'

'I know. Look at my hands.'

Ursula had just returned from a weekend with her parents at home. We talked about it, that secure and companionable-seeming place (I used to go back there a lot. I don't any more and neither does Gregory. I don't like going away at all any more: I'm frightened something might happen behind my back. And home gives me the horrors, anyway). Apparently father's ankle had healed after his celebrated fall from the barn roof; he now claimed to be fleeter of foot than at any period of his life. Recent stories about him included his heckling of — and subsequent scuffle with — the left-wing vicar of the village church, his new passion for indoor bowls, his continued refusal to eat vegetables, his second wave this year of horrendous spending sprees, his third early-morning pass at the septuagenarian cleaning-lady, and his decision to erect a wigwam in the main sitting-room.

'Christ, everything's falling apart these days,' I said. 'I suppose he really must be a bit mad, mustn't he?'

Ursula's expression — like mine, one of vestigial amusement — did not change. 'Of course. He always has been. All of us lot always have been. You're the lucky one, Ginger.'

'Oh *that's* what I am. I was wondering what I was. But you're posh, you lot. It makes no odds if posh people go mad. They're all mad anyway.'

'That's why you're the lucky one — you're not posh.'

'Yes I am. I'm posh too now.'

'No you're not.'

'What am I then?'

'You're a yob.'

No I'm not. I'm posh. I know everything there is to know about class, and about how you can locate it. I was present that historic evening five years ago when the girl sitting opposite me now came into the television room of Rivers Hall, where the family was watching a series about pre-war servants and their mistresses and masters, and unthinkingly curled up on her nanny's lap. The nanny (since retd.) did not move as she accepted the weight of her fourteen-year-old charge. *At no point did they take their eyes off the screen.* I know all there is to know about class. I say sofa, what?, pepper-and-salt, lavatory, vale*t* (I could even say behind instead of ass if I liked). When *I* was fourteen I did a quiz in a magazine: anyone who completed this quiz, the idea was, would know at once how posh they were. Halfway through — yes, I tipped the soup bowl away from me; no, I didn't put the milk in first — I could tell I was going to be very posh indeed. The last question was about what you had called your children, or what you would call them if you ever had any (this was when people could still afford them). Would you call your son (a) Sebastian, Clarence, Montague, or (b) Michael, James, Robert, or ... As I poised to give the (b) section an imperious tick (I hadn't fallen for all that (a) bullshit), my eye trailed over the (c) section, which ran: (c) Norman, Keith, Terry. The biro tinkled from my hand. So my dad was a yob. So what else is new? (Do you still think any of that matters, class and so on? It doesn't. It's crap. It's *crap*.)

'Yobs go *tonto* too, you know,' I said.

'Oh no they don't,' said Ursula.

'Oh yes they do. What's it like?' I asked dully, ' — I mean leaving home and stopping being at school and being in a town and jobs and everything? I've been doing it for ages now and I still can't tell what it's like. There's something ... '

'Well, I wouldn't know yet, would I? Cos I'm still at school. What do you think it is? More nerves?'

'Yes, more of them all right. But that's not it. Good. I'm drunk. About bloody time too. I just wonder what all the fuss was about — spend your life getting ready for *this*. No one has a good time after they're ten just worrying about it. It's, I think it's just — '

' ... How's Gregory?'

'How is he ever? A monster of conceit. And a hustler. And a faggot.'

'Oh, come on, Ginger. Anyway, what's a faggot?'

'Look. Don't ever call me Ginger again, okay?'

'I thought you liked being called Ginger.'

'Well I don't.'

'I thought you did. I'm sorry.'

'What made you think that? I don't like it at all. I don't like it one bit.'

'I'm sorry.'

I looked round in bewilderment, at the girls, at the couples. During such moments my ugliness hangs on me like cheap heavy clothes. I looked at Ursula. What good was she to me? I didn't even want to fuck her — I wanted to hurt her, to do her harm, to lash out at her shins with my boot, to swipe my wine glass across her face, to grind out my cigarette on her fluttering hand. Oh, what's going on here?

'Oh, what's going on here? I'm sorry. Let's go. I'm sorry.'

We walked in silence to Gloucester Road Underground.

'I'll see you home,' I said. We took a train crowded with drunks to Sloane Square. We walked in silence down tapering, underlit streets.

'This is it,' she said. 'I ring the bell now.'

'Well, that's sorted *you* out for life.'

'Mm?'

'I'm no good at all this any more. I've got to lock myself away until I'm fit to live.'

We kissed, in the usual style — so that the centre of my lips rested at a slight angle on the corner of hers.

'Terry,' she said, 'you must stop all that. You'll make yourself just how you pretend to be.'

'I know I will.'

Then she held me closer, with a kind of girlish authority, and we kissed again, mildly but firmly, on the lips.

'Thank you,' I said.

She put her mouth to my ear. 'I hear voices,' she whispered. 'In my head.'

'What sort of voices. What do you mean?'

'In my head.'

'What do they say?'

'Never mind. But I do hear them.'

'Hey look, I'll ring you tomorrow, all right?'

'All right.'

'Good night. Look after yourself.'

'Sweet dreams,' she called, moving up the steps to her door.

And it all peopled my mind along the moist avenues, during the vivid tube-journey, and in the rain and shadows of my own familiar streets. The rain, that kiss, those voices. Just think about it, boy, I tell myself — you can do it. Ursula-fuck, sister-fuck ... *foster*-fuck? No, I can't do it — I can't even think about it. That skein of corny decadence I leave to the suburbs of Gregory's imagination. *He's* always enjoyed hystericizing the few junior touch-up sessions he had with Ursula in his teens (I had a few with her too, in a sense). But I've been through all that, I've done all that and it's all too complicated. And I'm touchy about sisters generally. I had one who died and I'm sentimental about them. Let's forget about sisters. I've had enough of sisters. Fuck *sisters*.

I stood on the landing outside our flat. There is a wall-to-wall, floor-to-ceiling window there that creaks and bends when the air gets turbulent. It wobbles in the wind. It shivers in the cold. It hates stormy weather (it isn't up to its job). I saw my reflection in the pane. Raindrops were dribbling down my face in lugubrious rivulets. I listened to the traffic; I thought of me, and all of you out there, laughing at my losses. I pressed my head against the glass. It gave an inch. I pressed harder. I felt at any moment I might hear it crack.

This is the way it began.

Whoosh. I am six — my sister is hardly there yet, a hot wad of freckles and tears in the neighbour room. Two or three times a month, in the kitchen at supper time, seven o'clock, a slight, tickling, migraine haze would envelop and gradually retard our evening meal. Uh-oh, the air was saying. My father, a tall, lumpy, sober-looking man with flat red smalltown hair, a bent little slot of a mouth and stark protuberant eyes, sits to my right, saying nothing, eating his eggs, chips, beans and tomatoes with fastidious dispatch, paying shrewd justice to every food-stuff on each forkful, so that he will be left with, say, a sliver of yolk, a stub of chip, two baked beans and the pipped crimson gook of the tomato for the final prim swallow. My mother, a lean, nervous and intelligent woman with nutcrackerish features (she lost her teeth; she never did find them again), sits tight on my left, saying nothing, mashing her skiddy eggs, beans and tomatoes into thin brothy spoonfuls. Sitting between them — and looking, I should think, about the same as I look now — is me, Terry at six, the long-ago boy. I work at my fishfingers; no one speaks, though you feel everyone is trying to, everyone would if they could, and the air gets itchier and itchier until the sound of our irons on the plates is like the alarum of advancing kettle-drums which swells up to fill the room, then dies down again, then gathers once more.

And it's a completely normal evening — we all think it's a completely normal evening — except for this curious, unpleasant headache haze and this strange false clarity of sound. But perhaps, too, we can all sense something else, an extra thing, activity starting to occur somewhere in my father's brain, and maybe in my mother's mind also a perverse, insidious reciprocity has begun.

Time for you to go to bed, Terry, says my father to the air. Don't forget to clean your teeth, my mother adds, stacking the plates, her head bowed. I walk to the door and turn. For a moment I feel I am on the edge of their exhausted, frightening, migraine world, and feel that I could deliver them from it, tell them something quickly about the other side. But I say,

Good night.

Good night.

Good night.

And I walk softly upstairs, use the bathroom in watery porcelain silence, undress shivering and slide between the heavy blankets, crush the pillow to my head — and hear the house start to come alive like a big machine: the walls shudder and sweat, the ceiling splits, the floor bounces my bed high in the air, the cold sheets hug me in their fire.

When I was a bit older – taller, stronger, more aware that my parents were up to no good — I used to think that by simply appearing, by simply showing them I was there, that they would have to stop, and stop straight away and never do it again. (I had an absurd faith in the sacramental power of my own presence. What happened to that?) See! I'm here while you're doing this. Can't you tell what it must be like for *me*?

I stood waiting in my room. I wanted to hide, hide, but I made no move to get undressed. There had been that dizzying tingle again, and that sharp low threshold of sound, and I knew it would have to happen soon. Then the stirrings began, random and intermittent at first, like the collapse of distant breakers, harsh music over choppy water. Out on the shaken landing, the walls veering about me, down the stairs which creak by on a slowing treadle, part of the old machine the house becomes as I head for its heart, the back room, a place of dangling black pans, sooty cisterns and something I've never seen before. In the downstairs passage the noise is almost unbearable — and not the discrete, inanimate noise of battle and wreckage, but warm, sweaty, human sounds, as of pain and distress, of something far too intense to be seen. I enter the kitchen; I cross the room and push the half-glass scullery door; it swings open and I stare. At what? At my father's eyes as they focus incuriously on my face. Eyes without a trace of hatred or anger or surprise or any emotion I have felt myself or seen in another, pure and abstracted eyes gazing up from some impossible task. *Whoosh.* The room is full of migraine and I hardly make out my mother where she bends on the plastic floor: the headache air seems to bulge up to expel me, gusting me out and cracking the door shut inches from my face. Then the world and I retreat, recede from the back room, and the soft machinery begins to stir again, again cautious and intermittent, choppy music over distant breakers.

Everything would be all right the next day, more or less. My mother would look appreciably more fucked up than usual over breakfast but visibly relieved, my father preoccupied, vague, but at peace — an air of heavy compromise. Why did it have to get so much worse? I could have taken any number of those nights of migraine, and the appeasing quiet of those mornings. But things fell apart — I suppose they had to — ending in a few shrill seconds of panic, when my mother got killed and then it was my sister's turn and he never hit me. Why?

Ursula was wrong. Yobs *do* go *tonto*. I'm going it a

63

different way to my father, but I'm going it. I think everyone is going it a bit these days (I wish I knew somebody, so I could check the theory out). I'm going it, and *I'm* one of the people whom people like you see in the streets and think, 'Sometimes I wouldn't mind being like him — no joys, no pains, no soul to vex you.' But I have got a soul (and it wants to be kissed same as any other soul). Madness is being democratized too, you know. You people can't go on hogging it forever. We want our share too.

I finally had it out with that wastepaper-basket. I thought I'd rid myself of one bad thing. I got a whole packet of special black rubbish-bags from the supermarket (I reckoned they'd be handy for carrying my laundry in as well). I got drunk on a Saturday lunchtime and emptied the wastepaper-basket into one of these special bags. It was rough, but I handled it (it went on forever, like the strata of a Pompeian latrine). While I was in the mood I put a cache of dirty socks, underpants and shirts into another of these special black bags. I dropped the rubbish in the dustbin and went on to the launderette in Ladbroke Grove, where I left my stuff with the old woman who does it for you if you pay her (other people, most of them foreigners, are poorer than me and wash their stuff themselves. I feel quite flash, I feel like Gregory, in the launderette). When I turned up to collect my clean clothes on Monday morning, a disgusted manageress returned my special black bag to me. 'Do you want us to wash that?' she asked. 'How many dries, sir?' The bag was full of rubbish, of course. I ran back to the flat. The dustmen had been that morning. Four shirts, five pairs of underpants, six pairs of socks. Another bad thing. Thanks for that. I think I'm losing my bottle. I think I'm going *tonto*.

A fucked-up hippie lives in the streets near us. I see him two or three times a week. He looks more fucked-up every day. He lies wedged in the doorway of a barricaded shop in Moscow Road. He has a suitcase and some carrier-

64

bags. His orange-peel face is scored with trickly yellow lines from crying in the cold sun. I'm going to speak to him soon and ask him what it's like.

(ii) I had a dozen oysters ... followed
by François's triumphant *faisan à la mode de Champagne* – GREGORY

Of course, it's all nonsense about 'incest', you know.

In this country at any rate, *incest* ('the crime of sexual intercourse or cohabitation between persons related within the degrees within which marriage is prohibited by law' – *OED*) wasn't even considered a misdemeanour until 1650, when, quite out of the blue and grouped willy-nilly with various other delinquencies, it was arbitrarily promoted to a capital offence. Following the glorious second dawn of the Restoration, naturally, the suppression of the 'crime' fell to what the self-righteous Blackstone ruefully called 'the feeble coercion of the spiritual courts', though Bills to re-establish it as a felony were repeatedly introduced in Parliament – only to be laughed out of the House every time.

In 1908, however, legislation was sneaked through (the Punishment of Incest Act) under which sexual intercourse of a male with his daughter, mother, sister or granddaughter (*sic*!) was made punishable by up to seven years' imprisonment. And did it matter in the slightest whether intercourse was committed with or without the female's consent? Not a bit of it. Indeed, the consenting female was on conviction liable to the same punishment as the male. (Formerly all proceedings under the Act were held *in camera*, but this provision was repealed by the Criminal Law Amendment Act in 1922. In *Rex* v. *Ball* [22CX, cc366] it was held by the Lords that evidence of previous intercourse was sufficient to establish guilty passion and rebut innocent association. Well, it would be, wouldn't it?)

The terms 'brother' and 'sister', by the way, included 'half-brother' and 'half-sister', whether or not the relationship could be traced through lawful wedlock.

Such dithering needn't obscure the fact — may even serve to highlight it — that we're dealing with one of those taboos which society inherits as a piece of half-forgotten lumber, whereby the quite practical rules of a past community are fearfully revived by an anxious or repressive age. As Dr J. G. V. Kruk, in his recent monograph *Incest* (Michel Albin, 1976) has shown to my satisfaction (and to those of the experts: 'A convincing and scholarly exercise in de-mythology' — *TLS*), the whole notion was just an oldster ruse for luring fresh sons into the family unit. Clearly, you wouldn't want your shiftless daughters compacting the familial bastion by marrying your own sons — when in the next hut or hovel there languished some strapping ploughboy who would be only too happy to move in and help you farm, hunt, chop wood, stop other people fucking you up, and whatnot. That was the sole reason for the quarantine. Inferior genes, true, are more likely to proliferate in closed marriages, but then so are healthy ones. Take, for example, the superb Egyptian dynasty (Cleopatra, Rameses II, etc.): for several generations a series of siblings ruled; they were dazzlingly cultivated, physically perfect, talented, beautiful and strong. No, it won't do, I'm afraid: 'incest' is a strip of warped lead from the gutter presses, a twitch in the responses of philistines and suburbanites, a 'sin' only in the eyes of the hated and the mean.

Besides, we only did it once.

This is the way it began.

My sister and I are seven and nine respectively. It is summer, and we are playing on the D-Pond, a broad, somewhat neglected semi-circular lake at the northern prong of our vast estate. It is one of those shimmery, light-headed, pollen afternoons; ripples slowly flee across the dandelion waters, the wind hot on their heels. Can I find the bits of my lost childhood? Can I gather them up again? Where are they? Ursula cuts a tomboyishly suntanned figure, her tingling blonde hair hung loose on her shoulders; she wears but a pair of spotless white underpants. I am perhaps a head the taller, and already my body shows those qualities of athleticism and economy of movement which were later to serve me so well in the gymnasium and on the games field; I too am pleasantly bronzed in the afterglow of this long late summer (my new tennis shoes and clinging white shorts agree with me). We are playing with our raft, an uneven and treacherous affair roped together out of logs, cracked doors, spare timber and fat petrol tubs. I propose to test it with a circumnavigation of the lake, and with skilful thrusts of the punt-pole I set off, while Ursula falters along the shore, shrieking imperious warning of every reed patch and low-slung branch, and begging me not to go out too far. Straining to keep my balance astride the soggy dipping floats — and careful not to ruin my new tennis shoes on the disgustingly slimy bank — I coolly complete the arc to Ursula's shouts of wonder and relief. 'How clever, how marvellous,' she said. 'Oh how wonderful.'

'Come on, up you get. We're going to the island,' I said, turning towards the bushy green lump in the centre of the lake. At this, of course, a look of almost heavenly woe besets Ursula's features. 'No. Too far, the island. Too *deep*.' 'I'll look after you. Come *on*.' She clung to me tremulously when I lifted her on board, but I managed to get her to sit down at the prow and remain still; after a few moments she even began to help with the paddling, contentedly spooning her hands through the jewelled waters. Drugged somewhat by the heat and exertion, I swirled the punt-pole lazily in our wake, my mind caught by the prisms of sky, liquid, the girl's glistening back, her many-coloured hair ... Our island turned out to be smarter than it looked — past the mucky outer rim were three fairly spruce shrubs enclosing a patch of remarkably firm grass, on which we were soon happily seated. Ursula gazed about herself, at the heavy water on all sides. 'Success. How wonderful, how beautiful,' she said. 'Shall we take off our things?' I asked. 'Yes, I think we should. Oh, how wonderful, how wonderful.' Ah, that lost world. Boiling images gathered and fled beneath our closed lids, the sun decanting into the sweet marine tang of our bodies — held up there in the motionless rotundity of the lake, while our island grew and spread and the land cowered to fill the four horizons. As I placed my hand on the plump rift between her thighs, Ursula looked up at me encouragingly, her face lit by a lake of dreams.

When we came to our senses, of course, we saw that our craft had slipped from the bank and drifted dumbly off some ten or fifteen feet, and — since neither of us could swim (I loathe swimming) — we found ourselves temporarily marooned. Within half-an-hour, though, a housemaid whom mother had sent out with some chilled squash appeared; a rowing boat was duly fetched from the Willow Lake by two of the obsequious senior gardeners, and the young castaways were promptly ferried back to shore (hot blushes from Ursula at being seen in her panties by the staff). Oh, it was nothing really, nothing at all. But for a moment we were out there naked and cold, frightened at the thought of being alone in the empty world we had striven to create.

Following this incident Ursula and I had no close physical contact for more than a year. Not that our love cooled in the slightest. From the start — from the moment we began to sense who and what we were — ours had been perhaps the rarest and most exalted of brother-sister bonds. I cannot remember a single instance of rancour or harshness, a single rivalry or untender word. (I well remember our consternation one day in the village when we witnessed an hysterical brawl between two yokel sibs. Our eyes conferred incredulously, as if to say, 'But they're brother and sister, aren't they? *We* are.') Ursula and I loved each other throughout the long Eden of our childhood with a cloudless, sure, quite unanxious love: her miseries were my miseries, my triumphs her triumphs. Our April shower of physical wariness was a period not of withdrawal so much as of reserve, of anticipation. For soon we were to embark on that poignant, sapling rediscovery of our own bodies, a journey which continued for many years until its sudden and shattering end — but that was after Father got sick, and Terence came, and things started to fall apart.

Early in the month my sister telephoned me at the gallery. I had been steering some gravid squaw round the new one-man show and was heartily relieved when Odette Styles, her common face divulging an heroic minimum of disapproval, beckoned me into the netherland of her office to receive the call. Old Jason was in there too somewhere, and I felt the torpid weight of their lust on my shoulders as I said,
    'Gregory Riding.'
    'Hello, it's *me*. Who was that awful woman?'
    'My love, how are you? Well, that would be telling.'
    'The fat one who keeps trying to kiss you?'
    'Precisely.'
    'Gregory, may I come to lunch?'
    'Of course you may! At *once*.'
    I replaced the receiver — and swivelled. Old Ma Styles, having made an unprecedentedly shameless lunge at me in the lower passage that morning, was staring through the glass hatch into the gallery, moodily smoking one of her foul French cigarettes. I turned and saw Jason's eyes glinting at me through the shadows.
    'I'm going out now,' I announced.
    'Not another of your long lunches,' I heard her sigh as I picked up my cape and gadded across the floor.
    Now for Ursula, of course, everything has to be *just so* — and I, of course, infallibly ensure that it is. My usual table has been reserved at Le Coq d'Or, and good Emil

is on hand as ever when Ursula and I surge through the great double-doors. (Ursula and I love grand restaurants.) As I unswirl my cape like a balletic stingray and Ursula surrenders her fashionable white mackintosh to a pair of vying flunkeys, our nostrils are already flaring to the settled, inviolable elegance which hangs like cinematic grain in the crystal dining-room: the cultured symmetries of cornice and chandelier, the incognito scurry of dark waiters contrasting with the fêted entrances of incendiary chefs, the at first indistinguishable foreground presence of various moneyed and modish diners, the suspended, underwater elegance of the whole.

'It *is* your usual table, sir, isn't it?'

'Yes of course, Emil,' I said, folding a five-pound note into his silky breast pocket.

'And your usual cocktail, sir, as you wait for your lunch to be prepared?'

By now we are cruising through the body of the dining-room — I call and wave at various people I know, even pausing to chat briefly with a well-known young actor (which Ursula always adores).

'Emil, *please*. My guest and I must be settled at our table before we can think about anything as complicated as *that*.'

'Of course, Mr Riding.'

We gained our table — quite the nicest in the place, with its grotto-like candles, its proximity to a superb Impressionist nude that I have long coveted, and its fine vantage on the restaurant's broad span. Ursula chose her usual passion-fruit cup (we were both giggling rather by this time) and —

'And for me, Emil, the vodka martini with — '

'Yes, sir. Two slices of lemon, straight up.'

'Excellent, Emil. I know I may rely on you.'

Now whenever we are out having one of our grand meals, and Ursula sits with her back to the restaurant and prompts me to sit facing the stylish throng, it is always for a very clear reason ... I leaned towards her, tenting my forearms on the white tablecloth — my fingertips millimetres from my mouth — and began:

'Over in the corner, by the door, is Sam Dunbar, the "sculptor". He does junky Giacomettis that look like stolen microphone stands, plus the odd steel cast of things like pregnant waifs — all Mopsa hair and intolerably sentimental curves. Dunbar keeps turning up at Torka's. With him lunches Mia Küper, absolutely *the* tackiest of all the main London hostesses — she's quite capable of giving her luncheon guests two whole lobsters each, such is her complete panic to impress. Two tables over, the yob architect Ernest Dayton — he perpetrated the South Bank adjunct — is arousing Celia Hannah, the fashion editress, with his fat-lipped whispers. Nearer home (don't turn round), Isaac Stamp, banker, entrepreneur and Jew, is clumsily drunkening what I take to be some species of escort girl. He's the lazy fraud who — '

— But soon the food had to be ordered, Emil materialized in cautious attendance, and Ursula was in any case by this time in stitches.

I had a dozen oysters — not *quite* up to the house standard — followed by François's triumphant *faisan à la mode de Champagne*; Ursula, after much ticklish deliberation with the menu, inevitably opted for the same. And, although my sister drinks very little and doesn't really know about wines, I insisted on a full bottle of their staggering '52 de Rothschild, winking at Emil and good-naturedly urging him to be sure to guzzle our dregs. Later, Ursula supped freely from the pudding table (the bit she likes best, I sometimes suspect) while I enjoyed a powerful liqueur with my coffee — and even toyed with a colossal Havana, just to please her.

It must have been, oh, four o'clock by the time we wandered out into the street. I ought to say that U. looked very beguiling in her white mackintosh, and when I lured her for a few moments into a quiet arcade we were soon smoothing up against each other and moaning like doves. At length I shooed her off to her class and strolled back to the comparative gloom of the gallery; its stately matron reared jealously out of her hole as I entered, but I evaded her, tripping nimbly down the stairs; I spent the rest of the afternoon in the stock-room, where I had a good cackle over some side-splitting new prints with which she had recently blundered back from The Hague.

I don't know, but perhaps if I were leading a less galvanic sexual life myself I might be able to tolerate, if not indulge, Mrs Styles's ever-bolder attentions. As it is, I feel like — like some prospective conquest of Terence's, permanently trailed and scrutinized by this damp, adoring need. Three days ago the witch surprised me in the lavatory — I was training my hair and for once had failed to take the precaution of double-locking the door. 'Why do *you* need to bother with that, Greg?' she gaily cried, *and actually took me in her arms from behind.* Oh yes, a 'motherly' gesture. But beneath the squashy pressure of her bosom on my back and her great swirling pelvis on my thighs, I felt the taut shudders of a nerveless animal.

For things are getting *rather* wild at Torka's these days, and Gregory Riding, Esquire, is finding himself very much in demand. It's chic now, I'm well aware, to look for ladders in the silk of decadence, to fret about the underside of the permissive drift, to summon up the nemeses of pleasure. It's all chippy drivel, of course. (Worth a laugh, too, is the idea that decadence is somehow culpably undemocratic. Just look at the lower classes — look at them seriously. Naturally they stick to themselves. Who else wants them? They're made for each other.) Nothing sordid ever happens at Torka's. His glossy apartment is without the sickly tang of some decadent venues I've glanced in on, the tang of rough trade and sado-masochism, the tang of concealed cameras and one-way mirrors, the tang of crime. No: it's all very luxurious, immensely civilized and definitively good fun.

Arrive at eight, springing from my costly car, the tepid filth of the underground showered from my body, which is now hugged by insolently provocative nightwear. Torka's sniggering houseboy removes my cape, I give my reflection in the giant hall mirror a serious stare, and am ushered with the usual bustle into the half-crowded drawing-room, whose open balcony windows glide off towards the mermaid lights of the Park. I move across, under a heavy fire of eyes, to the marble drinks table, pour myself a glass of expensive white wine, and join the celebrated Torka where he is ensconced on his favourite *chaise-longue* for a few minutes' shop before the first appraisals of the evening begin. Who's there? Adrian of course, Susannah of course (I'm not speaking to them at the moment), that intriguingly shaped American girl of whom everyone is so full of praise, the shy boy who can be very sweet if you nurse him along, the slab-chested Swede who was such a disaster the other night, that television producer and his wife who aren't *quite* up to standard, and know it, and always get left till last, Johnnie (Torka's latest find), the twins (oriental sisters whom I put through their paces the previous evening — fascinating mirror-image stuff), Mary-Jane, who you'd think was a bit antique but is really very proficient in her over-adoring way, Montague, who only ever wants to watch, thank God, two new boys (one hunky cowboy — how did *he* get here? — and one rather more promising blond, who has a nice panthery look), and three new girls (one leathery bikie, one titled tearaway who I'm told isn't up to much, and one agreeably athletic redhead, who has just the kind of firm, tanned, hard-packed body I like).

It's all done with the eyes. At nine or so the pockets of conversation begin their languid dying fall — glasses remain unfilled, cocaine nostril-spoons are put away, the air gets heady with resinous smoke — and people have started to send their gazes wandering round the room. They are conjectural, uncommitted gazes which offer, spurn, flaunt, sustain, advance until they are met by gazes they like and say hello to, and talk about certain

73

other gazes in a critical way and agree about them or fall out about them or realign in new conjunctions. Then we slip away.

It was with three of the newcomers — panthery blond, leather bike-girl, athletic redhead — that I eventually repaired to the grandest of Torka's five bedrooms. (I believe, too, that the veteran Mary-Jane tagged along or at least put in an appearance, on the off-chance that an unattended orifice might at some point hove into view.) Inevitably, one imagines, I soon became the cynosure of their eyes, lips and hands. I was kissed by the redhead throughout as the leather girl unbuttoned my shirt and the panther helped peel away my clinging satin trousers. Much ungainly jostling when my brash virilia are displayed; an assortment of lips close and pop. Trickly unzipping noises from the leather girl and a sudden bouquet of healthy flesh as the redhead bursts from her white romper-suit and softly straddles my chest with her warm and freckly thighs, arching backwards as the panther boy cups her (perhaps rather too heavy) breasts from behind, thus admitting between them the busy mouth of the now-naked bikie, which bobs contentedly over my loins, and for a few seconds every cell in my body shakes with ravenous applause. That is the part I love most (though of course the whole thing goes on for ages). From then on, too often, it seems to be just skin and hair, membranes, worthless and familiar stuff, mere leftovers, junk.

One night towards the end of this wet and uncompanionable March I made an early exit from Torka's — causing a tedious furore — and betook myself home at a smart pace along the midnight streets. My hand-made car, always something of a prima donna in winter, had once again been summoned to the Garage of Thieves, and I relished not at all a late safari down the Bayswater Road and Queensway, that unpoliced, forsaken strip of cruising Mediterraneans, sick vagrants, wheeling drunks and rare taxis. Only the previous week I had witnessed a squalid and vicious scene in the overlit forecourts of the Three Square Garage on Smith Avenue corner. A stooped, intent figure was steadily clubbing another to the ground, while beside them a fat Alsatian padded nervously to and fro. Torka's had in any case been well below par that evening. I was simply smuggled into a bedroom by a reasonably attractive, and reasonably resourceful, new couple (that was all there was, actually), emerging ninety minutes later too wearied and replete to have much patience with Adrian's querulous reproaches. Torka himself was conducting a heated debate with some interior decorator or ballet critic in the kitchen, so I merely slipped away. (I should have gone with Kane and Skimmer on that Brighton jaunt of theirs.) I felt tired and numb, and it was cold outside in the streets. As I turned off the main road and started threading round the squares, a sour rain began to fall.

Then I saw him. The stairwell of my block has a glass wall fronting the street, thin bendy glass — it shudders when the wind is up. On the top floor, outside my penthouse, his body pressing on the rainy window, stood the squat martyred figure of my foster-brother. I halted. Slowly Terence spread his arms. He looked like an eager child, his face pushed flat against the shopfronts of night. What does he see out there? How is his life taking shape? I closed my eyes for a moment and saw him fall through the glass, spinning end over end through the dark air. I opened my eyes and he was gone. I shivered. Is there enough to keep him here? Careful, Terry, careful: please be careful you don't break anything.

4: April

(i) Dirty boy, they're coming to
seek you out — TERRY

Guess what? I fucked a beautiful girl the other day.
(Guess what? I didn't really. April fool.)

But listen. Don't get any ideas — I mean, I haven't a
clue how it's going to turn out — only I think things
might be looking up.

Of late, I've fallen into the habit of telling myself that
the reason I don't seem to pull any girls these days is that
I don't seem to meet any girls these days. How could I,
even indirectly? (I don't happen to know any human
beings. Suck on that.) There are women I'm allowed to
talk to like café waitresses and bus conductresses, but
that's about it. No. I've never had any friends really,
just as I've never had anything I could use against people
who might hate me. I'm on my own here.

What else is there supposed to be?

Ex-girlfriends? They've all outgrown or forgotten me
now, and I've simply destroyed any vestigial affection in
the few hearts that once found a place for me, what with
my clumsy needs and my shimmering hands. Girls in
the street, randomly approached? Promising at first,
though testing for the bottle — one phone number taken
(came to nothing) and one invitation to the pub accepted
(came to nothing) — but it obviously isn't done much any
more, (a) because most people seem to be able to fuck
whoever the hell they like without resorting to it, and (b)
because it's so incredibly humiliating when you fail (three

snubs running takes the spunk out of your stride; and a passer-by protectively intervened once, which was also very horrible). Girls brought back to the flat by Gregory? Well, *pace* whatever he may tell you, Gregory hasn't got many friends either — except for that talentless old poof Torka, the various bumboys, cocksuckers and muffdivers who comprise his entourage, and those two upper-class cunts Kane and 'Skimmer': if Greg brings a girl home it's for a brisk and fastidious coupling, and if he brings back a party I feel strictly below-stairs and don't dare go up.

But listen. An amazing new temp has suddenly started working at the office. And I mean amazing by any standards, not just mine. The most striking thing about her, or at least one of the most striking things about her, is that she's got, for a start, these huge tits. But they aren't huge in any vulgar sense; they aren't 'high' or 'proud' or anything pushy like that. In fact they're entirely incongruous and endearing, merged as they are on to this disproportionately puny thorax, small hollow-looking waist, almost embarrassingly pert bottom, and reindeer legs. She often walks with her arms folded demurely over them, as if they oughtn't to be there, as if she didn't want them (I'll have them). I think she's got a really beautiful face. It looks at first like a hard, fashionable, affectless face, with its wide halo of tangly hennaed hair, stick-on nose, dark-daubed eyes, dimpled chin and wide but ungenerous-seeming mouth. If you go on studying her, though, which of course I go on doing all the time, you come to see many kinds of softened and soulful shapes beneath that sharp telegenic sheen. Her eyes, in particular, genuinely are violet — playful and tender-natured eyes too.

It all happened one morning last week. I was at my desk, tricked out with an unusually desperate hangover (I had even bought a tomato-takeaway as opposed to a coffee-no from Dino's, always a bad sign) and conducting a jangled, queasy hate-talk with Wark, the mad Stalinist. His floppy bum parked on my low filing-cabinet, and with a more than averagely plastic-and-offal lilt in his mealy new voice, Wark was deploring at length the proven inability of the urbane Lloyd-Jackson to make any stand against John Hain over the coming rationalization. I was just about to agree with him when the pooh-poohing ex-copywriter himself pushed open my cubicle door and, a shapely half-smile on his neat little lips, announced,

'Ah. Two birds with one stone — or "rationalization", as it's now called. We have a new temp. Now this is Geoffrey Wark ... and this is Terence Service.'

And this is she: in tight jeans and loose T-shirt, slouching (her arms folded, a habit of hers, as I said), a shy scowl on her face and a short-sighted ripple between her indigo eyes.

'And this,' he said, 'is *Jan*.'

How like Gregory he sometimes is, I thought, straightening in my chair. Wark nodded with emphasis in the direction of the doorway, then turned to gaze unflappably out of the window. What could I say that would adequately indicate my disaffection from the values here personified by Wark and the intelligent Lloyd-Jackson, my shrewd sympathy (and it wasn't a hypocritical one, either) with the casual, more strictly functional nature of her position here, the fact that I was nice, extremely friendly, and would make a fine husband? Leaning forward with arrested gusto, I said,

'Hi.'

'Hi,' she said, and smiled.

'How long,' I asked her, 'how long do you expect to stay here?'

Jan flared her oval nostrils. 'Weeell. A month or two.'

'That ought to do the trick. Come along, two more to meet,' said Lloyd-Jackson indulgently, preceding Jan through my door.

'See you,' I said to her.

'Right you are,' she said back.

'I'll take you through the motions in a few minutes,' Wark damply added.

Which is how it all began. Later that same morning I strolled from my hot tube into the main office, pretending to be in search of the back-invoices to check off against the sales-sheets I had nonchalantly brought along with me — 'Ooh, I don't know where those are yet,' Jan pleaded — 'Here, I'll show you,' I said — and together we stood over the cardboard concertina for perhaps ninety seconds, the air about us full of zestless currents, sudden shadows and pinpoints of bright humming dust ... Oh boy.

Do I dare? There's nothing for it.

A donnish, twinkly 'Let me take you to a place where cash can be exchanged for alcohol'? A frank yet slightly literary 'Why not let me take you to the pub'? A casually speculative 'Coming over The Crown'? An abruptly plebeian 'Fancy a drink?'?

It was 5.25 precisely. Wearing a smartly cut Forties suit and purple stockings (the first time we'd got a proper look at her legs), Jan was ransacking her nosebag-like reticule in the unsystematic, indeed purposeless fashion which habitually preceded her exit from the office; any moment now she would stand up, stretch and yawn, and march round the central table hooting goodbyes. Jan got on famously with the lame young permanent secretary and the old fucked-up permanent secretary, and she tended to hobnob with them briefly before flouncing off. This was her eighth day here: it was also, therefore, the eighth evening I had spent gazing at her in gingery longing from behind my half-shut door. On the previous seven occasions she had been firmly engaged in chat with her two friends, which had of course rendered any kind of direct approach utterly inconceivable (you're not in the Underground now, you know, or in the streets. 'You can't have a drink? You don't *want* to have a drink? Fine, fine. Well, see you all in the morning!'). On this occasion, though, Jan lingered vexedly over a seized-up powder case while Anne and Muriel backed out of the office door. They were gone. All clear. Oh no.

Any gentleman would have got up from his chair and sauntered out to Jan's table. You yourself would have leant over and offered to attempt the recalcitrant pink cask at which Jan's long fingers pried. The next guy would surely have taken it from her hand, clenched his jaw and turned to the girl with diffident surprise when the aromatic clam split open. No one human wouldn't have slumped with emotion when she looked up, smiled, and cried, 'Tarzan!'

'Fancy a drink?' I said.

She came. We went to The Enterprise in Fox Street, a popular, cavernous, ramshackle pub with dark marble walls and sad windows. I completed my grotesque routine of standing on tiptoe several drinkers from the bar, pound-note cocked, failing to attract the attention of the fantastically slow-moving and resentful landlord, turning to Jan every few seconds to tell her things like 'Just be a sec' or 'He didn't see me' or 'Christ', until, equipped with a pint of bitter, a whisky-and-lemonade for the lady, and no change, I followed Jan through the crowd of tall suited men, established her at an advantageous corner-seat, and raced down the stairs for a frenzied pee and bald-patch adjustment before rejoining her and our drinks at the table.

'All set?' she asked.

And I don't care what anybody says — I think I hit bloody good form and made a really very favourable impression. I was, quite fortuitously, wearing my best (i.e. newest) clothes, and it happened also to be one of those days when I felt I could look my face in the eye: less blanched in texture, fewer munch-scars on the lips, my hair behaving itself. Nor were my hands shaking that much — why, I lit three cigarettes for her, panting in gentle appreciation as I marked the relative staticity of the flame — and my voice was without the spastic tremolo it opts for in times of stress, shame or yearning. (As for Jan, by the way — she was a wet dream throughout.) And conversation? Well, it came and went. It came and went, but it seemed to be there.

God, it was so *nice*. Absurd — I felt changed almost straightaway. On the way home that night (the bridge, the Underground, the streets) I no longer stared ravenously at every girl I passed, as if their very existence were a wounding *fait accompli* directed at myself and the remains of my dignity. The pretty black lady who does the exit gate at Queensway, normally the theme of some jungly fantasy or other, accepted my ticket with an exchange of thankyous: I might have been anybody else, I might have been you. Turning off the main strip, I saw a couple canoodling in a dusty hotel porch and veered away in automatic repugnance and anger — until I slowed my pace, and thought about it, and wished them well. The streets themselves, which felt last week like a dead newsreel reshown nightly in my path, seemed softer and full of more varied shadows. I paused in the square, friendly leaves hurrying across my feet, and watched the bedsitter lights start to come on. 'Yes, I know,' I said. 'Of course she won't. I know, I know. But still.'

I even met Gregory in the kitchen (this is real high-society); he was looking very spruced-up and places-to-go but showed willing to linger while I poured myself a drink.

'How's life?' I said.

'Busy busy busy. How's yours shaping up?'

'It isn't. Everyone's paralysed at work still. And no one's fucked me recently, if that's what you mean.'

'Didn't you try that little one with big ears again?'

'Gita? Yes, I did. And she didn't want to again.'

'Bitch. Why on earth not? Who does she think she is?'

'Actually, I think I know why she won't now. She's so thick that she's forgotten she ever fucked me in the first place.'

'They are hell, aren't they. What do they think is the point of them if they won't do that?'

'Where are you off to?'

'Torka the town,' he said.

'Have a good time. Perhaps I ought to go queer like you.'

'Thanks. Are you staying in?'

'Yeah, I — ' But he picked up his cape and waved. 'Good night,' I said.

I stayed in. I drank whisky until ten, dined on packet ham and cold baked beans, had a long swampy bath, and went to bed. Hot, exhilarating dreams of striving and crisis, a short wakeful period between five and six, more dreams, and something else in the bed while I smoked an early-morning cigarette, as if my neglected body were at last coming alive again.

That day, too, I asked her to the pub, and she came.

Another really cute ploy I've hit upon is this: through a tissue of hints, mild playacting, duplicity, reticence, subterfuge and lies, I have managed to give Jan the impression that I'm fucking, or used to be fucking, or at any rate have at some point definitely fucked, Ursula! Such precepts are arguable, I know, but I've always gone along with the view that, first, the surest guarantee of sexual success is sexual success (you can't have one without the other and you can't have the other without the one), and, second, that the trappings of sexual success are only fleetingly distinguishable from sexual success itself. (Third, I'm all fucked up anyway, and this can't do me any harm. I am not a sexual success with women. I just *am not*. Gregory isn't either, particularly. He's just a success with sex.) So: the fecklessly beautiful Jan is swivelling on her swivel chair in the focal office area: leaning easily on the table by her side, his blue eyes bright, his strong arms folded, his ginger hair falling out, is the Trainee Seller, Terence Service, talking with vim and without a trace of condescension to the flower of the clerical staff — when, at exactly 12.45, in walks this other girl of mine, this chick, this broad called Ursula, whose curious, up-market good looks I allow Jan time to register as I blurt *Uh-oh* out of the corner of my mouth and spring up guiltily to introduce them (first names only), in confused apology, before sailing out with Urs — to buy her a large and nourishing meal. (And that's more, by the way, than Gregory does these days. The other week, apparently, they had a very depressing half-hour together in some sandwich bar near the gallery — he wasn't meant to stay out any longer, he said, and he even had to borrow 60p off Ursula to help pay for the lunch. Most heartening. Ought to find out the truth about that job of his.)

I suspect, anyway, that this Ursula ploy is telling soundly on young Jan, who has not once but twice questioned me about her (unjealously, alas, but with respectful interest) and has several times remarked on how 'really pretty' she was. (Girls always like the way Ursula looks, doubtless because she's got no tits.) I go hurt and wistful whenever she's mentioned. 'Yes,' I said yesterday, chewing on a large creased lip, 'it's sad that things aren't quite ... clicking between us the way they once used to.' Jan said, 'Oh dear.' I gazed out of the drizzly window. 'Yeah. But, hell, at least we're still friends.' (I feel tremendous when I say things like that; I feel like a mountain. It's far and away the sexiest I've been all year.)

And surely Jan's fast-escalating alcoholism must continue to hold me in good stead, must continue to be a source of true security and encouragement. *Christ* can that girl drink. She makes me feel virtually teetotal, and I'm fighting drunk, falling-down drunk, drunk out of my mind all the time these days. I now grant the full potency of the cliché, *as if it were water*. I've seen her drink three pints and four glasses of wine at lunchtime — and she's efficient and ethereal throughout the afternoon. She can drink seven or eight whisky-and-lemonades after work without blinking — then race out of the pub like a schoolgirl to catch her train. (She lives in Barnet, with her parents, thank God. 'Jan' is short not for Janice or Janet, as I'd assumed, but for Jane — she's posher than she lets on. A certain little fuck called Dave is mentioned more often than I'd like, but always in the perfect or pluperfect tense, and never except in retrospective subordinate clauses.) I'm entirely adamant about paying for every single drink she has in my company, of course — in order to nurse her guilt about not sleeping with me — and I've computed that I could take her to the pub *twice a day* for three-and-a-half months before going bankrupt. (I'm very scared about going broke, incidentally. 'Broke don't scare me,' I sometimes say. But broke does. Broke scares me shitless.) It won't be that long, though, will it? One way or the other, it can't be that long.

Jesus, I'm mad about her. Sometimes, when she smiles at me or calls my name without looking up, I just want to burst into hot tears of gratitude. I can feel the husky saline need trying to well up out of me, trying to get away. Sometimes, when I hear her muttering to herself as she sorts through her handbag, or letting out a little grunt of effort as she shifts her heavy typewriter, I sit tight in here, my teeth bared, actually wringing my hands. Apart from anything else she's incredibly funny, as well as inexhaustibly good-natured: for instance, she can mimic the ulcerous, monosyllabic Damon to a T, yet she's far and away the least nasty to him of anyone in the office and even makes me hesitate before twitting him in front of the girls or obliging him to run some pointless and humiliating errand. (Everybody here loves her too, naturally. Burns hides his fish and vinegar in a desk drawer; Herbert is always bending her ear with his bullshit — fat chance *he's* got; mad Wark tenderly forgives her most egregious clerical errors; and John Hain himself takes a few seconds out from sly self-advancement to admire her as she swanks this way and that.) And, oh God, her face, her eyes, that silly hair. What if I reached for her hand and she took it in hers, what if I put my arms round her

shoulders and she stayed still, what if she let me kiss her ...
with tongues. Meet me, O Jesus, meet me — and what
can her breasts possibly be like? *Damn*, I have to know
this thing; I'd give all I own sooner than not know it.
And what if, say, she let me, you know, touch them (you
can see her thimble nipples when it's cold and she's
especially prone to folding her arms in modest diagonals
across her chest), touch them, just like that, then perhaps
move on to — why not? — her tight stomach and dinky
little weapon of a bum and *oh no* her (can't bring myself
to say that word any more) ... would it be singed auburn
like her hair or just plain black or what, and how much
of it would there be, a prim wisp or a great swirling
mother of a bush that teemed right over her midriff or
what? — and would I get to stroke it and ... yes, that's
what I'd do all right, I'd go down on her, for as long as
she bloody well liked, for months, for good, I'd really set
up camp down there and make bloody sure she had a
great time so it wouldn't matter that much when I
didn't get a bonk, unless of course she was particularly
skilled at dealing with this sort of problem or had mastered
some foreign technique or just treated me with unusual
gentleness and sympathy or if she were very excited
herself and ... Good God, it's never actually occurred to
me before: do you think she actually *wants* to?

Take it easy. That really *is* a bit fanciful. And what do
you give a shit, at this stage, whether she *wants* to or not?
How often, really, do girls go to bed with people because
they *want* to? (You won't get anywhere that way, fat boy.
You never have.) Just do it, do it. Wheedle, intimidate,
bully, bribe; beg, sob, goad, nag; curse, threaten, cheat,
lie: but do it.

We were, for example (though I say it myself), in the pub
together only last night.

It was an emotional dusk, so gradual and welcome that
no one had thought to put on the lights and chase it away.
We'd already had three each, in our corner, and a tear-

fully numinous haze had begun to form between ourselves and everything else. Moistly I peered at Jan as she talked on, thinking that perhaps the last thing in the world I should do was make a pass at her — because what if there were no more evenings like this one, warm and drunk at nightfall, surrounded by the talk of friends and, outside, by the sound of slow rain and confident cars. I began to speak. I looked at her again, the small clear nostrils, the curved-down mouth, the tangy trace of half-moles and freckles along the outlines of her lips.

'Listen,' I said. 'Come back and have a drink at the flat tomorrow. You'll meet my brother, my foster-brother. I was adopted by his parents when I was nine. I had parents of my own but they got fucked up. I share the flat with him. He's called Gregory. You'll probably like him' (and probably fancy him too. Do you imagine I haven't thought about that? I have. I'll talk to him. I'll fix it. He wouldn't do that to me if he knew how much it meant). 'He's odd. He's also a total faggot, by the way. We don't get on now — I can't remember what getting on with him was like — but there was a time, there certainly was a time when I loved him ... '

I hardly ever see him any more. I miss him. He's the only friend I've ever had.

There was a time when I loved Gregory. I did. I loved him in my own way — but then anyone would have. What a boy. You didn't have to be what I was to be able to see what he was. The one who could accomplish all things: with him it wasn't even a question of daring — his transgressions were merely the accoutrements of his unthinking self, the phraseology of his charm and luck. As if daring could exist, anyway, in that soft-tempered land of airy white rooms, afternoon toast, and fat housekeepers.

He stole with ambition, with casual acumen — and *without getting caught*. He would loiter in the exit-gates of supermarkets, his duffle-bag groaning with chocolate and pop. He once stole a *football* from Macmillan's in Church

Street — simply cruised out of the place patting it up and down on the ground. There was another time when, just for kicks (he doesn't smoke), Greg was leaning over the counter to steal some cigarettes at the dumplike sweetshop near my school and was caught in mid-theft by the huge owner, who barred the door and stonily informed us that he was going to call the police, get them round, dial 999. Naturally we both lapsed into tears — me with a throaty, regular, doomed sobbing (I knew they'd get me in the end), Gregory with pitiful high-pitched wails as he wretchedly surrendered the ten-packet of cheap filters in hysterical remorse, begging and begging the man to let us go. As soon as he'd shouted and sworn at us to his satisfaction, the tobacconist did just that, unbolting the door and shoving us disgustedly into the street. I was still deep in tears when, a hundred yards down the road, Gregory turned to me with delighted, cloudless eyes, a packet of twenty Pall Mall Kings gleaming in his palm.

Where did he get those nerves? Where did I get mine? I stole too, of course, rarely, amateurishly, compulsively, and from home. I would rifle through wallets and hand-bags in the pure, unadorned hope of not finding anything, but usually appropriating it if I did. Past the crowded sitting-room tables, each a glossy Lilliput of silver and quartz — and there I'd be, trotting in panic up the stairs with something valuable and heavy weighing my pocket down as monstrous as a billiard ball. If I saw my foster-mother's purse fanned open on the kitchen dresser, a sac of adult richesse — then suddenly my fingers would be burrowing in the leathery lips. I never hid the baubles with conviction, never spent the money I stole. Why did I do it? — there must be a textbookful of reasons why. Once I provoked an unprecedented furore by making off with some pricey cruet from the dining-room mantel-piece. Almost immediately — to my sweaty horror — the alarm was loudly raised. I put the burning insect on a first-floor passage table and fled to the attic, where I crawled under a collapsed bedstead and listened for the staccato threshes and sterling trebles of the advancing posse. Dirty boy, they're coming to seek you out. I wanted to *die*, to die ... Gregory was alone when he found me. I waited for him to rally the others with a whoop, but instead he paused, crouched at the side of the bedstead, and slowly edged beneath it towards me. His face was as wet with tears as my own. 'Come down, Terry,' he said. 'We're not cross any more. It's all over now.'

And he had tenderness then, and real radiance, an extraordinary flair for boyhood and youth, as if he had cleverly worked out that these were the licensed days of his life when there was nothing he couldn't do — and get away with it, and be liked, and that this could never last. Gregory, Gregory, my opulent and legendary brother. I feel sentimental about your childhood because I can't feel it about mine. I see you streaking down the village road on your drop-handlebar bike as the girls come out from school, no hands; I see you at your birthday party, in your first long trousers too, joy flooding your eyes when all twelve candleflames turned into threads of leaning smoke, as if the four horizons were converging for your delight; I see you being driven off to your school in autumn, not waving, your head held up high, going without fear into that world of harm beyond the garden gates. It was wonderful, and I loved it as much as anyone.

What fucked you up? What changed you? Something did. Something has robbed you of all soulfulness and feeling and heart and left you the thing you are now, the little bundle of contempt, vanity and stock-response you pass yourself off as, all the stuff that simply got to you before anything else could.

Look at you, *cock*sucker, *scum*, with your bloody stupid twee old heap of a car, your laughingstock poof clothes, your worthless layabout job, your cretinous faggot friends, your sullen and ravening *money* worries, your pathetic outdated swank, your endless lies. Gregory is a liar. Don't believe a word he says. He is the author of lies.

Listen, if he fucks Jan I shall just have to arrange for him to be dead. I'll kill him, and her (I'll leave the country and start over). Oh Christ, perhaps the safest thing is for me to pay him not to, make him an offer (he'd take it — he's very broke). Or threaten him (I know I can beat him up. He's bigger than I am, but I don't care what damage is done to me. He does). Or agree to move out if he doesn't. Or promise to kill myself if he does. Hear this: if he fucks Jan — a casual athleticism, one on his list, might as well — my hatred will find some way to injure his life, to do his body harm, or to make him mad.

(ii) April is the coolest month
     for people like myself — GREGORY

I really must say a few words about this rather marvellously tarty girl that Terence has taken to bringing home with him from the office. Joan? Janice? Janet? — something ridiculous like that. A secretary, of course, or the discharger of untaxing clerical duties at his blacking-factory, dreadful ragdoll manner and wilfully barmaidenly voice, just the sort of slouching nobody one half-registers among you all in the clamorous streetscapes but hardly expects actually to meet. Interesting, I suppose, to see these city-ciphers in the flesh, and some minor refund for having a nonentity as a flatmate.

She's got one of those corkscrew haircuts ... Now it's normally axiomatic that the *slightest hint* of 'frizz' is enough to have me reaching for my thickest dark glasses. But I playfully admit that with young Janice here the effect really is quite fun in a hackneyed, sentimental way, combining with her small stupid features and clogged goldfish mouth to provide that look of orb-like vacuity striven for by portraitists of the Woolworth school — you know, unbearably cute mites, all gaze and pout, whose likenesses are hung, mostly, by representatives of the criminal classes on taffeta walls. (They're enjoying a camp revival at the moment, sponsored by such slow-witted phonies as Du Pré at the Merton Gallery. Three weeks? Four weeks?) Yet Janet's face has withal several symptoms of an interesting hardness — the tough creasing round the eyes, the occasional mean tightening of those lips — which, in my vast experience, argues for great daring and know-how in bed.

And then I expect Terence has told you about her absurd figure? Now normally, again, I like girls to have *small* breasts: the breasts I like are mild round concavities which unobtrusively swell to gossamer petallic teats. I can't bear women who push out all over the shop, like one-man bands. Great plates of blancmange the size of knapsacks, topped by curlicued sausage stubs — oh, wonderful; thanks awfully. I will at once concede, however, that Joan's breasts are frankly colossal (so big that she wears a brassière) and would be utterly sick-making on any other girl (Susannah, Mrs Styles, Miranda, etc., etc.). But there is an air of sweet disproportion about Joan's body, as indeed there is about everything to do with her. Such breasts shouldn't be where they are really, gawkily perched on a frail lattice of ribcage over that poor waist (thumbs up from the waist down, incidentally: long lean thighs, boyishly dinky derrière). She carries it all off with a certain style and, no, I admit it, I'm rather amused by her.

Take the first time Terence brought her back to my flat. It was a glorious mid-April evening and a burgundy dusk was slowly decanting itself through the high windows. I lay musingly on my bed, a goblet of Tio Pepe balanced on the muscular tabletop of my stomach, freshly showered, midway between taking off my day clothes and putting on my evening ones — i.e., naked, except for some fairly daring and extremely eventful white scants — and generally readying myself to whizz off to Torka's in my aggressive green car, which had that day been returned from the Garage of Thieves with a staggering bill. I sensed the usual drunken scuffling at the front door and was about to put down my glass and feign handsomely profiled sleep — until I heard voices, and a light female cockney mingling with Terence's didactic baritone. I sat up in wry anticipation as they climbed the stairs to my room: Terence, carrying a shiny bag full of cheap drink, and the Joan, a frizzy presence in his wake.

'Oh, sorry, Greg,' he said, tugging his eyes away from my barely clad form. 'Thought you'd be out. Just wanted some ice.'

'Come in, come in,' I indulgently drawled.

'Oh ... thanks.'

'Introduce, introduce.'

'Oh — uh, this is Joan, Joan, this is Gregory.' He turned to me helplessly. 'She works at work,' he said.

'Yur, what a dump. Never temped anywhere so *dead*.' And in she strode, past my bed right up to the penthouse window, on whose sill she coolly leaned, running her screwed-up eyes over my torso in candid appreciation. I in turn, meanwhile, allowed my stare to praise the contents of her billowing T-shirt, the stripe of brownishly exposed midriff between it and her bejeaned, sharp-boned pelvis (noted also, with distaste, the abnormally plump pubic hillock).

'Cor,' said Joan in that mock-common voice of hers, 'what a flash flat. How much's it cost you?'

I waved a hand in the air. '*Rien*. An heirloom. I merely pay the rates.'

'What do you pay then, Tel?' she asked her colleague. Tel? *Tel*?

'Half the rates,' he mumbled. Terence really was looking something like his very worst that night. His unpleasant face, with its long upper lip and crushed nose-bridge, seemed drained of all colour and life, further highlighting the remains of his hair, which fell in fishy red tails down his brow. His clothes were the usual bellowing *mardi gras*. He appeared to be quite pleased with himself, however; he was smiling furtively, and a dirty glint played in one of his revoltingly bright eyes.

'Well well well,' said Janice, turning to me, *'isn't* this posh.'

I held her gaze — and, as Terence lurched away into the kitchen, and as a defiant half-smile offcentred Janice's round mouth, I felt a familiar tremor riding down the paths between our eyes: suddenly the room was full of burgundy light, and suddenly it would have seemed the most natural and decorous thing in the world if Joan, slipping her T-shirt over her head, had knelt unsmilingly on the bed to delve with her hard lips in the busy curvatures of my scants. Had it not been for Terence, slopping explosively about in the neighbour room, she would have done so without the slightest hesitation. Of that I entertained no serious doubt. And neither did she, the slut.

'I'm so glad you like it,' I murmured, whisking her pussy to the boil. 'I do think it's rather beautiful.'

'Oh I do too. Beautiful,' she said slowly (and we all know where her eyes were now), 'beautiful, beautiful.'

'What a charming friend you have found!' I cried when Terence appeared in the doorway, holding the two glasses aloft like a waiter. 'Do bring her back here as often as she is prepared to come.'

'Sorry, Greg, can I get you a — '

But at that I sprang to my full height and, with smooth indifference, started to dress. Terence squired poor Janet down the stairs in alarm — he won't make it, I thought: no chance — and I shot off to Torka's, found the great man asleep and his flat almost deserted, teased Adrian until he went off to his room for a sulk, and then imaginatively ground myself empty (compliments of young Janice) to the bland flicks of Susannah's boring, amphetamine-verdured and in my view rather sandpapery tongue.

April is the coolest month for people like myself. Down comes the roof of my ritzy green car. Out burgeons my spring wardrobe. I have a £20 haircut. Champagne is more often than not to be found in my refrigerator.

Flowers garland my room. I walk in the park. Dreams of legendary summers hang about me in the air.

I leave the gallery early when it's fine — enfeebled protests notwithstanding — so that I can enjoy to the full these lengthening days before the burnt months take the town in their clammy hug. I motoi out with Kane and Skimmer to country hostelries. We get rich girls to bring picnics along, or if it's warm we all eat late on the pavements of Charlotte Street. At weekends there's houseparty after houseparty — croquet, tennis, Pimms on aromatic lawns. Ursula and I keep meaning to drive up to Rivers Court for a few days while the weather holds (she loves the open car), but my diary is far too full, as hers must be by now: April is when the debs are making friends. Henry Brine wanted to take me to Paris for his opening and I couldn't make room even for that. It's right, I think, to crowd one's youth like this. I hardly sleep at all once the season is underway, but everyone says I look as fresh as always. How do you do it? they say. There's no answer.

I only wish I could entertain more here in my flat. You've guessed why I can't, naturally ... I've *considered* making a virtue of him, featuring him as a kind of court dwarf, a mascot, a curiosity; I wouldn't need to dress him up, after all. Too embarrassing, though, and people would be sure to ask questions. Quite often, of course, I simply instruct him to get the hell out for the evening. But the ghastly thing is that he has absolutely nowhere to go, and I can't bear to think of him in some coffee-bar all night staring at his watch. It's far too depressing for me. God, what am I supposed to do with him? (I'd like to evict him. That's what I'd like to do. Now how would I manage that?) Perhaps, at my next thrash, he could come with that nice Janice of his, as a sort of double-act; Skimmer would be wild for her, I know — he adores tarts. She's even made the odd appearance in my own thoughts too, as a retrospective visual aid, during dull sessions at Torka's ...

Watch out, Terry, or I may have to have her!

Well, he never shall — so much is clear. Good Lord, has the boy any conception of what is happening to him these days? Has he no idea of the kind of impression he has started to make? And I don't just mean the more effusively horrible aspects of his appearance, the aspects he can't do much about. It's not hard to read certain people's lives in the way they look, and something dreadful and lasting and deep is going wrong with Terence Service. I didn't mind him last year, for some reason — he was like a big friendly dog to come home to. Now he's like a reptile, a quiescent, loathsome thing. He's drunk. He's drunk all the time, and he thinks you can't tell. He returns from the office at eight — he can hardly walk. His smile is sick and smug; his face is numb and slightly luminous — it seems dead (you can tell life is getting to him). You feel he must be hating something very much nearly all the time. Something is sizzling behind his eyes.

How has he made me hate him like this? Do you know? How has he landed me with this concerted, headache hate which makes me frown as if in pain when I pass him on the stairs or hear the fat-thighed *swish* of his cheap denim trousers, when we jockey head-on within the bathroom doorway and I go on into the land of his smells, when we sit up here together and the room slowly fills with the sound of his breath. Why do I let him roost on my life? Why don't I swat him from my brain like the flea he is? Why do I care?

You know why.

There was a time when I felt very differently about Terence. Yes, I loved him — and who wouldn't have? Trite though the sufferings of his early life seemed, they had reality enough; when he first came to our house they still clung to him like sad heavy clothes, and he never quite shook them off. Poor Terence, poor Terence, my dear old friend. I see you running from the school bus in tears, clutching your satchel to your side as if it were some worthless extension of your body to which you had by now grown miserably used. I see you being led back to your room by servants at midnight, your face exhausted by the staying-power of your dreams. I see you kneeling on the curved lawn, your body bent over with the strain of the past and your own colossal efforts to expunge it, the grass rippling scarily all about you, the trees wringing their hands behind your back, the clouds scudding away above your head, scudding away from you and all the terrors of childhood and hell. Here is my pity, duly wettened with your brother's tears — take it, take it.

I naturally expected to be teaming up with a compact, urban, taut-nerved little tike: not a bit of it (one reaches for one's Penguin Freud). Although he later turned out to be a frightful thief and sneak, Terry was from the start an abject, pant-wetting supplicant of the most token forms of authority. All the spirit, all the *licence* of childhood, seemed to have been confiscated from his imagination before he knew what childhood was, before he saw it couldn't last. There I would be — up on a glass-spiked wall stealing apples, out on the Green baiting the village yobs, off on my ten-gear racing-bike pursued by scandalized schoolgirls — and there would be Terence, uncertain, retreating, distressed that sudden possibilities had opened up in the world of harm about him. While I tossed hissing cherry-bombs in the air, flicked them through the letter-boxes of the disadvantaged and distraught, or buried them in soft dog-messes beside scrubbed and splendid cars, Terence would be off behind some wall or tree, his wrinkled eyes clenched shut, his hands held flat over his ears as if to keep his whole head from flying apart. While I, standing tall on private property, rained splintery death on neighbouring greenhouses and conservatories, he would look on in the posture of one cocked for flight; and while I laughingly lingered in the lane to relish the fury of gardener or housewife, away Terence would scramble to the fields, and one would then have the tedious job of coaxing him out of some ditch where he cowered and blinked.

Curious, inconsequential things spooked him: parkies, too-tall buildings, dressing up, boarded shopfronts, any sudden noise or movement. Curious, inconsequential things steadied him and made him feel at peace: small rooms, buses, very old people, policemen ...

Whereas I stole with care, precision and superbly classy daring — from shops, from institutions, from enemies — the young Terence's thefts were grubby, doomed and exclusively domestic. With him, plainly, it was all part of some bungling anal compulsion, quite at odds with the expressive chutzpah of my own romantic capers (in several ways I think I'm still a victim of Terry's potty-training). I remember one particularly uproarious bit of banditry involving a rather fine Cellini salt-cellar which Terence the Menace scooped into his hot pocket soon after I had returned from Repworth, my expensive prep school, for the Christmas holidays. Instantly the disappearance of the piece was established, the culprit wearily agreed upon to be Terence, and a servant sent to get the boy and bring him forthwith to the Ridings, sternly arrayed in the library, wondering about some vague form of punishment — and all trying like mad to keep straight faces. But wait: the larval Moriarty had gone into hiding! We undertook a search of the house and quickly cornered Public Enemy Number One in the north attics, where he had crawled beneath the chassis of a warped bed. I was the first to discover him and raise the cry. His explosive confession and bawled apologies soon had us all in stitches.

Of the many singular and disconcerting things about my foster-brother — his graphic sense of his own inadequacies, his dreary obsession with psychological weather, his resentful craving for approval and affection, the way his nature seems to vulgarize even the very real horrors that shaped it — I immediately settled on one trait as being absolutely fundamental to his make-up. His humour was, from the start, always ironic. Ironic — never gay, fantastic, mirthful, relieved, outrageous: but ironic.

(Not that he was ever actually *funny*, mind you.) 'My shoes, they're too tight — they hurt more every day,' I said one morning. 'Growing pains,' Terence murmured. Once he and I managed to shirk some Sunday School outing and Mama self-righteously made us go and visit a retired nanny of mine in the village. 'Well, what do you expect?' he said as I grizzled all the way there: 'This isn't a Sunday School outing, you know.' Allied to that, I assume, was his instinctive and unthinking fidelity to truth, as if to lie were to guarantee one's personal cubicle in hell. Whereas I made no secret of my love of fabrication, my unquenchable thirst for falsehood, the truth would come blurting out of his mouth, no matter the circumstances, no matter the cost. On the few occasions when veracity would have been actually suicidal as well as morbidly perverse, adrenalin-heavy fibs crept from him like persecuted nomads, and his eyes became woebegone and doomed. He never could lie. No one believed him. This was yet another sickly precocity in the denatured world that took the place of his boyhood.

Who stole it from him? Somebody did. Or he gave it away. While you and I, the children, pushed off into the sea, into the thunder and the sunshine, he remained a melancholy, beckoning figure on the shore, lost in the abrasive hiss of shingles. There you are, Terence — I assimilate your past, its pathos and its fears. But now your past is of no use to you or to anyone, a hindrance, second-hand, trash; your pathos is an unmanly and demeaning thing, mawkish, banal and sour. It is why you have no friends or anyone who would protect you; it is why you will never be good at your job or anything else you try to do; it is why you're so neurotic, so very nearly mad; it is why your hair falls out and your teeth die; it is compounded of self-pity, self-disgust and self-love, and it is why *nobody likes you.*

Moreover: 1. His messiness. A common enough sight, the

sedentary Terry poking a cigarette out into a quite untarnished ashtray. Where can all the ash-droppings be? On the floor, on the chair, in his lap, hair, ears? 2. What you might call the flexibility of his personal hygiene. He scums up the bath no more than two or three times a week — though always, hilariously, on Fridays. I'm pretty certain he smells. Witness, if you please, the shattering pong from his room. 3. His climbing alcoholism. The drinks I don't mind having about the place include champagne, Tio Pepe, the lighter liqueurs and certain costly wines. And what is my flat cluttered up with? *Beer*, disgustingly cheap plonk, 'barley wines', domestic sherry, cut-price spirits — and Terence himself, boring, burping, blundering, baying. 4. His insolent sloth. *He's* the one who's forever preparing those plastic snacks — I always eat out — but does he ever clear up his mired tins and splayed cutlery? *He's* the one with rotting clothes, caked boots, and dandruff, but does he ever wield the hoover? (And imagine, too, my startled revulsion when an item of his chaotic laundry invades the pristine galaxy of my own.) 5. His vile drugs. As an *aficionado* of hashish — which he (wouldn't you know?) calls 'shit' — rank and incriminating odours are in perpetual flux from his room, which is itself a Hades of resin-scrapings, twisted cigarette-papers and nicotine-moist tubelets of cardboard. (The drugs I like are cocaine and mandrax — both far too expensive for Terry.) 6. His presence, the fact of it, the continuing fact of it.

Why doesn't he just get out. Get out. Get out, Terry. Get out of my room, get out of my flat, get out of my town, get out of my world, get out of my life and never come back again.

5: May

(i) Perhaps there *is* a solid bottom to
my life beneath which I will never
be allowed to fall — TERRY

Summer is well and truly on its way, which means I've
been an adult for almost two years now. And for the first
time it's all starting to look faintly possible. Waking early
in my northbound bed, I smoke cigarettes and watch the
morning shadows rearrange themselves across the rooftops.
In the evenings I sit and read and drink at my desk until
the dregs of the day have been tapped from the room.
Then, sometimes, I go out for a walk, last thing, to watch
the foreigners. Yes, I think, I can cope with a certain
amount more of this — not much more, maybe, but more.
Even the rush-hour streets look purposeful nowadays;
everyone willingly connives at this seasonal trick the world
has of seeming to start all over again.
   Last Saturday morning I was at the street market in
the Portobello Road, in search of a cheap electric kettle
for my room (Gregory bitches when I use the kitchen
early. He says he needs his sleep. Big deal. Who doesn't?
I even need mine). That fucked-up hippie I've seen about
the place was there too. He stood by my side at the tinker's
stall with two roped suitcases in his hands. Did they buy
tools? he asked the scarved gyppo behind the barrow. No,
they never bought tools. *Never.* Some sort of dehydrated
protest tottered from the fucked-up hippie; his chapped
lips were stained with flecks of vomit and undigested food
(and I thought *my* hangovers were bad). He wandered off
in his damp overcoat down the crowded streets, my age,

another whole shelf of his life just given away. I thought: I am not like that; that will never happen to me. Who knows? Perhaps there *is* a solid bottom to my life beneath which I will never be allowed to fall. And so for the time being I no longer wonder who will protect me when I am poor and bald and mad.

'Here, I'll tell you what you want to do,' said Mr Stanley Veale, the Union Regional Secretary, in his immensely calm and sinister voice.

'What do I want to do?' I asked.

Veale looked cursorily at Mr Godfrey Bray, the Union Regional Under-Secretary, and continued, 'You want to become Clerk of the Chapel here.'

'Why do I want to do that?'

'Because you want to not get fuckin' sacked, is one thing you want.'

This is making me nervous. As it is I'm sitting here in my cubicle with a mouthful of chewing-gum, a fag in either nostril, a paperclip on every finger-nail (and a ruler up my bum). 'Won't I?'

'No way. Not for three years you won't be, until re-election, and you'll be in line for Father then if you don't fuck it up. That's a long time for us here, the redundancies we got here already.'

'Twenty per cent in this Region,' said Mr Bray.

'This is right, Mr Veale, isn't it,' I said, 'that if we get Unionized a couple of us are going to get aimed?'

'Course. At least two of your five Sellers will be aimed. Definitely. They've got to be aimed so the rest of you can get Union rates. If they were already in the Union they couldn't be aimed. That's why you want to do things for us now. Do things for us now and there's no way you'll get aimed when you go Union.'

'Really? Does John Hain know about all this?'

Veale laughed. 'Who's he?'

'John Hain. The Controller.'

'Oh yeah?'

At this point Mr Bray, who was clearly so thick that he could hardly breathe, produced a notebook from his lumpy patch-pocket and said, 'What about training?'

' ... What about it?' I asked.

'Have you had any?' said Veale.

'Well, I'm sort of a trainee here.'

'We *know* that. It says it on your form. Look: "Trainee". Gor, he's really brilliant, this one. I mean you don't have to be ... Keir Hardie to work that one out.'

'Sorry.'

'Have you received a training course in Selling?' continued Mr Bray.

'No.'

'Shorthand and typing, anything of that kind?'

'No.'

'Apprentice work in the provinces?'

'No.'

'Anything?'

'No.' But I've got ginger hair and my dad killed my sis.

'That's bad,' said Mr Bray. 'Stanley?'

'Of course it's bad,' said Mr Veale. He closed his wet lustrous eyes. 'They're all bad here — no offence, Terry. None of you here should be fuckin' Selling. You know that. You're keeping real Sellers out of work. You, this lot couldn't sell a pass without having a conference about it. People you got here, makes me sick, you know? Tumblebum can pick up the phone without his ear aching, so what does he become. He becomes a Seller. That's his profession. That's what he does.'

'Why me?' I said.

Mr Veale stood up. He gazed out into the alley, his albinoid but coarse features puffed by the yellowy light. 'I come here, I got to see everybody here. I got to see the Dep. Controller, Mr Lloyd-Jackson. He sits back in his chair, you know? — he can deal with people like me, dealt with people like me all his life. Sarcastic, having a little laugh on us. He thinks we're thinking: "Mr Lloyd-Jackson, difficult gentleman to deal with, always was."

But we're not any more. We're thinking: "Ooh, saucy little fucker, eh? Hullo, we got a saucy little fucker here, have we?" ' He held his hand up to his cheek and squinted down an erect forefinger, which twitched. 'Bang bang,' he said. 'Think about it. I'll phone you.'

I said, 'Thanks. Thanks a lot. I feel the same way, you know? These people — ' I gestured vaguely ' — what do I give a shit about them.' They won't protect me. 'You want rights for people who don't have any rights. I want that as well. I'll do all I can for us.'

I will, too. I don't know what it is he wants me to do yet. But whatever it is I'll do it.

On top of all this, I've managed to kick wanking, which is a great relief for me and my cock both. Now I don't say that I'm never going to wank again (I mean, who the hell knows?); it's just that I've allowed my libido to lapse into the kind of unpicked-on quiescence that it seems to be demanding of me these days. 'Okay,' I've told my cock, 'you win.' For the time being anyway (until I really need you). I won't bully you any more. I won't wake you up nights and give you a bad time. I won't beef and moan and nag when you don't do like I say. You go your way — me, I'll go mine. No hard feelings.

(No feelings at all.) But it was getting ridiculous — the recriminations, the scenes. I remembered all those wanking contests I used to have with Gregory and others when I was young. Ready? Go! It was like squeezing a pee along a tube, nothing to do with desire at all, just a thing that your body was ever-willing to do for you. Later on, of course — after you've had real sex — wanking becomes largely a matter of substitution, but it still has its own role, its own autonomy. (Like I always maintain, a wank is bound to be slightly disappointing if what you really want is a fuck. But it's unbeatable if what you really want is a *wank*.) 'Honestly!' I would shout at it, 'I don't want a fuck, I swear. I want a *wank*.' 'You're just saying that,' it would reply — and of course it was absolutely right. I tried to think (as I always used to do when I wanked) about those ten or eleven strange girls who had let me go to bed with them — had let me put this bit of tendon right up inside their bodies for no other reason than that they wanted me to. Where were they all now? What had they all become? It wasn't sexy; it was extraordinary and heartbreaking that they had left me so far behind. I could remember their bodies — I could remember what each one's face, tits and cunt had been like; but I couldn't remember, couldn't even lyingly imagine, why they had wanted me enough to let me do that to them. (They won't any longer. I know. I checked.) And it was sad like sad sex is sad — all that as well. Naturally, I gave pornography a whirl, gave pornography a pretty thorough outing (in a consultative capacity, as it were). I spent practically half my wages on nude magazines. I went to bed in a great glistening sea of those law-breaking bestiaries. But who *were* all these people? I don't know them, they don't like me, we won't meet, that won't work. Plus I couldn't get a bonk, which didn't help.

Do I sound at all steadier? Probably not, but I feel it. For the first time in months — for the first time since that day when all the women on the planet got together and made a rule never to fuck me, and all the men gathered somewhere else to see if they could make me a tramp — I feel that I've stopped sliding, found a toe-hold on the last rung, on the last patch of briars before fuck-up gulch.

I think Jan is going to go to bed with me. Now I know that sounds rash, I know I'll probably regret ever having said it, but *I think Jan is going to go to bed with me.*

Until last week, progress was being made at more or less the usual rate (i.e., hardly at all, hardly any progress), with me as relentlessly considerate and generous as ever — and as awkward, and as ineffectual — and with Jan showing me no more, really, than a single facet of her sunny and straightforward nature. Obliquely but often did I attempt to gouge some past trauma or present misery out of her (some item that the Fear and Loathing Kid could plausibly be impressive about), yet it soon became clear that her life was disastrously free of neurotic content — got on with her parents, no particular worries about boys it seemed, the job would do for a while, she just wanted a bit of fun. Well, *fun* is hardly what I was brought here to give people. Fun I'm not — that much is certain. What am I then? What have I got going for myself? I don't know, but such things must have been quietly intruding on my thoughts last Wednesday evening, when this extraordinary scene took place.

As a matter of course — it being past 5.30 — we were in the pub, and, no less routinely, it being past 6.30, both utterly polluted with drink. Jan appeared to be telling me a very funny story about her younger brother Simon. Evidently Simon was in big trouble at home because, having just been given his first bank-account, he was already £10 overdrawn; after a long interrogation from Jan's dad, this Simon admitted that he'd spent his entire term's allowance on the boarding-school whore — and got the *clap*, too. (Sexy talk, this, I thought.) 'How old is he, your brother?' I said when I had stopped laughing. 'Fifteen!' said Jan, as she also completed her laugh. 'That's how old my sister would have been,' I said, without volition (it isn't even true, damn it). 'What happened to your sister?' said Jan. 'My dad killed her,' I said.

Whoosh. On the two or three occasions when I have said that in my life, I've always cried, inevitably, as inevitably as I wince at sudden pain or gasp at the splash of cold water. I didn't cry now. Perhaps I planned it. (I don't blame me.) Tears queued up. I said,

'Yes, he killed her.'

'Oh no,' said Jan.

Yes, he killed Rosie. He used to hit her from the moment she was old enough to hit. You would hear her crying then, *whack*, him hitting her. And so of course she stops crying. That's what babies do when you hit them.

They go quiet at once, shuts them up straightaway. But *she* cries louder, he's obviously on to a good thing here, plenty of reasons to go on hitting her. When she had grown up a bit, when she'd become a person instead of a thing in a crib, I thought he would stop. He didn't stop. She was so good-natured and no trouble — you couldn't see any reason for it. People knew. She was on the At Risk list from the age of four. But they didn't stop him.

'Oh God,' said Jan.

On the last day I met her from school. I knew it was the last day, she knew it was the last day. She always knew. I saw her running across the playground clutching her satchel like some extra bit of her. She ran everywhere. We didn't talk about it, we never did — we were too ashamed — but we both knew. I just said I'd go home first — she had somewhere else to go before she went home. She seemed cheerful, as she always did. She bit her lip for a moment, but only because she could tell I was hating it all. Then, clutching her satchel, she *ran off*. I felt panic for the first time. Stop running! I shouted after her. Why are you *running*? But she waved and went on running. That night he killed her. What sort of people do that?

'Oh, *fuck*,' said Jan.

— Then something broke and I lurched back in my chair. I stared at her with what felt from my end like pure consternation. 'I'm sorry,' I said. 'I'm going now.' And I stumbled from the pub into the wet air, already crying, and for whom? For my lousy self. (Oh, I've got so little resilience in my nature. This being alive, it's killing me. I'm just not up to it.)

I sat on a bench in the piazza. It was raining. She wouldn't come then. Windblown newspapers got too drunk to move in the wet. She wouldn't come. What about her hair? What about *mine*? The rain intensified, stroking the square in gusts.

'I'm all fucked up,' I said.

She put a hand on my cheek and I leant against her. 'Oh no,' she said, 'oh God, oh fuck.'

And since then — well, she's just been wonderfully sweet to me, is all. And I can see it's changed now. In the office, she looks at me with such gentle concern, such protective care, that I almost gag with emotion, and have to duck quickly into my cubicle and feel the thick rotundity of the earth melting all about me. I'm so sentimental these days that I squelch when I walk. We still have our drinks together, move past each other twenty times a day without our eyes meeting, but it's all changed now (thanks, Rosie. Is there anything I can do for you?). We're going to have a big night out on Friday week. It's Jan's last day here (she's moving on. Temps do that — they move on. Temps *fugunt*). They fuck, as well, sometimes, apparently. She's agreed to come back with me to the flat after our big night out. You might say that, in some respects, it's all fixed.

Except that Gregory has got *flu* — a real lulu of a flu too, I'm delighted to say. It was all quite hilarious. One morning early this month I had popped upstairs for some milk, and as I moved unseeingly past Greg's bed I heard this long theatrical *groan* from behind me. I turned (wondering how good I looked, which is always the first thing I wonder when I see him). Comically, he had half-levered himself from the caress of his satin sheets, and was spasticly spreadeagled over the edge of the bed, his weak knuckles almost grazing the carpet. 'Gug,' he said; his shiny, downward-hanging hair swayed in the early sunlight. 'Urgh,' he added. 'Echt.'

'Gregory!' I said.

He looked up at me like an old man in a film about the pitilessness of the jungle. 'Terence ... What's happening to me?'

I helped him back into his cot (what silkily bisexual skin he has) and obeyed his croaked request to call a doctor. I called the surgery of Willie Miller, the facetious private practitioner who handles both of us (I'm quite posh when I'm ill) and who promised Gregory a visit that day. Then, in a likeable onset of frank and sudden greed, my foster-brother blandly asked me to make him some breakfast before I left for the office. Quite flattering, I thought, affectionately explaining that I would be late if I did (Greg generally has some faggot mixture of yoghurt, prunes, saffron, perfume, etc., but he's too broke for that now and has resorted to a slice of toast and a 'coddled' egg. About as faggot as you can get with eggs, this dish involves skilful use of a wet dishcloth and takes about fifteen baffling minutes to prepare).

'I'm sorry,' I said. 'Are you sure you'll be okay?'

'Sure? I've no idea. I haven't a clue.'

I offered to make him a cup of instant coffee, but he flailed his arms at the very mention. 'I'm really sorry,' I said. 'I *have* to go.' I held my breath for a moment. 'But if you really need something in the middle of the day, ring me, and I'll come back from the office at lunchtime.' He frowned, not unkindly. The room gradually went red. 'Prescriptions or something you might need,' I added.

'That's very sweet of you,' said Gregory.

I love it when he's ill. Watch the way he treats me. His looks, impressive for their testimony to good health as much as for their formal beauty and proportion, recede to the back-benches of his presence, and the wistful, white-lying, weak, incestuous, decadent, hopelessly impractical self edges out like an alien into the strange air. *My* looks suddenly seem sensible and hard-wearing. From a faltering, sparse-feathered vulture I am transformed into a game and stalwart sparrow, with my efficient short legs, heavy-duty trunk and no-nonsense face. Not only do I feel quite good, I feel quite nice — and tremendously reassured, of course, that he still likes me sometimes, that I still have a handclasp with a family, that there are still some people on the planet who would prefer me not to be a tramp.

I seem, anyway, to be behaving quite flashly with him these days, partly out of genuine high spirits. What is it that makes us want to see our loved ones done down? That day, as cool as you like, I did not ring Gregory from work, but what I did do was ring Ursula and tell her to ring him. (Ursula sounded all right, by the way, apart from appearing to be out of her fucking mind with every second thing she said. I've got to talk to that girl, or talk to someone about her.) Jan was away that day as it was, and I could hardly contain my eagerness to be out of the office and home. In addition, John Hain was in hiding, and the officious Wark had been taken to the Dental Hospital (practically on a stretcher) to have the horrifying and deeply mysterious condition of his mouth attended to, so it was quite simple for me to strut nervously away at five.

I had entered the flat and was taking off my coat and reorganizing my hair when Gregory called piteously down the stairs,

'Terry — is that you … ?'

'You bet,' I said.

'Come up,' he moaned.

I expected him to be splayed dramatically on the bed, or clawing for that last vital pill, but he was reclining drolly on what he calls his *chaise-longue*, his arms folded across the poof-pageboy ruffles of his kaftan, and looking, as they say, thoroughly sorry for himself. It was a spotless evening, and many aeroplanes strained cheerfully through the empty sky.

'Hello,' I said. 'How are you? How was your day?'

'What day?' he asked.

'That bad, eh?'

'Perfectly frightful. This morning seems as far away as childhood. I'm so weak I can't do anything to pass the time. And so the time won't pass.'

Quite bucked enough by this agreeably rehearsed-sounding plaint, I nearly dropped my Wine Mart bag when Gregory then said, with an interrogative lilt,

'Terry, stay up here this evening and cheer me up. Go on. I can't tell you how depressed I am. Tell me about your day, for instance. How was it? Now get yourself a drink and sit down properly. Tell me everything about your day from the moment you walked out of the door to the moment you walked in again. Right. You walked out of the door. What happened next? God, this is better already. Tell me — '

So I tell him about the day, obedient to my usual policy of making everything sound slightly more humiliating and prospectless than it actually is (for ironic purposes, and so as not to dispirit him about his own job, which sounds really awful despite Greg's terrifying hints that he might, at any moment, inherit the entire concern), recounting my modest vicissitudes, unpeeling this segment of my life to his oblique and only half-curious gaze, opening up the hackneyed trials of my life to amuse a sick prince for an hour at evening. Then we played backgammon (I won, natch — £2·40 — but he never pays and I don't mind), ate the kebabs I went out to buy (I treated him), watched television, talked.

'When you're well again, Gregory,' I said, uncapping my second litre of Château Alcoholic, 'will you do me a favour? Will you let me have the flat to myself one evening?'

'And to what end?' he asked, rather grandly, sipping his Perrier water. It was late, and by this time we were friends again.

'Well, as a matter of fact, I was thinking of entertaining a young ladyfriend here.'

'Ah. Whom? Young Joan?'

'Not Joan, you fool. Jan.'

'Yes, she is rather fine, I must say. Have you not ... already?'

'Have you gone out of your mind? I mean, no, I haven't. Where could I, anyway? She lives with her parents in the sticks somewhere.'

'Yes, I do see. But she's given you reason to believe you could have your way with her, granted an enclosed space and something to lie down on? I must say, she doesn't look like the sort of girl you'd have to take to the opera *too* many times.'

'What do you mean?'

Then he said, '*She* won't give you any trouble. She's been playing hide-the-salami since she was five. You can always tell. My God, that night you brought her back here and I was lying on the bed? I've never seen anything so brazen. You could *smell* it. I tell you, Terry, she was absolutely *dripping*.'

And for a moment he was the one who looked ugly and mad, and if I could have rendered him dead at that moment I would have done so with a snap of my fingers. '*Christ*, Gregory,' I said, 'what the hell are you talking about?'

'Just stop pussyfooting, you ass. There's no problem with girls like that. Just get there before somebody else does.'

'It won't be you, will it,' I said quickly. 'Promise me.'

'Oh don't be so wet.'

'Promise me.'

'Oh all right. Now let's talk about something else.'

'Ursula.'

He turned away. 'I don't want to talk about Ursula,' said Gregory.

(ii) What other things will happen
     to you now you're old? — GREGORY

Summer is well and truly on its way, it bores me to report. A span of trite sun heats me awake each morning in my vast bed. The empty afternoons fill the world with beach fatigue as the sun completes its slow lob across the sky. At evening, in the thin final glow, the skyline takes forever to become itself, as if the vapidly grinning day had drained it of all life, all secrets. Cities are winter things.

And I've got the flu which I think is bloody unfair

considering I took all my vitamins throughout the winter and successfully spurned the foul ethnic bugs that kept poleaxing Terence and everyone else I know. It is, moreover, a vicious little weapon of a flu, the most resourceful and tenacious flu ever to have made me its home. Five days ago I awoke with a body full of heavy water, as if my internal mass had condensed overnight. At first, staked out there among the satin cushions, I rather halfheartedly put it down to the alcoholic and hallucinogenic excesses of the previous evening (Muscadet and mescalin too freely quaffed). Likewise the intensified aura of lassitude and disgust which was the last guest to leave my memory of the night before (Adrian and the redhead too freely indulged). But when I tried to hoist my body out of bed, a great dark hand reached out from behind and tugged me back on to the pillows. I couldn't move! Providentially Terence was busy in the kitchen — doubtless it was his transit that woke me — so I cried out to him, and got him to ring the doctor at once, cook me my breakfast, dash out for the papers, fetch me the card table and generally make me comfortable. I had to ring the gallery myself: the Styles woman groaned rudely on, and kept saying how 'inconvenient' it all was. Bitch. (Willie, our London GP, was on the other hand very sweet and reassuring, and gave me lots of those strong sleeping-pills I like.) And since then I've been absolutely out! I just haven't any strength! Mountains crack as I bear the cup to my lips. The building holds its breath when I reach for my dressing-gown. The walk to the lavatory is an insomniac hike through ulterior corridors and runic rooms.

I'm so *bored*. I've read all the readable books in the flat — including some from Terence's lurid shelves — and playing patience is far too effortful. I look all day at the telephone but it just beams and beams, its arms smugly folded. Skimmer is abroad, and Kane is working away at that merchant bank of his. I rang Adrian, who said it served me right and gloated idiotically about the whole thing. Susannah said she didn't want to catch it herself, and of course I couldn't imperil the distinguished Torka. Yesterday afternoon, when I was feeling particularly sorry for myself, I rang Mama, who naturally offered to come to London on the next train; but after a long chat about her foolish husband — it's potholing now — I felt up to going it alone. One boon. With that weird prevision, with that almost supernatural empathy which she and I have always enjoyed, Ursula rang me *on the very morning that the flu struck.* She has been coming in every day to cook me my lunch, tidy my room, fatten my cushions and whatnot. She is in marvellous form, and sometimes, if she happens to be pottering round my bed and I happen to be feeling rather frisky, I clutch at her tiny hips and we tumble about giggling and grappling as of old. For the rest of these slow spring days, however, it is just me and the windows, a pale, affectless world of ceilings, skies, and my heartbeat.

It is perhaps, then, in the spirit of false humility that illness and isolation produce that I have started allowing Terence up here in the evenings.

It is six o'clock. I am finished with any dozing that the afternoon might have let slip, and now stare moonily out of the penthouse window. At ninety-second intervals, tinselly aeroplanes wobble upwards through the bland air. The room darkens and I make no move for the light. The world curls up and dies. Only sad memories linger. The silence is climbing, climbing — as if at any moment it might burst into harsh laughter.

Terence comes home — with a sigh of the lift, the determined approach of his footsteps, the hello of his key in the door, the arc of light that comes up the stairs as he flicks on the hall lamp and noisily divests himself of duffle-coat, brolly, satchel.

'Greg, are you awake?' he'll call.

'I think so,' I reply.

'Hi. How are you? How are you feeling?'

'Come up.'

Rather touching, this. My illness seems to make it easier for Terry to express his full concern for me. All the other things that clutter up our dealings, all the envy, awe and hero-worship, have taken a back seat for a while.

'How was your day?' he asks, chugging up the stairs so that he enters my vision like a figure being wound on to a film reel. The creased ginger hair, the face (which at least looks quite honest and decent, apart from those disgustingly fizzy eyes), the boxy shoulders and upper torso, the sovereign of pee-stain on the crotch of his jeans, the incredibly short legs (I'm amazed they reach the ground), the 'shoes'.

'Dull and long. How was yours?'

'Dull and long. Except there was this quite funny bit in the afternoon when — '

And then he's off — off on some hectic anecdote about one or other of the cretins, louts and pseuds who work in that frightful dump of his. Terence really does catch them all quite well, and often amuses me with scarcely credible tales of the resentment and obstructiveness that characterize his strange little life (the firm is joining Yobs' United: it all sounds risibly squalid). He drinks his undrinkable wine and gets me my Tio Pepe or Abroja with crushed ice, I make him cook me an omelette — or send him running, as fast as his legs will carry him, to the take-home bistros and kebab-houses in Queensway — we watch television on my powerful Grundig, I take a few pounds off him at backgammon (my game is fast, fluent and aggressive, his paranoid and cramped), he drinks on, we play chess, we talk.

'Tell me,' I asked him the other night, 'have you made any progress with young Joan.'

'It's not *Joan*. It's *June*.'

'June then,' I murmured. I was building up a witty attack on Terence's left flank. He had fianchettoed, and as usual all his pieces were clustered inertly round his king.

'Well, I haven't had much of a chance. I was going to ask you about that, actually.'

'Oh?' I brought my second rook into play, revealing a delightful combination with the white-square bishop.

'I wondered if, when you're well, you might let me have the place to myself one evening.'

'I expect that could be arranged.' By this time Terence's king had been poked out of its nook and was making its usual distracted diagonal dash across the board towards me. 'I take it she's willing. She looks a complete pushover to me.'

'Gregory,' said Terence seriously, 'will you promise me one thing?'

'What's that?' I interrupted a series of brutal checks to fork and capture his queen with my knight.

'You won't make a pitch at her yourself.'

'Oh don't be so wet. And so ridiculous. I don't fuck the lower classes. Now let's talk about something else.'

'All right. Let's talk about — '

'Wrong play,' I said calmly. 'Grigoric suggests taking the pawn.'

In my view, of course, the whole idea of Ursula coming down to London like this was an utterly preposterous one, and I think Mama should have sat on Mr Dick in no uncertain manner when he first hatched his frisky little scheme. One way or another, though, a large part of life at Rivers Court has involved remoulding, intercepting or sometimes just 'going along with' my father's banal whims simply in order to get things done. The family needs a holiday and we all decide on Greece: a book or pamphlet on this clime is left by his bed and the next morning he is loudly making reservations into a brandished telephone. He suddenly gets a passion for woodwork and handicraft: instead of allowing the French furniture to be cannibalized, we have him help with the retimbering of our scheduled barn, where he harmlessly makes a fool of himself among the stooped village carpenters. And so when he claimed that he'd need a secretary for this absurd book of his — I think the project has already been abandoned — it seemed cleverly opportunist at the time to offer Ursula herself as his future clerical auxiliary. At least she would gain some sort of qualification, which as we all know 'helps' these days, and at least the plan put paid to the intolerable notion of having some overpaid frump sitting about the place all day with nothing to do. The old boy was as easy to talk round as ever, and in fact Ursula was a good deal less keen on the idea than he was by the time she was dispatched to the Great Wen. That was six months ago ...

During the semi-delirious phase of my illness I dreamed of her almost constantly, hurtful and saddening dreams that left me with a sense of irretrievable loss, as if something had gone wrong with the world while I slept which could never be put right again. Occasionally I would wake during her actual visits to my flat (she has her own key, the darling), and I would be unable to tell if she was really there and talk nonsensically — the words all in the letter A of dreams — until she hurried to my side. One morning last week, the sight of my suffering distressed her so much that she melted into tears; I held her painful, shuddering body in my great arms as her bones contracted into exhaustion and as I watched the clever new dreams marshal themselves once more on the white ceiling.

I can't bear to dream of her small and unprotected evenings over there by the river, that lonely district of tall, set-back houses and the treacly nocturnal glaze under which the Thames seeps, that beetling drainpipe-splinted hostel, past whose yellowish windows flit the wraiths of pale factotums, dust-whorled typists and submarine stenographers. She is too small for any of that, the labelled refrigerator trays, the rooms containing three asymmetrical beds (it always looks wrong, like a ward), the scattered underthings and rubbled make-up, the pungent, towny bickering of it all.

When she used to come to me, at night (I dream this daily), in the lost world of our childhood at Rivers Court, it was with a slow tweak of the doorknob, the thin wake of the landing light playing on the alert, skeletal silhouette within her nightdress, the watchful glance over her shoulder which showed me her hair, like a Guppy-doll, the quick tiptoe through the darkness to my bed, the soft kittenish spring landing her knees first by my pillow, and the nervous burrowing slither that in one movement exchanged her nightdress for my sheets and left her warm breath and cold skin gradually osmoting with my cold breath and warm skin. 'Success,' she would whisper. 'You're a very clever girl,' I would whisper back. Before, during, and − if less regularly − after my pubescence, and then, ultimately, through hers, did brother and sister indulge these childish pleasures, until time stood back and made way for that sudden afternoon.

Puberty for me, of course, came like some brisk and thrilling benediction. One week my voice was a piping treble, the next it had descended without incident to its present mellifluous bass; one week my genitals comprised the pouch and knobble of any young boy's, the next my enflossed virilia were craning wantonly in bathtub and bedroom; one week my physical movements had all the natural grace of a healthy child, the next they had taken on the full authority and calm of an athletic adult. (In easy contrast, Terence's clamber-up into manhood was the usual sprawling three-year nightmare of stubbed toes, pimples volcanic, leaping octaves and cat-flux.)

Well, I've never been really sure how long it took Ursula to notice the difference. Our fledgling nights together had naturally often featured startling tumescences on my part, and I enjoyed many delicious pre-adolescent orgasms under Ursula's inquisitive little auspices; but there had until then been nothing in the slightest bit carnal about it all. *You* know: we would exhaustively caress each other, inspect each other's private parts with a kind of giggly revulsion; a lot of hair-stroking, I seem to remember, took place. We never kissed, funnily enough. In all my life I have never kissed my sister − not on the lips, not on those lips.

Gregory, she said one night, you're getting all awful and hairy down there. You don't like it? I asked. Well, she said, amused, I preferred it small and smooth. What other things will happen to you now you're old? Why, I jolly well showed her, the minx. Look at all this *stuff*, she said: how clever. A month later her thin moist face poked up from beneath the sheets; she rested her chin on my chest and frowned. I believe it's very nutritious, I whispered with a smile. She crinkled her nose – a gesture which in her indicated uncertainty rather than distaste. I'll probably get used to it, she said, and added: What will you do when I go like Mama? – But I had sent my sweetheart packing down the bed again, and I lay back with my hands stitched behind my head, as the Cinderella birds encouraged the dawn to peep in past the frayed edges of the window, and as my sister salted my stomach with her sacramental tears.

Why does she cry so much *now*? What else can she be crying for but the lost world of our childhood, when it didn't seem to matter what we did?

Uproarious scenes on my return to the gallery. How these good plain people do without me for a millisecond is a complete and enduring marvel.

Eventually, I suppose, it was sheer boredom rather than any dramatic recuperation that lifted me from my sick-bed. Also the impertinent Styles woman had been agitating in the most unforgivable fashion – braying telephone calls, facetious get-well-soon cards of a predictably vulgar stamp, and I believe there has even been some suggestion of docking my handsome salary if I don't return forthwith! In addition, Terence – dour, attentive, heavy-breathing Terence – has been tenderly nagging me to get well on account of his wonderfully comic bid to seduce that tarty June of his, in accordance with which I have provisionally agreed to stay on late at Torka's one night towards the end of next week. Fair's fair, I do see the boy's point – from the sublime to the ridiculous and so forth.

I elected to return to work on the Friday, in order to give myself the weekend to recover. Putting on all my clothes so early felt strange, exemplary, like getting dressed up for some mythic ball or hunt, or like preparing, at an impossibly tiny hour, to begin a holiday. For the moment I found it pleasurable, and was excited by the touch of my expensive and unfamiliar clothes. It looked hot outside. I stood up, amazed, alive again.

'Good morning, sir, good morning!' fluted the toadies in lift and hallway. 'It's good to see you on your feet again, sir,' said the porter, deferentially holding the doors open for me as I cruised past.

... My, but the world changes quickly these days. How long can I have been away? Where am I — Munich, Florence, Calcutta? Among the snorting buses and the thronged porches of the sudden hotels, whole races, entire cultures, seem to gather and disperse. As I walk, like a foreigner, like Rip Van Winkle, down the diasporadic Moscow Road, I weave through boisterous peninsulae of Pakistanis, step aside for vast cohorts of panting, flaxen Scandinavians, negotiate Jumbo-loads of torpid, Italianate trudgers, forge through great continents of Middle-Eastern immigrant workers. Up-ended dustbins and capsized vegetable barrows are being sick all over the pavement; rubbish bags slump like tramps against shop windows; rabid pigeons, too fat to fly, squawk among the filth. I turn into Queensway and it could be anywhere. A shock-haired nig-nog is selling fresh orange-juice from a colourful, two-wheeled refrigerator. Across the road, the stickered visage of a new building announces CAMBIO — WECHSEL — CHANGE — 24 HOURS (I look around for a sign saying ENGLISH SPOKEN HERE). Everyone in the street but me is clutching a map.

After this the underground is almost a haven: I complete the shunting, frangible journey pressed flat in the crushed carriage, wondering with amused detachment whether these people can really be my kind (there are so *many* of you all. What will become of you? How will you cope?). The better-kept precincts of Mayfair, with their tub-like Americans, costly women and velvety window displays, are the theme of some reassurance as I purchase my tulip and saunter up Albemarle Street to Berkeley Square. There is the gallery, the Odette and Jason Styles Gallery, the place where I work.

'Gregory! How do you spell "Metamorphosis"?'

The poor dears wonder how they kept going without me. As I sit at my desk, trying to suppress an uncontrollable fit of giggles, I wonder how they got *started* without me.

'M, e, t, a ... ' I manage to blurt.

Do you know what they've gone and done while I've been away with my flu? Only commissioned, set up and hung the most ghastly, hideous —

'Gregory! How do you spell "Euthanasia"?'

'E, u, t ... ' I gasp.

— one-man show from *an interior decorator in Bond Street.* I walked in here to find the walls vandalized by abstracts of what I call the Perforce School ('I paint in abstracts, perforce, so that no one, not even me, can tell I can't paint'), dreadful kaleidoscopic slap-ups in brown and ochre, with a kind of —

'Gregory! How do you spell "Extraterrestrial"?'

'E, x, t ... ' I moan.

— simple-minded oriental motif, inducing in the fit viewer a tendency to think he needs his eyes fixed or his stomach seen to, a gust of existential nausea, a deranged insult to all one's —

'Gregory! How do you spell "Embryonic"?'

'E, m, b ... ' I plead.

— most intimate hopes and dreams. Reeling through the gallery towards the Styleses' fetid grotto, I saw that the Creator, the First Author himself, was present, hunched worriedly over the catalogue draft; Old Ma Styles stood in hirsute attendance while Jason fumbled with the coffee cups behind them. Apparently the fraudulent little oik was very anxious about the catalogue, partly because he couldn't dream up any 'titles' for the oblongs of homogeneous drivel which now smothered the gallery walls. 'Less think,' he says. 'What about "Sensuality" for this one. Or for that one. Or for that one.' I crept away to my desk, suffering Madame Styles to give me a bellow if —

'Gregory! How do you spell "Schizophrenia"?'

'Oh, you'll have to look that one up,' I said wearily.

The show is a flop, of course. Throughout the following week the gallery remains deserted, save for the odd mad-eyed Nipponese, in whom the canvasses seem to awaken a momentary, tribal pang. Odette and Jason are depressed. They are losing more money than they usually lose. They stay in their pit all day, and I can hear their morbid whispers. The interior decorator comes in less often now; nobody tries to look cheerful when he does.

But the week is slow. I have nothing to do. I sit at my glass desk here as the afternoons stretch and yawn, and by the time I get home I feel tired and wretched and don't go out. The dreams have not gone. Once I awoke with a jolt to find that I was in the gallery, which seemed shrill and hollow, like another kind of dream. So I just sit here with the feverish taste of rust in my mouth, sickening again, fading and fading, until the week stops.

6: June

(i) Busy busy busy. I don't know
why I make all this fuss, I'm
sure — TERRY

Twenty-four hours to go. Now let me see.

Gregory doesn't want to talk about Ursula. I don't blame
him. If she were my sister I wouldn't want to talk about
her either. It looks as though she has started to go mad,
I'm afraid. And she knows, too, just as my sister always
knew.

Of course, in *his* family there's a lot of it about. (There
must be some in mine as well, I suppose, but I feel so
unimplicated by that part of it: my stuff all comes from
without.) Greg's father, for instance, is, by almost anybody's standards, off his head — though in an entirely
benign and comic way (he is, I should say, a manic
depressive who never gets depressed. Everything about
him is light-hearted — even his occasional heart-attacks.
I like him: he has always tried hard to make things okay
for me). Greg's mother is, in my view, quite mad also —
though try telling *her* that (she is, I should say, slightly
paranoid, tending to delusions of pride rather than of
persecution. I don't like her much: she has always been
dutiful and correct with me, but no more). And now
Greg's sister Ursula is going mad too: she is 'getting'
schizophrenia, rather in the way that other people get
hay fever, or get rich quick, or get fucked up. I love her
(and she loves me, I think, which is some claim to

uniqueness), but I have no idea what to do about her.

Gregory himself has always been very cavalier on the subject, playfully tending to rattle the skeletons in the family cupboard rather than board them up. He has always enjoyed chronicling the *tonto* exploits of his ancestors, particularly those of his great-grandfather, who, among other idiosyncracies, used to like sleeping in the stables and once tore down two rooms of the house and dug up large parts of the garden in search of a mislaid marble, which was later discovered in his shoe. Brilliant. I further suspect that Gregory finds madness posh, like gout or incest. If you're sufficiently protected by family and cash (the argument runs) you *might as well* be mad, since nothing you do is ever going to matter a bugger anyway. Well, things aren't like that any longer, bub. The world is changing. You are not protected, your father is not rich any more, and what you do suddenly counts. Madness doesn't mean maybe these days.

Now that's passed some time. Twenty-three hours to go. I expect I'll give madness a try myself, if things don't work out tomorrow. It all seems to be fixed still. Keep your fingers crossed for me.

My foster-brother is up and about again, if rather groggily so. A week ago today, when I saw him before going off to work, he looked as complacently poorly as ever, crying out when I started to draw his curtains and fluttering a wristless hand at the mug of Cona coffee I had laboriously prepared. But what happens when I get home that evening? There he is, pallid and overdressed, feebly pacing his room. I expressed surprise, which annoyed him, and then lamely asked if he felt better. Greg said that he wasn't better so much as too bored with illness to go on countenancing it. He added something to the effect that the gallery 'couldn't do without' him any longer, and made it clear that he planned to attend work the next day. In fact he seemed so incredibly fucked up that I assumed Mr and Mrs Styles (both of whose mothers, so far as I can gather and guess, suck cocks in hell – I mean, they don't sound terribly nice) had been nagging him to return. This evening I went upstairs and, after a bit of nervous fawning, asked him if our plan was still intact. What plan? he asked. I rehearsed my dream that he might stay out until at least twelve o'clock the following night. Oh, and don't come into my room when you get back. He agreed again, shaking his head in friendly bemusement. Christ he looked rocky, but we're almost there now and I'm pretty sure he will keep his promise to me.

It's all fixed.

Ever since the epoch-making, Rosie-induced crying-jag, there had been a lot of breezy, offhand banter between Jan and me in the office about our 'big night out', our 'night on the razzle', our 'spree'. There would be expensive drinks, a posh dinner – 'hell, we might even take in a show', the Trainee had cracked in response to Jan's ironic cooing. Then, once, in the pub, I plucked up the bottle to say, 'And I'll make sure Gregory is out of the way so we can have the place to ourselves ... ' And *then*, instead of walking out of the pub, instead of slapping the sick grin off my face, instead of shouting, 'You've made sure of *what*? Why do you think I'm coming *back* there, fat boy?', instead, she leaned forward and whispered, 'And I'll fix with my folks to stay with a mate in Chelsea, so there'll be none of that last-train bit.' I was shocked, I don't mind telling you. Perhaps Gregory was right, perhaps she does fuck everyone. Perhaps all you've got to do is ask her and she will. ('Will you?' 'Yup.') Or perhaps she really likes me. Do you think that's at all possible?

Twenty-two hours to go. For the time being cleanliness preoccupies me. I shall need to have a marathon soak, obviously – and I even toy with the idea of actually sleeping in the bath. Jan and I are swanning straight out after work (we happen to be having cocktails at the Bar

Royale — a wallet-thinner, true, but it's a tremendously sexy place, I'm told), so there will be no time for pedantic, nitpicking ablutions immediately beforehand. Maybe I'll take some sort of kit with me to work and have some sort of session with it in the nasty lavatories there (and they're *very* nasty lavatories. The two cubicles are separated by partitions no bigger than cowboy-saloon swing doors, so not only do you hear the awful farting, plopping and grunting of your co-crapper, and he yours, with especially high fidelity, but also, on preparing to leave, it's quite possible to pull up *his* trousers instead of your own. It is even more horrible if you know who's next door. Wark always has a particularly bad time in there). The morale of my cock, incidentally, which was suavely sporting an erection this morning, albeit of a piss-proud, bladder-bolstered variety, is surprisingly good considering it's been lying very low these days and, well, we haven't been on what G. would call 'speakers' for some weeks now. I have given it, in all kinds of senses, a free hand, as a gesture, hoping that the trust I am so plainly reposing in it will spur it on to greater efforts on the night. No more henpecking: all right, you say you can handle the job, young fella — go ahead and handle it. I *think* my cock has fallen for the ruse. (I'm keeping my voice down here, so to speak — it might get wise. But the response so far has been encouraging. After all, it has a lot of prestige riding on tomorrow night.) My room is in superb shape since I aimed my wastepaper-basket. I even own a double-bed I see.

I had a soul-session between eight-thirty and nine — a fairly grateful one, which left my cheeks with a post-sneeze tingle — and then slipped out (all was quiet up there), to walk, perhaps to eat, perhaps to find someone else to fall in love with for when things went wrong. The sodium-illumined arcades of Queensway buzzed with the random, yapping faces of aliens enjoying their stay or actually living here now in the dirty and fire-prone tenements whose sparsely lit top storeys form a queasy mezzanine above the shop fronts (this was a street once, with houses). A coloured woman in a green-ribbed T-shirt with the biggest breasts I've ever seriously seen on anybody walks alongside her waiflike but massively pregnant girlfriend. Across the road a couple dance indolently to the weak strumming of a pavement guitarist. As I go by my nearest pornographer's — run by a greedy Greek who keeps the shop open practically round the clock — I see a very old woman stand becalmed between the pavement displays: for a moment she is weirdly framed by a montage of whopping breasts and proffered backsides. Busy busy busy. I don't know why I make all this fuss, I'm sure.

Deciding, after mature consideration, against the hamburger, ditto the pasty, the pasta, the pizza or the pastry — against any take-home variant of these — I found myself entering The Intrepid Fox, the semi-sinister pub in Moscow Road which sells everyone Particular Brews. Particular Brew, a potent domestic beer much favoured by my ubiquitously near-alcoholic contemporaries, tastes of soap and makes you totally pissed and *tonto* the instant it touches your lips (I'm sure that when the truth about these Brews breaks, when we all find out what they've really been doing to us, such things as the Thalidomide tragedy are going to look pretty trifling in comparison). By ten o'clock, everyone is either fighting or dancing or crying or all three in The Intrepid Fox, such is the pathetic paradigm of drunkenness that this beer sets in train. 'Never any trouble in my pub,' I've overheard the ketchup-cheeked landlord saying, and then adding, with a smug downward glissade, ' — except of course-with-the-Particular-Brews.'

I thought I'd have one, just to keep the cold out. I did, and most refreshing it was too.

As the landlord cheerfully poured out my second, I thought: success. It will be a success. My cock may not be in colossal form these days, but — Christ — we *like each other*, Jan and I. We have feelings to share, thank you. Excuse us, but we don't happen to be that interested in brisk, press-up, Seventies sex. Not us, my friend, *oh* no. Even if I goof, even if my cock retracts beyond recall into my loins, the evening will one way or another be a *success*.

As the landlord solicitously poured out my third, I thought: ... I thought about the extraordinary amounts of tenderness contained within the world, about all the scruffy pockets of everyday goodwill and desire to be nice, about the nobility and pain of growing up and never being young again. I thought of the frightening beauty of clouds, the fluffiness of kittens, little girls with big eyes.

As the landlord facelessly poured out my fourth (and the first tear of the evening plopped fatly on to the bar beside my drink), I thought: oh God, why is it this hard. Why does it have to be this hard. That poor fucked-up hippie never had a chance to become anything else. It can happen when you're young, or it can happen now, or it can happen at any point in the future. Who fucks us up? Who is it who makes our bottles crack?

As the landlord, using his old and violent hands with deliberation, uncapped my fifth, I thought: shiteaters like you, mack, with your horrible unsmiling ways. Look at these cocksuckers, I thought, swinging round from the bar and disgustedly surveying the people grouped about me in circles and rows, drinking, smoking, talking. What have *you* ever felt, what do *you* do, what has *your* life ever been but some sort of appetite. Look at that mindless asshole over there with the two girls — yes, you, you scumbag — what the hell are ... who the ... what do ...

As the landlord, after an interlude of noisy argument, finally agreed to sell me my sixth, I thought: I'm going to be sick. Very sick, very soon. Slumped over my high-octane washing-up liquid, I became the theme of derogatory remarks from both sides of the bar. Dirty boy. I couldn't finish my drink. Off with you, said someone, and good riddance, as I stumbled out into the eventful night, Terry the Tramp once more.

It must have been, oh, 11.30 by the time I came lurching and burping back to the flat. I shut the door brashly and executed a menacing wheel in the direction of the stairs. I'll go beat him up, I'll go cry on his shoulder, I'll go fuck him (the faggot), that'd be good, all that would be good.

I lurched and burped along the corridor to my room, swigged candidly from the whisky bottle, undressed, and, with a bale of nude-magazines stacked in front of my arched form — the fist of lav-paper beside me, the two pillows in the tell-tale L (one as prop, one as lectern) — had a bitter catfight with my cock, which hadn't the slightest intention of tumescing in the first place and was very bored and imperturbable about the whole thing. Well fuck *you*, I thought as the ceiling swung down on me, unwashed, whisky souring my teeth, drunk, battered, unloved, all fucked up.

Delightful behaviour, I think you'll agree? Tremendously sexy stuff, and the perfect prelude to the epiphany of the next day.

So this is what a hangover is, I said out loud when I woke up. All the others — they weren't hangovers. This is, though.

I overslept (or, rather, was unable to climb from the cot) until 9.45, and had to run, coffeeless and with someone else's head, an old monster's head, on my shoulders, to the dry cleaners', in whose canned heat I gaggingly queued for fifteen minutes before the information reached me that my suit had been mislaid in the van. Thence to the launderette (I've been a joke-figure there ever since I asked them to launder my rubbish — Pakkis look up and smile), thence home and into clean creased shirt, fresh pants and socks, and second-best clothes, thence the streets. Pausing for a spectacular hawk in the gutter (strata of ancient poisons lay in wait in my lungs), I dashed into the fumy hole of the Underground. For twenty surreal, nauseous minutes, no train arrived. When one did, it was naturally very crowded — I had to ooze my way into the wall of limbs and was practically frenching an elderly Chinaman all the way to Chancery Lane (I don't know how he bore it). Stopping for a panicky coffee-no at Dino's, I found I had only a £10 note, which, on top of winning me the unanimous venom of staff and clientele alike, delayed me a further eight minutes. It was *11.30* when I crept, more or less on all fours, into the office – undetected, I thought (except by Jan, who seemed to smile my way) – and found a note on my desk from the Controller saying, 'See me, when you get in.' Hated that comma.

'God, I'm incredibly sorry,' I said. 'It just happened.'

'It could happen to anybody,' said John Hain. 'Go and apologize to Wark. He's been taking your calls. And get on with it.'

I apologized to Wark, who looked up with abstracted scorn, as if my presence would only multiply his remaining tasks. Then I got on with it. *Two* sales-sheets lay by my telephone. Wark had self-righteously failed to indicate which calls had already been made. I didn't dare re-approach him. I started at the top and worked down. Was I buying or selling or neither or both? It seemed I was playing simultaneous chess blindfolded in a space-capsule. I felt like an animal, I felt like a god, I felt like the ghost of summer thunder.

Not until 12.15 did I make my first serious mistake. I ran out of the office and entered the pub in the side-street beneath my window, where for some reason I demanded a boilermaker (whisky and beer), having been told that this was especially good for hangovers. Fifteen seconds later I was vomiting convulsively in the alley, my forehead pressed on a length of rusted scaffolding. People were peering down the side-street at me, to check on how fucked up I was. Being sick did not have the effect it is often reputed to have: it did not make me feel better. It made me feel worse. I lit a cigarette, whose first inhalation caused me to cough up items so entirely revolting in their own right that I was sick again – independently, disinterestedly, in sober tribute to the goings-on inside my body. I bought an apple (noting, after the first bite, a squirt of blood on the pulp, from my lungs perhaps, or from some gum-bogey, for which many thanks), and regained my office, where I found (a) another sales-sheet, (b) a message confirming an order I hadn't ordered, and (c) a message cancelling a sale I hadn't sold. I dialled until two. I hiked to Holborn (couldn't face Dino's) and bought a takeaway pie and tomato soup, both of which were inedibly tepid by the time I got back to my desk. I dialled until four. I took my empty coffee carton to the nasty lavatories and filled it with warm soapy water; one of the cubicles was free, though sultry and aromatic; next door someone very ill (who no doubt set aside his tea-break for just this dreadful task) was parting company with substances that sounded like a sack of melons being poured down a well; I washed bits of myself as best I could; I looked terrible, and felt it; I cried some and ran back to my desk. I dialled until five. I spoke to Veale, who still wants me to do things for him. I dialled until six. I yelled for Damon (the boys from downstairs have started beating him up: he *asks* for it) and offered him the three completed sales-sheets. I leaned back, giving gangway to a neurotically smelly blast of vintage, hoofy wind.

'Well *hi*,' said Jan, who was standing at the door.

Ah but from that highpoint, let me tell you, from that proud peak, things definitely took a turn for the worse, things ceased to gel in the way they had been doing, things started to go wrong.

Not that I was actually jeered away from the Bar Royale's commissionaired portals (for being fucked up — 'Sorry, sir, I can't let you in.' 'Why?' 'You're too fucked up' — an eventuality I had anticipated and, in part, made alternative arrangements against): on the contrary, there was nobody there to stop us. We went to the Maverick Lounge, where we quaffed many Sidecars and Old Fashioneds, supped several Banana Daquiris and Harvey Wallbangers, drank deep of Whiskey Sours, Bullshots and

Screwdrivers, of Tequila Sunrises, of Vodka Gibsons and of Mint Juleps. I was totally delirious by this time, naturally, but still talking and so on, still acting in the manner of one who had hopes that he might indeed be going to go to bed with somebody or other that evening. Jan was cheerful and young-seeming, and of course blindingly beautiful. We then had dinner, I appear to recall, in an Italian restaurant in Greek Street (what was that doing there?). I tried hard to eat a lot, to shore up against the mutinous gang-warfare taking place within my body, but could manage only a slice of melon and a couple of burpfuls of risotto. I noticed with climbing awe, however, that Jan was inflexibly present when I paid the bill, obstinately by my side when I hit the street and looked for a cab, still in intransigent attendance when I poked the key into the front door, rode the lift and entered our flat.

'I know,' I said, leading the way upstairs, 'let's have a drink.'

'Up here?' said Jan. 'Where's your gorgeous mate?'

'My foster-brother,' I said.

'He's not in, is he?' said Jan.

'Oh no, he's out,' I said.

'Oh no he's not,' said Gregory. 'He's in.'

'Come on,' he had said. 'Please. Stay and chat with me for a while.'

'All right. Yes, let's all have a drink together,' I said, with some pride.

'Most frightful day. Had to steal back from the gallery and seek my crib. I tried to ring you, Terry, but you weren't there. It's this flu again.'

'What is it with that flu of yours?'

'I know. Well I think it's bloody unfair.'

'Ezza poor baby,' said Jan.

'Well I do. Bloody unfair.'

'So do I,' I said.

'I won't be in your way, don't worry. You can just

leave me up here at death's door, and go off and play
bodies together.'

Pretty sexy stuff, I thought, coming from his delicately
curled lips. If *he* thinks I can, maybe I *can*.

'Tell me,' he then asked us, 'what devilment have you
been up to tonight?'

'Well,' said Jan, 'we had some flash drinks. Lots of
flash drinks. And then we had a flash dinner. And then
we came back here.'

'To do what, pray?' said the twinkly Gregory as my
blood congealed.

Jan turned to me and said, in a brilliantly hurtful
imitation of Gregory's voice, an imitation that did full
justice to how pompous and prissy and coarse and queer
he sounded: ' ... To play *bod*ies.'

I laughed — I laughed hugely, with vicious abandon.
I laughed in pure triumph, delivered at last of all envy
and fear.

' ... Really, Terence,' said Gregory, 'isn't it about time
you coped with your teeth? They've gone green now, and
you *can* get them done on the National Health. You can
get toupées too, you know. In fact, Terry — '

Jan frowned. Then the telephone rang.

I stood outside on the street. It was raining now. I held
up an arm. I wondered how much the taxi would cost,
realizing I could never ask anyone for the money back.
I hated myself for thinking that, of course, but there were
so many new things I hated more: the gorgeous Gregory,
up there in bed, dry and clean; the beautiful Jan up there
with him, drunk and free; the ruined Ursula, abruptly
half-alive in an ambulance somewhere, being driven with
a *swish* through the glossy streets, kind uniformed hands
trying to make her feel all right, her brother on his way.

(ii) You know what it's like, of course, to
      be desired utterly by someone? — GREGORY

Oh dear.

It seems that I have misbehaved. It seems that I am in
disgrace. I have 'misbehaved'. I am *in disgrace*.
  Oh dear.

I must say, however, that Terence is behaving in the most
killingly stuffy way about it all. He's in a massive sulk.
Stupid boy. It's hardly as if I've run off with his wife,
and — as I told him quite frankly — it was far more her
idea than it was mine. Yet he is livid: I have never seen
those gingery features so intense and concerted, so resolute
and yoblike ... Nasty business.
  In a way, you know, I suppose I could argue that the
whole thing was simply a matter of habit. Insomuch as
our previous sexual dealings with women ever coincided,
there was never the slightest question of Terry having
any *say* in the issue of who got whom, who wanted whom,
who preferred whom. In fact his status then — and a
status unthinkingly embraced by T. himself — was one
of courier, of scampering pander, rather than of an auto-
nomous sexual unit, with its own needs, hurts and dignity.
'Terence, go and get those two girls over there ... There
are two girls over there, Terry — go and get them ... Go
and get them — those two girls over there, Terry ... ' That
sort of thing. Naturally enough, he would get the ugly one
(if that), or on those rare occasions when the girls were
equally desirable — and it is rare: beauties hunt with
beasts (why, look at Terence and me then) — he *might*, he
just *might* set his cap at the moody and disgruntled reject.
He accepted this. Now and then, inevitably, I would sense
the dull, adenoidal longing usher from him like a great
slow pulse — as, say, his grumpy dog looks on in resigned
wonder when my bronzed Viking staggers replete from
the bedroom — but really his demeanour was on the

132

whole one of extreme diffidence. Sex, anyway, equalled transgression to Terence, and he saw transgression at the heart of all life.

I even hatched complicated schemes to make Terry feel better about it. For instance: two rich, neglected girls appear in the village one spring. No sooner am I back on holiday from Peerforth than I am established as the elder's cosset, taking my tea there in the long, parentless afternoons. I bring little Terence along — partly for his own amusement, and partly also to deflect the bothersome younger sister, who has not taken my preference for her rival well (and who has too, I note, dark hairs on her legs crushed flat by her stockings, like a preparation ready for the microscope). Nevertheless she gives Terry no change, until I step in, promising secretly to service the trollop if she will look more kindly on my friend. *V* exhausting and almost gets me into trouble.

Or again: under my direction, Terence lures over two rather fine young shopgirls in the Cambridge bus-station. Within minutes both are stroking my shiny hair, and Terry is edging down the bench with a vacuous, qualmish smile on his ill-bred face. While he's off getting us Coca Colas, I playfully promise the tarts that the first one to be nice to my foster-brother shall also be the first to have an hour alone with me. (Promises, promises — besides, I was devoted to a school-friend at the time.)

That was the way it had always worked, the sort of odd-job arrangement we'd always had. By the same convention that he got my expensive clothes when I soared out of them, so he got the rejects, the table-droppings, the leave-offs, which he guiltily exhumed as if from a forbidden attic drawer.

Well what would *you* have done?

There I am. It's the end of an exhausting week, and after all I've been bloody ill, and I haven't been to my friend Torka's for yonks, and there's this perfectly acceptable girl absolutely hurling herself at me, and —

Listen. Terence had just made some fatuous joke or other when the telephone rang. It was past midnight and the three of us turned to the telephone — T.'s panting giggles subsiding — and stared in minor surprise. I held Joan's gaze, violet in the quarterlight, as Terence lurched drunkenly across the room and picked up the receiver, his back to our busy eyes ('Hullo? Pardon?'), eyes which were already seeking each other out along slick cool parallels ('Yes. Who?'), parallels which already seemed full of secret liquids ('She *what*? When?'), liquids which were already glistening like dew on duck feathers in the cusps of our bodies ('Where? Yes, yes. Well Christ of *course*'), bodies which already —

Terence reeled wildly round. He babbled something about Ursula and hospitals. 'I'll *have* to go,' he said incredulously, and stumbled towards the stairs. But were June and I really listening?

The door slammed.

I lifted a forefinger and slowly beckoned her to my bed. She obeyed, raptly swaying across the room, hypnotized, dazed, battered. She hovered above me, as on that first night, a sleepy voluptuous sneer on her half-open lips. Very well then.

'Sit.'

Now first — placing my hand among the sharp curls at the nape of her neck — I began to lower her face swooningly towards mine. Ah, but then, with a quick and contemptuous jerk on her head, I adroitly diverted her lips to the — what have we here? — superbly twanging erection which had long craned free from the folds of my kaftan (my kaftan is maroon, by the way, and it's got buttons all the way down the front and a curiously effective white ruffled pageboy collar). I don't know who was the more mesmerized as, with abstract stealth, her puckered mouth neared my palatinate dome: the face hovered, irreducibly close, kept in check by my rod-like hand, while, using natural heft only — I didn't even need to tense my buttocks — I scoured the perimeter of her

lips. Poor Joan's goldfish mouth was flaccid with yearning
by the time I let it have its slurpy, syrupy little way
(strictly controlled throughout, of course, by this warm
scribe my hand), and I let it sup full before I wrenched
her face back, pointed it at mine, and told it,

'I want you naked. Now.'

I do believe the girl had some trouble finding her feet.
Meanwhile, I propped my head on an elbow to enjoy
the view. She was wearing a downy patterned T-shirt
and spray-on dungarees. She kicked off her golden shoes.
I straightened a finger at her.

'The breasts last,' I specified.

Off, first, came Joan's jeans — taking the pink and
quite hygienic panties along with them in rather inelegant
fashion (I always like a good peer at the pristine puff
before confrontation with the jungly reality). But she still
looked very fine standing there, legs defiantly apart, her
fingers curling under the T-shirt's hem, inches above the
disappointingly sparse quiff of glistening henna. Now the
breasts. They did not, I'm afraid, produce in me that
tender, existential ache that occasionally comes with the
slow unbuttoning of a shirt, the sudden unloosening of a
gown strap, the sighing exhalation of a recalcitrant 'bra',
that sense of glazed despair of the world's staying alive
long enough to touch the skin naked. What June did was
to take hold of the hem with both hands and immediately
cat's cradle her arms, so that the material catapulted up
into the complex of her neck and elbows, hiding the face
and revealing with bizarre abruptness the two great
swinging eminences, which lapped confidently on the
summit of her ribcage. (We ought to remember that she
was drunk.) Once she had got the bally thing off, though,
and was peeling its sleeves from her arms, she shut her
eyes and laughed, and for a moment she looked touching,
pretty and extremely capable.

With just that negligent hint of brutality which all girls
adore, I tugged her down on to the bed. You know what
it's like, of course, to be desired utterly by someone? The

gluttonous all-over kisses, the swirling fluttery hands, the deep-secret shudders, the gasps of imploring volition? Perhaps not. Lying back, my arms folded behind my head, I let her initial frenzy run its course before taking decisive command. Then: I flattened her on her back and, straddling her waist with my thighs, placed *her* arms behind *her* head. Both stimulated and amused by her look of B-movie prostration, I began to slide peelingly up her midriff, and went on to make delightful play with the tumescent trio beneath me, digging, gliding and bending long after her nipples had started to throb for mercy. Inching up further, seated comfortably on the bench of her breasts and supporting my diagonal torso against the head-rest with my hands, I dipped at my own slow leisure into that ravenous O.

A quarter of an hour of that and, with another display of skilful athleticism, I had executed a 180-degree pivot, offering my face up to her hooked-over thighs (I had already reckied the area, naturally, paddling a finger and covertly sniffing it — it was warm, wet and sweet), while she continued to shower my dock with her saliva and her tears. Now mind you I wasn't down there just for the hell of it: after a few messy moments — adequately beguiled by her tonguey doings — I did another expert turnabout, swivelling my legs under my chest like a gymnast and concurrently upending the girl's body, so that in a flash she was on her tummy — haunches aloft — and I was tensed mightily behind her. She tensed too. She tensed too late.

After a perfectly civil, and in fact somewhat tedious, phased entry, I buggered her quite pitilessly for — oh — a good twenty-five minutes, wrenching at her hair whenever she made some coquettish attempt to wriggle free. Roots, roots. Why, the bottom sheet was looking like a butcher's apron by the time I flipped her on to her back, surged forward into the hot crush, and gouged myself empty to her screams.

It was two o'clock before I managed to boot the sobbing

husk out into the night. I had to walk through Terence's empty room to the airing-cupboard, then exhaustedly set about changing the linen.

Well even *I* felt a bit sheepish the next morning.

Asnooze on my storm-washed cot, having slept with the well-won fatigue of a returned warrior, I opened an eye to see the tremblingly self-righteous figure of Terence, who stood like some windy assassin at the foot of my bed. Oh Lor, I thought, I might as well hear him out. For once those fat little puds of his, the fingers gnawed down till they resembled ground-out cigarette butts, held all the 'moral' cards, and I decided to let him have the scene with good grace.

'Ursula is in hospital. St Mark's.'

'Well?'

'She's all right now, more or less.'

'Good. Stupid girl.'

'She slit her wrists, for Christ's sake ... She wants you to go and see her.'

'Where?'

'In hospital.'

'I dislike hospitals, she knows that. They depress me,' I said softly, examining my rings.

'Christ, did you realize what was happening last night?'

I made no reply.

'I said did you realize what was happening last night?'

'Look, I've been frightfully ill for some weeks now. I can't be ... '

Terence turned his back on me unsteadily. One hand clutched the table. Oh God (I thought), he's going to blub.

'When ... what time did she leave?'

'Who? June? Oh, about — '

'It's *Joan*, not June — you fucked her and you don't even know her fucking *name*.'

'Joan then,' I murmured.

' ... What time?'

'About two, two-thirty,' I said crisply, resolving to clear the air.

' ... What was it like then?'

'Rather fun,' I said in my manly way. 'You should try her yourself sometime.'

'Well thanks a fucking *heap*' was Terence's cryptic rejoinder as he clattered down the stairs.

That was a fortnight ago. And has his distress been healed by the soft massage of time? Not a bit of it. Indeed, I think he is getting angrier about it every day. Ho-hum. I'm afraid I simply had no idea of the (apparently) vast emotional investment he had placed on Joan's shapely but fickle shoulders. And, as one who is used to having, at a snap of his muscular fingers, any girl he looks on, it takes some effort on my part to squint through the undergrowth of others' needs and desires. Besides, I've been terribly ill. (I feel marvellous now; that work-out was just what I needed.)

Naturally I'm worried about Ursula. *Naturally* it was unfortunate that this aberration of hers struck so inconveniently. But there was nothing extra I could have contributed, after all, and between ourselves I happen to know that Ursula preferred me to be off having my fun. (We've already had a good hoot about the whole evening. She says, anyway, that Terence was impossibly drunk and tiresome at the hospital. All the nurses stared.) There is confident talk hereabouts that Ursula will soon be coming to stay with Terence and me, here in my flat. I have even offered her my dressing-room — a serviceable nook between Terence and the bathroom — which I now seldom use. Of course, she gets depressed. Of course she gets disorientated. Eighteen, nineteen — they're hell. It's not success we crave for then but youth, youth.

She will get better quickly. We're a highly-strung house, the Ridings, and many a princely caprice and noble foible has been let out to play in the large, tolerant rooms, lawns and walks of Rivers Court, Cambridgeshire.

My father's grandfather, Coventry Riding, insisted that he be carried everywhere from the age of twenty-one on, though he was as hale as is all our stock; my great-uncle Ivan played the fiddle and kept a vicious white mouse. Ursula will get better quickly, here with her tall and successful brother in his attractive flat. And, if she is as like me as I think she is, the example of Terence Service should prove a sobering commentary — and a very funny one, let me add — on the perils of seedy self-absorption: all that solicitude to one's neuroses, all that unsmiling concern with one's emotional ozone. I see her again as she once was, in that other world; the delicate piece of *petit point* slipping from her frocked lap to the foot of the velvet sofa as she half-rises, seemingly petrified with delight when the golden Gregory (just back from school, his poor suitcases abulge with trophies, rosettes, panegyrics) bursts away from the harassed housemaids and fussing footmen to throw open the drawing-room doors: my princess dashes down the length of the room — some fifty-five feet — and I catch the sinewy bullet of adoration in my arms, warm lips, warm tears, my heart everywhere at once.

7: *July*

(i) My calculations about how to
stay alive and sane on this particular
planet have clearly been at fault — TERRY

Thanks. Thanks for that, Jan. Thanks for that, Greg, my brother. That's it. Yes, you've really fucked me up now. You too, Ursula, you poor bitch.

'Did you fuck her, you bastard?'

Gregory continued to feign picturesque sleep. I kicked

the bed (it hurt). He opened a narrow, quizzical eye.

'I *said*: did you fuck her, you bastard?'

He sat up. His face looked completely clear now.

'Did you *fuck* her, you bastard?'

'Not exactly ... I, we ... '

'What do you mean, not exactly? Did you fuck her or didn't you fuck her?'

'We played bodies of a rather unconventional kind, young Joan and I.'

'You fucked her and you don't even know her fucking *name*.'

' ... Sorry.'

'Ursula,' I managed to say, 'cut her wrists last night.'

'My God! She didn't. Where is she?'

'You didn't even know what was going on, did you. She's ... at ... ' And, in a dribble, all the shame was mine again, as I stood there, in the right but small, poor, bald.

'You know what you've done,' I told him. 'You cut my cock off.'

All the shame is mine. Why? Somehow everything about the incident — in which, if you remember, my girlfriend and foster-brother copulated perfidiously while I went off without hesitation to do my (and his) fraternal duty — *diminishes me*. Why? If I should ever run into Jan again, in a pub, in a street, which of us will falter, mumble, turn away, and release a silent gasp of ignominy? When I said that pathetic thing to Gregory and stumbled down the stairs, whose face burnt the hotter with embarrassment and remorse? Mine, mine. Why? I'll tell you why. Because I have no pride, and they merely have no shame.

What does Ursula have?

At six o'clock, her classes for the day completed, Ursula Riding left her hostel and walked the quarter-mile to the King's Road, a laundry bag in her hand. She installed her cleaning at the Washeteria and strolled up and down the strip before entering a café, where she ordered and drank a lemon tea. She returned to the laundry, then started back to her hostel, stopping at the all-night drugstore in Royal Avenue to buy a packet of Wilkinson razor-blades. She went straight in to supper with the rest of the girls; afterwards she sat in her room chatting to friends until lights out at 10.30. She slipped away then. The night-monitor found her an hour later, deep in a cold red bath.

And when *I* found her an hour later — as I came lurching and burping into Ward B4, Casualty, St Mark's Hospital, past a boy with a fork in his knee, a screaming woman whose back had been split in a car crash, a fat tramp with a huge plastic hold-all in his hand and half a Guinness bottle in his crown, several evidently whole refugees who just liked the look of the place, a polite but unhelpful porter, a black nurse, a black matron, an orderly, a young skinhead doctor, and many white squares of light, sheets, flooring — there she lay, lost among cloudy pillows on her eerily high bed, an expression of scared, fully-conscious self-reproach on her half-hidden face, my first reaction was: I wanted to hit her, hit her hard, give her something to slash her wrists about, make her see what it was really like, make her cry. And I felt like crying too, I wasn't Gregory and she wanted him, everyone wanted him and what was he doing now, and me drunk and Ursula mad.

'Oh, Ginger, I'm sorry,' she said. 'You won't tell Mummy or Papa.'

'Jesus *Christ*, Ursula, what the hell did you do?'

'My wrists,' she said, holding out her bandages.

'What the hell did you do it *for*? What could have gone wrong with you yet? Look at all this here. It's nothing to do with *you*.'

'Ginger, you're drunk.'

'You bloody bet I am. So would you be. And don't call me *Ginger*.'

I stayed an hour, as agreed with the skinhead doctor. She was all right in the end.

'We're going to have to change the way you are,' I

said, leaning over to kiss her quickly good night. 'We're going to have to do something about it.'

'Why? Why not let it go?'

'You don't want that and the whole thing there,' I said.

And I can see, too, that I'm going to have to change the way I am. My calculations about how to stay alive and sane on this particular planet have clearly been at fault. Lots of people are plenty uglier and poorer than me without seeming to mind, without the self-hate and self-pity — the sentimentality, in a word — that makes me such a quivering condom of neurosis and ineptitude. I have never been *nice*, but from now on, boy, am I going to be nasty. I'll show you.

I'm standing by the tall bendy window outside our flat, the one that hates stormy weather. Greg is asleep. Jan has gone (I won't see her again). It is raining outside and the glass is full of tears, tears for the wrecked Rosie, but let that go, yes let that go and never come back again.

'Hello, may I speak to Mr Veale, please?'

'Veale speaking,' said Veale, in his calm and sinister voice.

'Oh, hello. Mr Veale, it's Terence Service here, from the —'

'Morning, Terry. What can you do for me?'

I hesitated (he's a sharp fuck, this one). ' ... Anything you tell me to do,' I said, and laughed.

'Pardon? Can't hear you. Talk louder.'

'*Sorry, it's this line.*'

'I know it's the line, brilliant. That's why I told you to talk louder. I mean, you don't have to be ... Marconi to tell it's the line.'

'*I said I'd do whatever you tell me to do.* Is that better?'

'Lots.'

He told me some things to do. They sounded innocuous enough, though I wasn't sure I'd like people to know I was doing them.

'Well, I could do that now,' I said. 'Wark, for a start. He's all — '

'Did I tell you to do it now? Did I?'

'No.'

'Well don't do it now then. Do it when I tell you, like I tell you.'

'What do I do now?'

'Wait.'

'Okay.'

'Take care of yourself, Terry-boy.'

I put the telephone down and yelled for Damon. 'Go and get me a coffe-no,' I said (I'm practising being nasty on Damon. This is extra tough for Damon. Damon doesn't need this. He looks as though he might drop dead any day now as it is). I gave him 12p. 'What's that you've got there?' I said. Silently Damon took a colourful paperback from his coat pocket. 'You're reading these days, are you?' I glanced at the cover, which showed two pantied girls in a sneering embrace. 'Dikes. You're into dikes?'

Damon shook his sickly head.

'You're not into them. You don't like dikes.'

Damon nodded his sickly head.

'Why not?'

'It disgusts me,' he said.

'Well why the hell do you read about it?'

Damon shrugged.

Christ, he looked ill. 'You don't half look rough, you know, Dame.'

'Yeah, I know,' he said.

'Go and get my coffee, go on.'

The office seems empty without her. Everyone keeps saying they miss her — except me. I wish they wouldn't talk about her in the way they all go on doing. I have to pretend I have fond memories of her. And they *are* fond. But I must change that too.

As I walked back from the Underground that night — briefcase, umbrella (you'd carry one if you had my hair) — I saw the fucked-up hippie again. I saw him by the back-door dump of The Intrepid Fox, slumped like a rubbish-bag himself among the shiny black sacks and ripped cardboard boxes. I crossed the road and stood near him. He wore an overcoat, strapped on with various belts. Obviously he dressed for the cold of night and just sweated helplessly through the day. His hair was in thick sloping handfuls here and there about his head. He was muttering; his hands flapped idly on the tarmac. I went over.

'Do you want a cigarette?'

'I don't beg from no cunt.'

'Who's begging?' I asked, impressed. 'I'm offering to give you one.'

'I don't take charity from no cunt.'

'How do you know I'm a cunt? We've only just met.'

'Cunt.'

' ... How the hell did you get fucked up like this? How the hell did you get so fucked up so soon?'

'Cos I hate all that shit there.'

'Oh come on. All what shit where?'

'All *you* shit. All *you* cunt.'

'Me? I'm practically as wrecked as you are. I'm practically a tramp myself.'

'No you're not.'

'What am I then?'

'You're just a shit.' He laughed. 'The biggest shit of all.'

'Listen, do you want some booze, or some turps or some after-shave or whatever the hell it is you drink? I'll give you a couple of quid if you want.'

'Fuck you,' he said.

'Well fuck you too.'

Perhaps he's right. Perhaps I am a shit — a big one too. I must say, it's all rather flattering.

Ursula moved in at the end of last week.

I helped. We got all her stuff out of the hostel and brought it round here in a taxi. It was a cool bright sabbath, clean after a night of rain, and it seemed to be one of those days when fresh cycles loom ambivalently in the air. We passed garden squares, in which lone couples played tennis under the shadows and men wearing whiter whites, standing out in the sun, wondered about a cricket match. Even Queensway appeared to have itself under control, as the taxi made its stertorous way down the strip, and the aeroplanes looked completely relaxed and at home in the featureless sky. Ursula paid, the young cabbie admiring her still-bandaged wrists.

Ursula attempted to give me a hand with her things, tripping and staggering under ridiculously tiny loads, but it was left to the beefy Terence to make three solo journeys in the lift. The 'dressing-room', which hardly gives you time to blink between me and the bathroom, merely a bit of passage, hardly a room at all, seemed about right for Ursula, with its scaled-down cot, narrow window-sill, and twenty-four square feet of carpet.

'I've always quite liked this room,' she said, unpacking one of her chaotic suitcases.

I gazed on laconically from my desk next door, hardly wondering at all how often I'd get to see her in the nude, or what bits of her in the nude I'd get to see.

'Where's Gregory?' she asked, but with very little emphasis.

'Off at that old bumboy's, Torka's.'

'Mm. Why does he go there so much?'

'Because he's a queer.'

She took me to lunch at the three-time-losers' wine bar off Westbourne Grove, a long low dark place full of Sunday desperadoes. I used to go there myself quite a bit, and I was pleased to note the looks of surprised — even slightly betrayed — resentment on the faces of the cravated sportscar-drivers and big-bummed hearties who precariously teamed up there for their weekly lunch. I held Ursula's arm, making some show of this courtesy, and felt fairly flash and shitty throughout the meal of soft quiche, dry salad, thin meat and old cheese. I insisted on paying for the wine, of which we had two bottles, of which she had two glasses.

Afterwards, under the leering sun, we walked up into Queensway, in search of something easy to take back for dinner. We successfully bought a couple of plastic pies, but I could feel Ursula growing troubled and skittish with all the heat and the filth and the boogies, so we went back to the flat and spent the leavings of the afternoon in Gregory's room (it's all right to, I reason, with a blood-relation there. For a while I tried to make him paranoid of me. I don't think it worked. Anyway, it was too tiring for the bottle, and I'm paranoid of him again now), flapping through the newspapers and watching his TV. At seven or so, Gregory returned. He looked more fatigued and disaffected than I had ever seen him look before (and very nice it was too), making no special response to Ursula's presence. He was suddenly quite unintimidating — and when he said a few words about wanting a nap, it seemed the most natural and unanxious thing in the world for Ursula and me to return together to our rooms below. I calmly relate that we there played records and talked until bedtime (we even forgot the pies). I used the bathroom first: when I came out she was sitting on her bed, inches away, her legs crossed like a squaw, wearing a light-grey nightdress, whose folds shone wispily in the overhead light. She reached up, I leaned down, she kissed me on the cheek.

'Why did you do it, by the way? Just for the record.'

'It was those voices.'

'Which voices?'

'Oh, the ones in my head.'

'What, they sort of told you to?'

'No, they never *say* anything. They just wouldn't go away.'

'Do you still hear them?'

'Sometimes.'

'Well don't do it again, for Christ's sake. And if the voices start going on at you, just come and tell me about it.'

'And what will you do?'

'I'll tell them to shut the fuck up.'

'They won't listen.'

'Oh yes they will.'

'Good night, Ginger. Oh, I'm not supposed to call you

Ginger any more, am I?'

'No, you're not. Good night. Not any more.'

Ursula moving in here with us has proved to be a bonus in all kinds of ways. One particularly heartening thing, of course, is that she is fucked up, clearly very fucked up indeed, much much more fucked up than I am for instance, possibly (who knows?) totally fucked up for ever, decisively fucked up for good; no matter how fucked up I get, she will always be that little bit more fucked up than I am: it is a virtual certainty that I will never be able to get quite as fucked up as she is fucked up already. This is good. Ursula is, in addition, fucked up in a way radically at odds with the way in which I am fucked up. Everything observable about me is fucked up — my face is fucked up, my body is fucked up, my hair is fucked up, my cock is fucked up, my family is all fucked up. Nothing observable about Ursula, on the other hand, is in the slightest bit fucked up: looks, ability, background, advantages — all this is, on the contrary, notably unfucked up. And yet Ursula, Ursula Riding, my foster-sister, is *fucked up*. She is *fucked up*. This is also good.

Why is it good? Remember that day at school when you were found out, caught doing whatever it was they caught you doing ... caught stealing the dinner-money after the boys had hung their jackets up for handicraft, caught flobbing on the classroom door-handle (so that the incoming master would, ideally, arrive with his soiled hand aloft in ecstatic disgust), caught scrawling cloacal obscenities in the Fat Boy's Letts Pupils' Diary (*April 21st*: Got spunk up tonight; *April 22nd*: Fucked my sister again today; *April 23rd*: Stole another £5 from Mum), when you got *found out*, remember how you longed for only one thing, not for release, not even for innocence, as you stood there solitary and foul at the head of the room while behind you your classmates, enjoying the disruption as you too would enjoy it, were lined up in rows, seeming to nod unanimous mocking assent to all the horrors of schooldays and death? Remember how you longed just for a guilty friend, someone like yourself, a partner in grime, a sharer of your shame? Remember that.

We have a rule now, Ursula and I, that whenever she starts to suffer from anxiety without an object, or whenever she says something that has nothing to do with anything anyone else has said recently, or whenever she suggests doing something impossible or incoherent or generally crappy, or whenever she locks herself in the bathroom and mumbles fanciful excuses through the door, or whenever she bursts into tears for no good reason that *I* can see — then one or other of us enunciates that word *tonto*. I say, warningly, '*Tonto*', or she says, humbly, 'Ton*to*', or we both chant 'Tonto!', and this seems to negotiate the delicate leap over the distance between how she sees things and how things actually are. To me that distance is a rut which any frog could straddle: I see things the way they are, and they are horrible. I live with this. She doesn't see things the way they are, and they are still horrible. But — '*Tonto*', I whisper warningly, and at once they are horrible no longer.

Can I help? Do I care? I don't really care if I help, do I, obviously? And how can I help if I don't really care? (I can't help not caring, but that's another matter.) I unfurtively admit that most of the time it fills me only with gloating irritation to see such fuddled, helpless solipsism (yes, act like an idiot. That's my girl, I think). *My* sister was neither rich nor pretty and she behaved with perfect normality right up to and including the moment she died — reacted, indeed, with exemplary sanity to the surely very *tonto* experience of getting murdered: it didn't seem to alienate *her*. Whereas it doesn't take shit to alienate Ursula. Any bugger can alienate Ursula. Ivied cemeteries are stacked with people you can blame. I just think she's *mad*.

I saw her mad tits the other night. They are mad but nice, like her and unlike me. Come on, I'm going under too. Remember. Forgive, forgive.

(ii) The world is going bad on
      us. I'm having nothing to do
      with it — GREGORY

July too hot, smelly and boring to merit much comment
from me.

The world is heating up. I've seen *three* oldsters drop
down dead already this month — just flicking over flat
in the street for ever. It used to be the winter they were
afraid of: now it's the summer that finds them out. The
world is boiling. You hardly dare open a paper these days:
the news is all of cataclysm and collapse. Tempers are
threadbare; the yobs are winning; everybody accepts
the fact that they've got to get nastier in order to survive.
The world is going bad on us. I'm having nothing to do
with it.

Notes in an artist's yearbook ...

Tuesday the 7th. Getting bored with the gallery. Unacceptably fraught and humid-breathed scene with Mrs Styles,
she of the fat freckly arms, copiously fringed upper lip
and embarrassing bald patch. Trim Jason had come
over all nauseous after lunch (with my clever little flu, I
trust), and had gone home, burping greenly, in his
hilarious new Homburg. I lay back, as nubile as ever,
on the sofa in their hot office, my sleeves rolled up after
some strenuous picture-packing, being fed tea and
expensive Chocolate Viennas by the matronly Odette.
Was wearing my deceptive new jeans, the ones that look
like incredibly smart and well-pressed cords (with sewn-on
crease. I know, but these really work. *Trust* me). Gallery
completely deserted, it being the final trickling lees of
the interior decorator's unsaleable lino designs. Abruptly,
and with a loud shimmy of her stockinged colossi, stale
Styles leaves her chair, returning half a minute later to
announce that she's just shut up shop! 'But look here
[you fat fool],' I cried, 'I haven't finished my tea and

biscuits yet.' Don't worry, says she, making a grab for my cup, you shall have all the tea you — and with a harsh bark of self-reproach she had upended the whole scalding mess over my brand-new jeans! (Oh, I see it now, I see it all now, you bungling hag.) In crisp, act-now terms, she instructed me to 'slip out' of my wrecked trousers, and, through concern for the fragile material, I hastily concurred. — Cut to the jockey-panted Gregory, reclining on the sofa in appalled petrification, as Mrs Odette Styles (36 yrs) kneels before him, caressing in murmurs the roots of his spread legs, and staring — with what she no doubt thought of as an hypnotic tug — at his sprawled manhood! Well, I simply had to smack her hand away, cross my arms and my legs in one deft wriggle, and talk wildly on as if nothing had happened. The huffy hen stalked off home, without a goodnight and, moreover, without doing anything about my £25 jeans. Had a tiresome fifteen minutes with soap and nail-brush downstairs and felt like some lunatic or incontinent drunk on the underground train home. Went to the Garage of Thieves. A swarthy yob looked up from cleaning his fingernails with a spanner to say that it would take six days and sixty pounds before he could cure my delicate green car. Asked the brute to Torka's, as a good mean joke.

Sunday the 19th. Getting bored with Torka's. Spent last night there, always a mistake. It's just that he's going in for ruffian-trade these days, which isn't my cup of tequila *at all*. Adrian has been given the push at last (serve him right, I agree), but has been grimly replaced by a cuboid, power-packed little hoodlum called 'Keith'! With girlish bell-bottoms swathing his ridiculously truncated legs, a purple T-shirt painted on to his brutal, slab-titted chest, coarse complexion and coarse bouffanted blond hair, tiny vicious eyes and a fur-lined stripe of a mouth, why, I find *Keith* about as attractive as I find Terence Service (and a lot less manipulable). Perhaps he's frightfully good at beating Torka up, or something.

And as for Keith's crew, which looms and glowers all over the apartment: loutish, sidling Norman, the pool-sharp with the 'quick' Zodiac and even quicker temper; Dilly-boy Derek, the near-toothless Scot who claims to have the mightiest member in the metrop (it *is* enormous, if shockingly scarred); petulant, ever-naked Yvette, who has the failed eyes of all dead blondes, plus an — I concede — extraordinary tongue; huge Hugo (pronounced *you-go*), who paces the floor in his eighteen-inch platforms recounting unbelievably evil tales of sexual humiliation and GBH; tiny Tessa, a would-be nymphet of at least fifteen to whom you can, admittedly, do whatever the hell you like (you can kill her if you like — it wouldn't bother her); wondering, hippyish, soft-faced Jerry, an Aries, a prose-poet, a dreamer ... And there are more where they came from ... All right — on a Saturday evening, wheedled by the right wines, coaxed by the correct stimulants, I too can take *some* pleasure in the honest heaving stink of these crude, troglodytic people (though the threat of disease is a pervasive nightmare), with their mean and dangerous bodies, their rather touching views on personal hygiene, the callow lasciviousness of their caresses and, above all, their immense talent for self-preservation. But the next morning! Ah for the olden days — a sleepy, bemused yet still-gorgeous confluence of half-naked bodies in the warm pined kitchen, toast and crispy bacon and a great cauldron of real coffee, all three baths thundering to their marble brims; while Torka fondly prepares the Bullshots and Bloody Ivans he knows I like, we skim the better Sundays, cackling at the clowns in the review sections, and talk of Proust, of Cavafy, of Antonio Machado — before streaking off in our cars to Thor's and its slow, slow Sunday lunch. And now? I awoke this morning to the damp smell of cabbage (what's this? a gravy brunch?), a smell akin to the tang of poverty and failure sometimes discernible in Terence's undersea quarters, a smell of cheap sad clothes and given-up-on bodies. I find I have slept in the smallest bedroom — the one formerly reserved for the most scorched and peed-on catamite — find also, to my horror, that I am sleeping with dreamy Jerry, *one-up one-down*, and that his fat dreamy feet are quivering gently on the pillow beside my head (what mangled *cauchemars* might they have witnessed?). Stumbling into a bathroom, I surprise the vested, spotty-backed Hugo, complacently shaving before the wide swing of the looking-glass with Torka's drum razor. 'Cheers,' he tells me. Radio One is having hysterics in the kitchen, and in the drawing-room blonde Yvette is clothed only by *The People*, with Derek the Denture still asleep in his underpants on the chesterfield beside her. Then unsmiling Keith appeared, wearing the spare kaftan I once used to wear, followed by the hunched Torka, devoted and bruised. — Luckily Susannah turns up and I whisk her off for a stirringly pessimistic lunch at Paupers'. Time of changes. Either Keith and his kind go, or Gregory does.

Friday the 24th. Getting bored, too, in a way, you know, with how things seem to be turning out in my flat, now that Ursula is here, and what with Terence still slightly fizzy (i.e., in a state of helpless, purple-gummed paranoia) about that absurd tart of his, June. My flat is an eldest son's flat: it is designed for one person: it is designed for me. The spacious drawing-room, with its high knobbly cornice, serried bookcases, and white blaze of window, was, in days of yore, an ample stage upon which the young Mr Ridings could muse and wander, wander and muse ... These days my civilized eyrie appears to have gone the way of the rest of the neighbourhood — a teeming subcontinent of alien voices, alien clothes, alien needs. Ursula *will* leave everything all over the place, and Terence, who is virtually a tramp these days anyhow, clearly feels that if a Riding can be untidy, you just watch a Service. Scenes of Rabelaisian squalor are commonplace now on the ground floor, and it takes a clear head and a strong stomach to forge one's way through that jangling rag-and-bone shop to the blighted bathroom. Ursula, mind you, is herself quite prettily installed in the little dressing-room: normally I shouldn't mind in the least her powdery pandemonium of discarded dresses and unrecycled laundry, her rockpools of jewels and bombsite necropoli of make-up. There's just something promiscuous and infra dig. about my sister's girlish, patrician (i.e., essentially maid-less) disarray mingling with Terence's apathetic slobbery: her used stockings are sandwiched in the wastepaper-basket by Terence's beer-bottles and pin-ups; his splayed, pyorrhoeac toothbrush and ginge-fleeced comb flank her lipstick tubes and hair clips. They have, moreover, got a definite little community going on down there, often pooling resources for take-home snacks from Queensway and brewing up hot drinks on that electric kettle I forced Terence to buy. I sometimes feel — coming in late to deposit my coat in the large cupboard I still use in Ursula's room — that *I* am the interloper; they'll be sitting on the bed chatting, or listening to Terence's absurd gramophone, or just pottering about, content in one another's proximity, and *I* seem out of place, too glamorous, too in-demand, too far ahead of them. (Extra disorientating, this, when you reflect that from puberty onwards the young Ridings' life had been a constant quest to evade their foster-brother, the weepy new-boy whose wrinkled socks never would stay up.) Why doesn't she go out more? How does she fill her days? Where is her life? I've completed the circuit, have myself adorned the endless soirées, outings and cocktail parties of her near-coevals. She should be off to Ascot and Wimbledon and Henley, or just having those teas with her friends (where *are* everyone's friends? A pity that no one's daughters 'come out' any more, or rather that only yids' daughters 'come out' any more). I don't think it's really on — is it? — that my sister should be permitted to slum in Terence's world of cheap eateries and drab bedsitterdom, that world of contingency and failure. Shall (a) make an effort to take her out more myself, (b) get her to sneak up here sometimes at night — fun for me and symbolic rescue from below-stairs, (c) forbid Terence to have her in his room. (T. is, by the way, pretty well his docile, winded old self again. I think he has now accepted the status that was always so clearly his true one. Don't you?)

Thursday the 30th. Staying bored, staying it, staying it. Last night attended an unavoidable — and virtually inedible — dinner with the Styleses at their repellent home. I don't know, perhaps I'll chuck up my job for something else, walk out on the gallery, ignore their promises and their pleas (they've already offered me more money. But *I* don't need money). Fresh careers fan out at me like a conjuror's playing-cards ... Diplomacy: rather fun, house abroad, a troupe of servants (absolute walkover for someone with my connections, social talent and flair for languages). Publishing? Quite amusing despite the derisory pay, and you might get halfway tolerable colleagues (also relish the prospect of, say, knocking an arts list into shape — would need a free hand, of course). Politics ... the charisma — *and* some — is already mine, salary good, secretaries, perks (but then all the fools, the fools). The City! No — not the City, definitely *not* the City. Writing holds some appeal; a few dashed-off prose-poems of mine have already won a small but resonant *succès* ... I don't know, perhaps I'll travel. The patchwork quilt of Europe, the rusty triangle of India, the green baize of Russia and the Urals, the lacquered prawn of Japan. See the world while the world is still there. Today I got home at twenty-to-seven drenched with the filth of the city and the filth of my boredom, and as I came out of the jaws of the under-ground and walked down the yapping hell of Queensway, the beercans, the youths eating muck in the street, I thought of my sister and my bath and my tea and my book and the congenial evening ahead (with maybe a little extra something after lights-out, courtesy of Ursula).

I took off my gloves and walked straight into Terence's room. No one there. The flat silent and dead. I moved into the smoky light of the dressing-room. Through the mist of my disappointment I saw the signs of a hasty and excited exit. The day's dress, left in a puddle on the floor, made me gulp. It hurt my heart to see the rejected shoes, placed together, saying twenty-past-six with their heels.

8: August

(i) But tell me a bit about the
     bit about having no clothes on — TERRY

August is the month when we both have our birthdays, his on the 18th, mine on the 19th. (This was one of the things that so appealed to my foster-father's quirky, musing nature; he loves all coincidences, flukes, windfalls, anything arbitrary.) Everyone seemed to think that the contiguity would cause me much abject distress, but in fact it was among the very few things that didn't bother me, at least not in itself; I didn't mind him having a better time than me (then. How would I dare?). They used to try and try and fuss and fuss, though, and of course I hated that. More than likely I would've preferred not to have birthdays at all; boys like the boy I was, I think, hate attention more than they hate anything. I enjoyed Gregory's celebrations, for instance, infinitely more than I enjoyed mine. No effort was needed to render it good — there was little of the sense of strain which marked the gatherings gathered round me. And my foster-brother made tremendous viewing, of course. It is hard to transmit the sheer lustre of the growing

Gregory, when you can see the uncertain and compromised figure he has since become.

Especially recently. Especially since Ursula has come here. She diminishes him in some important way that I cannot yet detect. Do you know what it is? Or does he still tell you lies?

Why doesn't he take her out more, give her more of his time, claim her as his own, which is what she is? At first, through craven habit, I inferred that he left Ursula and me together in an unthinking, disdainful way, as if to suggest that we were compatibly small-time and fucked up, the below-stairs losers who should not be allowed to impinge on the sparkling citadel of his own life. But that can't be right, somehow. He doesn't seem to be having a good time any more.

Did he actually fuck her ever, is what I want to establish. This must be important. I know she used to go to his room a lot at night (I thought she did it simply because she was better friends with him than she was with me, but I once surprised her in the bathroom afterwards, and she looked startled and ashamed for a second, and her nightdress was bunched and creased, and there was a salty odour about her that I had never smelled before), I know they had sexy jaunts together (there was one incident, for which they both had their ears soundly boxed, when they got marooned in the nude on a tiny island in the D-Pond), and I know they embraced every opportunity to touch each other up (I myself once wandered into the barn on a bright-shadowed spring afternoon and heard the cornily filmic noises of love among the hayricks, and crept towards the sounds of playful struggle and giggling reproach, and saw Ursula stretched backwards over an enormous saddle on the floor, her dress pulled up, the lower half of her body concealed by Gregory's busy shoulders and back, and he certainly did seem to be caressing her very thoroughly, I thought, as I ran silently away), but did he actually *fuck* her, is what I want to

156

establish. Because then things would be clearer, wouldn't they, not just for them but for me.

'Hey, Ursula,' I asked her the other evening, 'that time out on the D-Pond, when you and Greg got stranded without any clothes on — what actually happened?'

'Oh,' said Ursula, not looking up from some knit-by-numbers pattern she was working on, her thin, sensitive hair almost intermeshing on her lap with the cotton and her own nervous fingers, 'it was silly really.'

'I dare say it was silly, but what actually happened?'

'Oh, well, we went out on this raft Gregory had made and we didn't notice it slipping away from the island and grumpy old Mr Firble had to row us back.'

'But tell me a bit about the bit about having no clothes on.'

'Yes, we took them off.'

'Clearly. What for though?'

Her hands paused, and she glanced sideways towards her room. 'We just took them *off*.'

'Yes, I'm with you so far. I've mastered that bit of it. But sort of *why* did you take them off?'

'Because it was so *hot*. I'm no good at knitting and I'm going to stop it and never do it again.'

'*Tonto*, Ursula. Ursula — *ton*to,' I whispered warningly, and she looked up at last. She made what's known as a funny face, compressing her lips and bulging her eyes.

'Sorry,' she said.

'I bet,' I said, as she looked down again, 'I bet it was quite embarrassing, being rowed back by that old turd Firble with no clothes on.'

'Yes,' said Ursula, 'it jolly well was.'

Mad bitch ... Perhaps, then, the whole thing is altogether simpler. Perhaps it is *really* simple. If I'm right, the way to my revenge is now clear.

Has she fucked anyone since, I wonder idly, if indeed she ever fucked him in the first place? Has she fucked anyone ever? I haven't fucked anyone since I last fucked anyone.

I haven't fucked anyone ever either, or at least it feels that way by now. It just disappears from your life. I don't even go on about it as much as I used to, do I (though I still say *fuck* a lot)? That's in character too. You'd think it would get worse, wouldn't you? It doesn't, thank God. The loss just looms lunar and abstract, like a dog on a distant moon baying at the Earth.

I'm earning so much money these days that I hardly know what to do with it all. I'm earning so much money that I'm thinking of going to a whore, and a good one too. Good ones, they say, cost a lot of money but are good at giving you hard-ons. The more money you give them, the better at giving you hard-ons they get. She'd have to be a very good one, my one. Perhaps there aren't any that good. Perhaps, no matter how much money I earned, I'd never be able to afford one good enough to give me hard-ons. Who *could* give me hard-ons? Someone who liked me — I think that's all it would take. Perhaps there's a whore somewhere who is so good at giving you hard-ons that she likes you if you give her enough money. I'd better save up for her.

I'm earning so much money these days because Veale gimmicked it (why is Veale giving me all this money? Perhaps he likes me. Perhaps he could give me hard-ons too, if he wanted). Veale has already gimmicked it that I get tax relief and supplementary benefits for doing things about being Clerk (i.e., for doing things for him. I did them when he told me to. They only took a minute, and now I get all this money. I've got to do even more things for him later, but then I get even more money).

The rationalization proper hasn't taken place yet. Everyone at the office is in a state of inordinate apprehension — quite rightly. They all think they are going to get aimed. Most of them will get aimed. Whereas, six months ago, it seemed that only one or two of us would be, it now seems that only one or two of us won't be. I listen all day to Wark's mushy-mouthed forebodings, watch Herbert sit in quiet desperation at his desk, notice that Burns has got too paranoid to eat his fish in the office (Lloyd-Jackson has already resigned — there's true bottle for you). Only the Controller is calm, though Veale says he oughtn't to be. I am nervous, though Veale says I oughtn't to be. I am as nervous as anyone here.

All this money I get. I feel most nervous when, every Friday morning at half-past ten, I go to get it. I feel nervous when I take my place in the slouching queue at the pay-bay downstairs, among all the stooped clerks, foul-mouthed van-drivers, and prismatic secretaries, when I announce my horrible name (Service, T. — 'Here's old tea service again', 'Two lumps with milk, please', 'Don't like his pot, do you?', etc. etc.) and the fat woman or the thin man flick through the ranked packets, when, to my weekly consternation, my envelope is not only there but actually gets handed over to me, and when I walk back along the line of alternately exuberant and catatonic employees, holding in my fist a heavy brown wallet containing seventy-three quid! Even before all these bonuses started pouring in, I had calculated that I would always be able to afford my daily three packets of fags and my daily litre-and-a-half of Spanish wine — which was all I seemed to need to live and not go mad on. Now there's all this extra stuff: I have a drawer at home, my tramp drawer, silting up with fivers I can't spend; I keep coming across forgotten notes in odd pockets; I weed out the coppers from my change and stack them contemptuously on the window-sill; I took a taxi somewhere the other day, just for the hell of it; la, sir, I might even buy some new clothes. (It would be hard to go broke now, though broke still scares me. Broke always will, I think.)

I've fallen into the habit of leaving my pay-slips in prominent places round my room. The hieroglyphed ribbons are to be found on desk and bed, on bookcase and table. I think he must have seen one by now, because the other Saturday he asked me, in rather appalled tones, whether I could lend him £15; I did so, with negligent panache, and left him staring at the notes as if they'd just materialized in his hand. And naturally I take Ursula out a lot now, in the most ostentatious manner possible, similarly arraying the many restaurant book-matches and expensive cinema-ticket stubs. I like taking Ursula out because it fools the world that I have a girlfriend. It's beginning to fool him. It's beginning to fool me. It's beginning to fool her.

Listen.

Yesterday a sinister and wonderful thing started to happen to me. *Suddenly* (I got home at six-thirty. Ursula and I had one of our quiet evenings together, me drinking and reading and going bald in my room, her knitting and muttering and going mad in hers, but the door between us ever-open) *I knew what I had to do.* Ursula had used the bathroom and was contentedly sitting up in bed by 9.45. About an hour later, Gregory wandered vaguely through to use the bathroom himself, pausing for a rare chat with his sister before wandering vaguely back upstairs. I went through soon afterwards for my own discreet trickles and swabs. On the way back I stood over Ursula's bed, as usual, and leaned forward to kiss her chastely good night.

'Come to my room,' I then said.

'Mm?'

'I said come to my room. Come to my room,' I said.

I switched off my bedside lamp and lay there in tingling naked incredulity, the colourful darkness thudding against my eyes, my heartbeat filling the room, my nose sniffing at the aromatic vacuum, my eardrums peeled for the answering ruffle of blankets and the creak of the adjoining hinges. Before any sound could impose itself on the silent thunder — there she was beside me, a warm downy presence of skin and light cotton. *Christ.* I made no move but then she furled her arms about me in a confident, childish, deeply unsexual embrace and for a time we lay there like sleepers, hardly daring to breathe, her jawline snug in my pit, the caps of her knees oddly cold against my thigh. (Is this it, I thought, or is there more?) I made an almost imperceptible gesture, as if to kiss her, turning on my axis hardly a tenth of an inch, and sensed her stiffen — likewise when I brought a hand up and placed it fraternally on her forearm. Momentarily I felt a sticky uncertainty at the centre of my being — like the panic-second of readjustment after frightening dreams, or like a trivial, charmless memory that says hello every day — but then the little secret clicked and suddenly I knew again what I had to do. I let the secret out.

'Do it,' I said.

'Mm?'

'I said do it,' I said.

'Oh.' At once her thin hand appeared on my chest. Briskly it trailed downwards. With an unthinking grunt she propped up her head on an elbow and slid a few inches down the bed to improve her purchase. I heard her yawn complaisantly, and parted my trembling lids to see the angled, downward-pointing face, the mouth set in feature-less concentration.

And she likes me. At first I half-expected a schoolgirl *tsk tsk* from my no-nonsense bedmate, but after a few patient caresses I found that I was able to offer myself up to those small fingers. Although her movements were strictly mechanical (and never more so than in the trills and graces she executed with her knuckles and nails), it didn't seem at all like distaste — more like affectionate conscientiousness. I lost myself until I felt my muscles tighten and Ursula came closer in response to give me the full action of her arm. Confusedly I made as if to take her hand away (you needn't, you needn't) but her hand was resolute and unsqueamish and I voided with a *whoosh* of hilarious remorse.

'There,' said Ursula firmly, like a nurse, and whispered, 'I think I'd better go back to my room now.'

I turned awkwardly to kiss her and her mouth was nowhere to be found.

'No kisses. Never on the lips.'

'Oh, love, love.'

'You'll never leave me, will you,' she stated.

'No, never, never.'

'You won't tell Gregory, will you.'

'No, I won't, I won't.'

'Good night, Ginger. Whoops. I can't call you that, can I?'

'Yes, you can, you can.'

Happy birthday, Terry. It doesn't take much to make you better.

That morning I brought Ursula tea in bed ('Happy birthday, Terry'), kissed her on her lineless forehead and gave her a note saying that I loved her and would always protect her (one thing about incest − there's no point in playing it cool. They cannot get away. They cannot hide out. They just cannot hide out), and strolled like a mawkish schoolboy up a freshly discovered mews to the Underground. I paused for two whole minutes to watch a high-flying, string-trailing jet, no more than a glinting crucifix in the deep blue above the thin salty clouds. Even the bang and shudder of the Underground kept saying a new thing to me: purpose (there are reasons why people go to work). As soon as I was in the office I rang her, frantic for assent that my life had changed. How are *you*? Are you all right? I'm fine, fine. How are *you*? Are you sure you're all right? It wasn't enough: I rang back ten minutes later. Did you read my note? It's true what I said. It is. Don't worry about anything ever again. And it was the same that afternoon: I couldn't keep away. Me again. Sorry. Can I buy you a nice dinner tonight? I love you. Why? I always have. Don't ask why. I love you.

Why? Because she gave me my cock back, is why. I felt so changed, so brazenly transformed, that I kept expecting mad Wark, or whoever, to come up and say, 'Hey, what's happened to you? Did somebody give you your cock back or something?' Yes, somebody sure did. In several respects, I grant you, it's far from ideal. Ursula is more or less my sister, for instance, and she often seems to be unclear about what exactly is going on. This introduces an arbitrary element — I feel like the Jacobean trickster who impersonates an absent husband in the dark bedroom, or like the lucky sailor who gets to go first in the gang-bang queue: if they knew what I knew (I feel), they wouldn't be *quite* so keen. But, Christ, Gregory did it too (didn't he?), and he really *is* her brother. And it's a start. And who am I to be critical?

I wanted to sprint home that night, but even in the routine delays and prevarications of the afternoon there was something cool and erotic. I loved the man who sold me my evening paper, and I returned the hello of the tobacconist with courtly particularity. The yellow lights of the tube-entrance machines, with their embossed patterns of fares and destinations, made a dusk of the indoors, and as I rode the descending staircase into the grey vault I felt as if a large and watchful creature were welcoming me to its deep preserve. My train raced beneath the city, bursting out of tunnels, creeping back in and bursting out again.

All kinds of surprises awaited me. When I came bounding and barking into the flat, holding two presents for Ursula in my mouth, my tail thumping on the carpet, who should I encounter but fucking *Gregory* (who the fuck is *he*?), sitting with Ursula in her room. But — down, boy, down, and it was such a piquant joke on the past to have *her* making covert, placating gestures at *me*. I offered, greatheartedly and at once, to take them both out to the expensive French place in Dawn Street (I got a birthday bonus from work, too. £25. Happy birthday, Terry). After we had dispersed to change I fawningly offered Ursula her presents — a cashmere jersey and some scent — which she accepted with grave delight, placing a quick kiss on my forehead. Dinner made me feel secure, even pampered, a prince for a day — Greg silently gluttonous

163

(much inspired, no doubt, by the shimmering prospect of not paying for what he ate and drank), Ursula calm and attentive, as I guided the meal along.

'I suppose this is our joint birthday party,' I said at one point.

'Yes,' Gregory agreed, 'I suppose it is.'

We walked home three-abreast, Ursula between her brothers. To my grateful relief, Greg gloomily proposed going to bed straightaway, so Ursula and I walked in single file down the passage (Good night, Good night, Good night) and wordlessly, unsmilingly, we set about our motions of storage and ablution, like people who had lived together all their lives. I walked out of the bathroom, dressing-gowned, and moved past her bed with hardly a backward glance. I lay there, waiting, a last cigarette my taper. She came (with a quick tiptoe through the darkness, the soft kittenish spring landing her knees-first by my pillow, the nervous burrowing slither). And so did I.

(ii) There are many more secrets I
      must tell you — GREGORY

August is the month when we both have our birthdays — the shattering, Nostradaman coincidence that so excited my father. Do you know, by the way, what the twinkly old twerp is up to now? According to Mama, he is landscaping a useless field in some corner of our estate, at colossal expense, with ha-has, mirages, the lot. Mama and I are formulating long-overdue plans to have him *put away*, yes *put away*, before he pauperizes us all.

This proximity of our birthdays was always, naturally, the cause of much gruelling pain for Terence and even of some rather poignant embarrassment for me. Thirty or forty friends usually seemed about right for my parties, and since most of my friends were delivered to Rivers Court by their parents, and since most of my friends' parents were my parents' friends, why, the house was more or less thrown open and a carnival, holiday air blessed the entire estate — the tap-tap of marquees being erected on the lawns, every passageway junction zig-zagging with precipitate, grim-faced servants, the good cottagers (folding their caps in their hands like newspapers) getting their low-octane punch at the side door, the vast driveway rimmed by fat silent cars like rhinoceros at a river-bed, the cacophonous clatter of the hired steel band, the fruity *zoot* of kazoos, whistles and streamers, that flowery throng of high summer. Poor old Terence! I believe it was at my suggestion that we once put through the disastrous scheme of combining the two celebrations. Picture, if you will, the contrasting piles of presents in the drawing-room — T.'s humble rubble of half-a-dozen family tokens next to my fabulous, piratical haul. Imagine, if you can, the wincing introductions — 'And this is little Terence (the boy we've adopted), whose birthday it also is today, well, not today exactly — it's just that ... ' And contemplate, if you must, the split-screen spectacle of the chosen son, metaphorically aloft on the shoulders of the crowd, in a blizzard of confetti and love, and the nauseous, cowering, hot-faced interloper who was always hiding, always hiding. Thereafter we reverted to the standard arrangement, my mythic *mardi gras* being preceded by a small, domestic tea-and-crackers affair in which the servants were bribed to play a prominent part. (Terence attended the village school, and had no doubt formed some sort of preference for a selection of his colleagues there. But we couldn't have the spore of, say, the local street-cleaners, rat-killers, shit-shovellers, and so on, up to the Manor Hall. Now could we?) Ursula and I suffered the mandatory low spirits which such an inequality would tend to enforce, yet frankly we were far too absorbed in one another for Terence's miseries to be truly ours. You see, those years entirely belonged to Ursula and me — Ursula, whose growing body I knew as well as I knew the shape of my own teeth — and the huff-and-puff of Terence's doomed and squalid life, with all its humiliation and hate, seemed an infinitely postponable thing, merely an image of the frenzied greed, stupidity and filth which suddenly beleaguers us now.

I wonder what will happen this year (last birthday I went to the Court, but I'm far too tied up these days) ... I expect I shall take a couple of dozen friends out for a slap-up dinner at Privates', that new place in Chelsea. Then, too, Torka will no doubt throw some extravagant party round one. There'll be the usual salvo of presents and telegrams, and that large cheque from Mama. Wonder what Terence will do for his ... Nothing, is the most appealing possibility, though perhaps he's hoping not to become a tramp until the day *after*! (I don't imagine you realize that Terence pees in the washbasin? Well, he does. On several occasions recently I have found the porcelain stained − at loin height − by a slug's trail of yellow. It's only a hypothesis at the moment, but one that will shortly, I am confident, turn out to be susceptible of proof.)

Now − say quickly: What do you think of me? What do you think of me, Gregory, Gregory Riding, the being I am? Let's hear it − haughty, vain, florid, contemptuous, lordly, superficial, corrupt, conceited, queer − and insensitive, above all insensitive (look how he gives himself away). Actually I'm extremely self-aware. You fool, do you think I don't know all that, all *that*? You fool, I know it, I know it all, you *fool*.

Listen.

Yesterday a sad and irretrievable thing started to happen to me.

I rose at nine. It was sunny. I had a cup of tea and a square of toast. I walked to the underground station in Queensway. The lift was taking one of its frequent days off; I descended the endless steel staircase, my hair scattered by dirty winds from the earth's core. At once the metal train rushed from its hole, an ugly beast sprung from a trap. I entered the half-full carriage and stood, as usual, in one of the door-bays. Everything was as it always is, the suspended hand-holds wiggling at the car's every lurch, the sodium lights fading and strengthening again with a blink, the powerful whine of the undercurrent, the muck on the floors, the heat, the passengers sitting stupidly face to face. Then it started to happen. As the train surged with a *whoosh* out of Lancaster Gate, as the tunnel walls went black and the lights fluttered, then (like the thud of air from a nearby explosion, like the *excuse me* of a sick memory, like the sizzle of mixing chemicals) I felt it, felt it in an instant, felt as if I'd been mad for years, as mad as a mad old sheep in a drizzling field under sodden skies. No, don't do this to me, don't do this to me, no. I got out at the next stop. I climbed to the colourful surface and stood scratching my hair in the mad motion sculpture of Marble Arch, the traffic going on and on, the clouds scudding away above my head.

What happened to me down there? Something did. Physically it was real enough all right — cold sweat, shortness of breath as if my heart were fighting to get out, a bodily tremor too deep to reveal itself in shaking or in shouting either. I saw at once that, like a prentice bicyclist or a first-time-flung equestrian, I would have to go straight back, back into the underground, the nethers, the underside, and I turned, repurchased a ticket, and stood like a doll on the descending staircase as the hammers pounded louder and the dark air swirled and my body (the sweat, the tremor, the heart) again picked up its rhythms. It took every neutrino of my resolve not to turn and race back up the moving steel treadmill like a crazed hamster. And to go on, deeper into all that? — no, no, not a chance. I walked swiftly from the *down* to the *up* staircase and with huge strides raced out into the light.

I tried again that evening. The same. A nightmare succession of slow, smelly, packed, jerking buses ferried me home by seven-thirty. Ursula and Terence were

having one of their sickly little evenings together downstairs, and I couldn't face them anyway. I lay on my bed
until about eleven, then braved the bathroom. Terence,
looking sly and reptilian in an absurd new shirt, sat
crouched at his desk over a fathom of whisky. We never
know how to greet each other these days. Good night.
Hello. See you tomorrow. Ursula was in bed, knitting,
and I paused for a rare chat — yes, she was fine, and had
no trouble filling the days. Alone among the steel and
glass of the bathroom, I found myself toying once more
with the idea of instructing Ursula to visit me later in my
bed. But no — that would be just as frightening in its
way. I went upstairs again and took a strong pill, and
another, and let them all fight it out like blind tribes
inside my head. Somewhere in a room near by, in one of
the forsaken tenements along the street, a demented
foreigner bawled on hysterically into the night. What was
it he kept screaming? ... *Shut the doors* — *shut the doors* —
shut the doors ... At one point I sleepwalked to the open
window and looked out. The doors of the black ambulance
that had come for him were certainly open; but even when
someone closed the doors after him he went on shrieking
mechanically, *Shut the doors* — *shut the doors* ... Which
doors could he have meant, I wondered as I returned to
my bed. It might as well have been morning by the time
I wound down into sleep, the pillow grey and wet, the
dawn grey and soiled behind my curtains.

I tried again this morning. The same. As soon as the
brutal lift doors cracked shut I knew that there was
absolutely no chance, not the puniest most blighted hair
of hope. I walked quite solemnly up the great steel staircase. I took a cab this morning. But I can't afford it.
I must adapt my life.

Who is there to talk to? I rang Torka from the gallery —
rude Keith answered and was impossibly offensive when
I asked him to make Torka call me back. I rang Mama
from a telephone-box at lunchtime — but she was preoccupied and vague and too far away. Skimmer and

Kane — they're idiots really, just upper-class yobs (you never did meet them, did you?); they wouldn't understand anything like this. God, sometimes you turn round to test the rope-holds of your life and realize how tenuous they are. Now I've got this new thing in my life called panic. It was only a word to me until yesterday. What do I want with panic? Why can't panic go and pick on somebody else?

After a confused talk with Ursula, I returned home by surface mail, edged along the queueing city with all the others in the sluggish reshuffle of evening. Ursula — and Terence, if you please — were waiting up in my room, both looking pathetically dependent on me to transform their day, to relieve their series of tired little compacts below-stairs. I had intended to take Ursula out to dinner, and now felt too drained to prevent Terence from joining us; when I decided on the French place in Dawn Street and Ursula ran off to get ready, I made no real effort to stop him tagging along. We walked there zestlessly. The restaurant was crowded and far too dark (practically requiring usherettes to guide the diners to their tables). Once I had secured an aperitif and decided on my meal I abstractedly relinquished the job of ordering it to Terence; this he stutteringly did, with much gauche deference to the waiters (and how badly he pronounced the names of the French wines). I let them both chatter through dinner, and then, after two large Benedictines, forced Terence to pay, by way of recompense for giving him an evening out. But it afforded me no genuine pleasure, even when I saw that huge tab whisked away, smothered with Service's fivers. We walked home three-abreast (T. on the outside, one foot in the gutter, dodging trees); it was suggested we have some 'coffee' together, a scheme I briskly quashed. They scuttled off to their beds downstairs, to the calm cycles of their calm lives, while I, with the help of some pills and that liquor, searched for the letter A in the random alphabet of sleep.

*   *   *

What happened to me down there?

Everything has changed. That was all it took. A whole layer of protective casing has been ripped off my life. Nothing looks the way it used to look. Familiar objects now writhe with their own furtive being (I think they do things behind my back). When my eyes pass over the trogs, the yobs, the animals in the street — people who were hardly there at all before — I get sucked in by them helplessly and see the hell *they* are too. I take nothing for granted any more: the tiniest action or thought is broken down into a million contingencies. I have come out. I am one of you now. Where did I catch all this?

There are many more secrets I must tell you. But go easy on me. It's my birthday. Let's take things one at a time. (I know. I caught it from him.)

9: September

(i) This is one of the ways you get them
at your mercy — TERRY

There is now something leprous and inexorable about my nights. Things have progressed with steady certainty, with the slow cohering logic of a genre novel, or a chess combination, or a family game. Already I know how it will end — things will suddenly get much worse for two of us and never get better again — but I cannot break out. I don't want to break out. I will go on until it happens. That seems to be the only thing I can do.

I went out with a blind girl for a while, you know — that's right, totally, congenitally blind: she even sported dark glasses and a white stick, which used to look like a floating chalk mark or a trail of smoke in the streets at night, an irrelevant thing when we were all blind too. Plenty of attractions, then, for the concerned, duffle-coated student, with his plastic bag of books and his experimental ginger beard (I soon aimed *that*). She was small, Jewish and slender; she had dazzling black hair, a large tragic nose, damp-sand complexion and wide lips almost as brown as her skin; she was regretfully agreed by all to be pretty. Think, also, of the poignancy of that brave but hesitant figure, strolling relaxed and cheerful with her friends between lectures, yet an uncertain sleepwalker when you glimpsed her alone in the town, her tread trying to be firm, her expression changing with scary rapidity as she moved down unknown paths. Consider, in addition, the fact that (a) she was a girl, and (b) she couldn't see what I looked like, and you begin to appreciate the full potency of her spell.

She was tremendously easy to negotiate. I merely helped her across the road one day in town, asked her where she was going, and announced my intention to accompany her. There's nothing they can do about it, you see: that's the point of them. I was as nice as I possibly could be to her for a very long time. In due course she started almost going to bed with me (yes, she was one of the girls I wrote to when nobody would go anywhere near going to bed with me. She is a married woman now, or dead, or *tonto* in a home. Can't quite remember if she ever replied). I knew it was going to turn nasty the moment her blindness became something I could use: and, sure enough, one evening, in her room, when she removed the freckly hand that was shimmering flat-palmed up her thigh and placed it primly back on my lap, I raised my hand again and waggled two fat splayed fingers underneath her nose. Suddenly the door was open. I took to hovering behind the sofa on which she sat, peering without relish into the slanting triangle of her shirt; I used to return on all fours from putting on a record, staring the while up her skirt (they don't know how to sit right, these blind girls); I would make faces at her constantly, finding particular enjoyment in belying my words with my facial expression, so that, say, everyday cordialities would be synchronized with gazes of rapt ardour, tender endearments chaperoned by contortions of sneering hate, etc. Finally, as we lay naked in her bed one evening (that was okay. But she was into non-penetration), I produced, with some effort, the sound-effects of a crying-jag, piteously honing that she could not really love me, that I would die if I did not possess her, and suchlike mendacities. In the end she complied, shedding more tears than I ever shed that night. We didn't see each other again. The point was, you understand, that she *knew* I was faking, but couldn't say she knew. Because that would have been much too frightening, wouldn't it?

This is one of the ways you get them at your mercy.

Shudder shudder.

'What else did you do?' I ask, arresting with a twitch of my haunches the downward trend of Ursula's hand.

'Mm?'

She has just slid into bed with me for the eighteenth night running and seems by now quite blasée about the routine, showing a tendency, indeed, to get down to her task with what I take to be insulting dispatch (not that my cock gives a shit one way or the other. It does just like I tell it these days).

'You and him. What else did you do?' Stiffly I place an arm round her shoulders, raising the timbre of my voice to make things sound friendly.

'Well, yes,' she muses to my armpit (I don't know how she can bear me during these revolting interludes), 'as a matter of fact there were other things we did.'

' ... Oh yes? Like what?'

She wriggles slightly. 'Can't *say* them.'

'Do it then,' I hear myself tell her, in the impervious monotone I have developed for such requests: 'Do it.'

Again with a non-committal grunt, as of some dead-end toiler asked to switch from one equally meaningless chore to another, my foster-sister shinnied down the bed. There was no contact between her skin and mine until I felt the firm, distinct clamp of her lips.

'Was that all right?' I asked in awed disbelief when she resurfaced.

'I think I'll get used to it,' said Ursula, crinkling her her nose in distaste.

Hardly perfect, is it?

After each one of these nightly acts — after Ursula's self-satisfied 'There', uttered in the tone of the truly experienced virgin — my immediate and prevailing instinct has been one of grateful, yearning reciprocation. On the first night I slithered down the bed like a fool, and only after a humiliating struggle — Ursula half-slithering down the bed with me — did I blinkingly re-emerge. Clearly, that wasn't the idea. For the next few nights I reached out for the body in the bed beside me with a kind of ecstatic circumspection, as if it were a friend's baby or a critical nuclear pile, only for my fingers to find it dead, dead, a frozen log on a gusty night. Once she jerked away with crude abruptness, and I snarled silently in the darkness. For a moment there, I was back where I was before. I haven't tried since. But I'm going to try again soon. I've been thinking what's best to do.

Is Gregory on to us? (Has he said anything?) I would guess not. I would guess he has other things on his mind. Natural conceit protects him, of course, but now there are other things, and I'm pretty sure I know what they are. He looks scared (look at him! *He* looks *scared*). He looks as if the very air might turn on him in fury ... When we were young, I was always the scared one, always getting fucked up and peed on at school, always getting stomped and creamed by the townies, always getting belted and hollered at by the parkies, always in tears over some trifling slight, always scared. Gregory hardly ever cried as a child — only at the distress of others (yes, that's true).

Now he goes about with the ripe, tremulous smile of someone with too much emotion in his nostrils. He is really scared.

I don't think I need do anything about him after all. Something else is doing it for me. I think things are being taken care of very nicely.

'Ah, hullo. Come in, Terry.'

' ... Which way?'

I stood in the sweeping drive of Mr Stanley Veale's Fulham home, an auburn three-storey Victorian residence against whose broad husk various gleaming super-structures leaned and crouched. Veale addressed me through the slide-up window of one of these dinky little afterthoughts, what looked like an oval breakfast-room full of pink chairs and motley scatter-cushions. His great white face remained expressionless.

'Through the car-ports.'

Oh, you have more than one car-port, do you, I thought, having already noticed the three cars lying in their ruts of gravel — the heavy Ford Granada, the van, the Mini.

'Which car-port?' I asked.

'There's only one car-ports,' said Veale gravely. 'I keep the Granada down the road. It's for the runabouts. Round the side.'

Oh, you have more than one runabout, do — 'Oh, right,' I said, tardily realizing that Veale's lust for the plural was a shrill result only of his posh emphasis on the terminal *t* (a decade ago, no doubt, he would have said *car-por'* and *runabar'*. But then again he wouldn't have needed to say those words a decade ago). Hence also, presumably, his fondness for the husky initial *h*. Veale said *hello* like a resolute halitotic sounding out a friendship.

I set off round the side — Veale's head gingerly with-drawing — between the fireman's poles of the car-port, and into an open-air vestibule where a large selection of cloaks, capes and bike-ponchos stood hooked to the wall, shrivelled prisoners in a northern camp. A heap of lopped feet, in the form of discarded wellingtons, lay on the tiled floor. A glass wall slid back: Veale turned away down a wide passage that immediately spanned out into a double-level sitting-room — fluffy white rugs like snow on moss, facing sofas as long as cinema rows, a fireplace the size of a back-entrance to Versailles, a kidney-shaped bar against the shelved walls of bottles.

'Scotch?' said Veale. 'It had better be. That's all there is for now. Unless you want that sweet shit,' he added, gesturing with contempt at the bottles of Parfait Amour and Chocolate Mint Cream, ranked about him. 'My wife drinks that sweet shits. *Before lunch.* You watch her.'

'Incredible place you've got,' I said. Veale took a gilt paper-knife and ground it into one of the four cases stamped WHISKY behind the bar. 'Christ. Do you buy in bulk?'

'You could put it that way,' said Veale urbanely. 'The vodka and that's not indoors yet. Here — four cases of whisky, four vodka, four gin, four rum, four campari, four vermouth, four brandy: one-eighty cash.'

'Really? What, you get it cheap?'

'No, I pay extra, don't I? I mean, you don't have to be … Maynard Keynes to work that one out. Course I get it cheap.'

'Sorry.'

'Can't remember when I last paid full for anything. Only a prick would pay full for anything these days. All cash. Up front.'

'Really?' I perched on a stool, accepting the largest whisky I had ever seen, heard or read about.

'Yur. Course it's not what it was.'

'You used to get other stuff?'

'Wine, sherry, ports — the lots. See the Granada in the drive? Got that less than half showroom price.'

'How?'

He sniffed. 'Now how do you think?'

Clamour from the direction of the far door preceded

the entry of two small boys (one of them, in fairness, about twice the size of the other). In a tone of benign formality Veale asked what he could do for them.

'Orange, please, Dad,' said the smaller, in unreclaimed Cockney.

'Pepsi, please, Dad,' said the larger, in comparatively courtly accents.

Veale served his sons.

'Thanks, Dad.'

'Thanks, Dad.'

'That's one thing I *do* pay full for,' said Veale when they had gone. 'Costs me a grand-and-a-half to send that little bugger to school.'

'What, he goes to a sort of private school, does he?'

'No, it all goes on bus-fares. It's the bus-fares to the Comprehensive that's really crippling. I don't know why I bother with you, sometimes, Terry. I mean, it doesn't take ... Maffyou Arnold to work that one out.'

'Sorry. I'm drunk.'

'So am I, mate. Drunk Friday night to Monday morning — always am.'

'This private school bit. Isn't that all rather' — I coughed — 'against your principles?'

'No. It's nots. It's not against my principles at all. What do you think we're after, eh? Steakhouses, transistors, Costa Brava holidays? That ratcrap?

'Now listen. Have you seen the Branch man yet?'

'Yup.'

'Good. So have I. He's friendly, but he says you've got to do the Course.'

'Damn. I thought he would. Which Course?'

'Four nights a week for a month. No trouble. At the City College. It's just protection.'

'What will it cost.'

'That'll come from funds, don't worry. Here.' He rebrimmed my glass. 'Anything going at the office?'

'Nah. They wouldn't get organized even if they could. It's not in them.'

Veale gazed neutrally at me. 'Cunts,' he said.

The session ended soon after the beguiling entrance of Veale's wife, a rather marvellously tarty woman called Meg — Miggie? Mags? — something ridiculous like that. She wore astonishing white trousers. The bits of them that weren't already halfway up her bum were as transparent as polythene: you could see the line of her panties, and their tender blue check. A woman with tremendously large breasts, she paid me a terrifying amount of attention, all of it under Veale's pensive, grey-eyed stare. (I think he *must* think I'm posh.) I probably drank, oh, I don't know — about three-quarters of a bottle?

'Stay for lunch next time,' said Mags.

'Cheers,' said Veale.

I walked happily in the sun to Fulham Broadway Underground. I thought:

I want all that and I want all that. And I want all *that* and I want all *that*. And I want *all* that and I want *all* that. I don't want what he has. But I want what he wants.

'Why, hello there, fair sir. Hello there, sweet prince,' I said forty minutes later (all these new people I know).

The fucked-up hippie lay roasting in the small car park behind The Intrepid Fox. He was spreadeagled hellishly on the hot macadam, as if he had been staked out there by Indians. Most of his teeth were gone now, and his skin was old rope. 'How the hell are things?' I asked.

'I don't talk to shits like you,' said the fucked-up hippie.

'I love all this about me being a shit. How do *you* know, brilliant?'

'I don't talk to shits.'

'You're the real Fool on the Hill, aren't you? You show the shits what the hell it's all about.'

'Fuck off, shit.'

'Yup. Well! Everything looks okay here. Everything seems hunky-dory with you. Nice place you got, nice long winter to look forward to — lots of happy-go-lucky months ahead.'

'Don't worry about me, shit. I do all right.'

'Oh, you do, you do, you certainly do. No, I can tell that. Better than us fat boys, who have to sit in a nice office all day, and come home and cuddle up nights. You bring your chicks back here?'

'Yeah.'

'Put on the hi-fi, out comes the scotch, and so on. Mm, I bet they're suckers for someone like you, a heartbreaker like you. For a start you look about eighty, no teeth and so on, and we all know they go for that. Plus you crap in your clothes, also very popular I believe. And — '

'Go back to work, you little shit.'

'Look at you, you dumb hippie. You could go to jail for smelling like you smell. Look at you, you dumb tramp.'

'Don't talk to me, shit. Find another shit to talk to. Why d'you talk to me?'

'Because I love it,' I said. 'I ... *love* it.'

To the careless observer, at least, the night of September 30th would have looked like any typical U and I evening. Everything quite normal and under control: my prompt return from work, Ursula knitting and pondering while I changed and boozed, Gregory's incurious roam through our rooms (he goes to wash off the taint of other people's air), the meal at the three-time-losers' wine bar, the walk home — no hands — along Queensway (loud shop windows but it's dark behind, the odd tramp or spinning, gesticulating drunk — all nice and nasty for Ursula), then the reassuring dimness of our suite: the little fan-heater belching rhythmically in the corner, the thick curtains shut, the dividing door wide open until it is time to go to bed. I visit the bathroom second (where I catch my eye in the mirror. I pee, by the way, in the basin these days; it's quieter like that, plus which it reminds you to wash your cock). 'Come soon,' I say, on the way back, as usual.

Ah, but things are different tonight and I think she knows it (I hope she does). For my manner has changed —

subtly yet radically my manner has changed. No longer am I the shrugging, grateful, ironic foster-brother, the cowed denizen of a changing city, the young man who is just about holding on. No, tonight he is calm. His words are few and far between. He listens to Ursula's directionless and interminable commentary on her day (the one that can only end: Then I came here. Now I'm talking to you about it) with the air of a preoccupied parent. He is authoritative, even rather cold perhaps, in the dark restaurant, ordering straightaway for this young girl he has brought with him; he settles the bill and stands to leave, his gaze elsewhere. And when he escorts her down the overlit shaft of Queensway, his demeanour and stride have something of the epic serenity of the child murderer — the assumed prerogative of adulthood, nothing bad can happen if you stay at my side, the offer of toffees through his whisky breath, come with me little one — tickled and thrilled by the audacity of his needs, the ravenous applause in his brain.

She is beside him, in her nightdress.
Take if off, he says.
I'm cold.
Take it off.
I'm *cold*, Ginger.
Don't call me Ginger.
You said I could.
I was lying. You can't. Take it off.
Oh ...
That's better. No. No, not yet. Wait ... Be *still*.
... No, don't do that.
Why not?
Please.
Why not?
Just don't.
Why not?
Oh please don't.
That's very childish, Ursula. And extremely unnatural.

Why don't you want me to do to you what you do to me? Eh? Eh?

I just don't.

That's the way a child answers, Ursula. And that's the way a child behaves.

Oh, I'm going back to bed.

You certainly are not! Now that's what I mean. Ursula, how do you expect people to love and protect you when you behave like this? Tell me, Ursula, please — I'd really like to know. There are people who will look after you, and I am one of them, but if you go on behaving like this we will all go away. We will all go away because you are behaving unnaturally, because you are *tonto* ... Now, yes ... that's right, that's all you have to do — see? — just lie back, no need to cry now, just want you to — ah-ah-ah, *tonto*, Ursula, *tonto* ... Yes that's right, that's right, that's right.

He is down there feeling like an exultant gargoyle, probing, sniffing, staring, feasting, when Ursula shudders and jerks, half-crossing her legs (and dealing him a mighty crack on the chin with her bony kneecap), as if she has heard someone coming in the distance. He is about to spit some crudely high-minded rebuke — when he hears it too. Snap. In a spurt of clumsy terror, he has wriggled galvanically from the bed. The light comes on like a flashbulb and the dirty boy crouches stranded in the middle of the room as the door swings open.

(ii) I used to love the man I
      would become — GREGORY

Who'd have thought it?

Yesterday morning I happened to stroll past the Underground station on my way to the bus-stop. I was looking in superb form, with my cape fanned out behind me like Superman's, wearing some crackly new snakeskin boots, my hair spruced high by an expensive haircut. On an impulse, I paused and peered into the black and yellow grot of paper-stalls and ticket machines. A big-shouldered Scandinavian hitch-hikerette, crippled by a lumpy green knapsack the size of a rolled double-mattress (no doubt housing a kitchen range and a three-storey tent), gazed at me with listless desire. A middle-aged American couple — they *had* to be American: how else the matching Pickwickian check of their trousers? — wheeled about arm in arm, looking for a sign ... — Why not? I thought. I marched straight in, purchased a ticket and a *Times*, entered the half-full lift (some monkey checking my ticket over), and descended without incident to the platform, into which the silvery bullet at once exploded. I got in — and read a quite shrewd leader on the economic collapse as the train zipped beneath the city. When I emerged into a great wash of sunlight at Green Park, and stood bantering with the deliciously sideburnt flower-boy (who gave me my Camberwell rose for free), I turned and looked into the pit of harm from which I had triumphantly climbed. Well, I thought, that's put paid to *that*.

Recognize the style (I suppose I'd better change that too now)?

If you believed it, you'll believe anything. It was a lie. The very entrance to the Underground makes me want to pee with dread. I cross the street to avoid it, as one might to avoid a boring friend, or a foaming dog, or a flailing drunk. I'm not going back there ever again. Ever.

It was a lie. I tell lies. I'm a liar. I always have been. I'm sorry. Here come the secrets.

My job, for instance, is, and always has been (to put it mildly), *fucking awful*. It is a round of boredom and humiliation, with no prospects and no rewards. I have to make the tea now (I always did have to, actually), and clean the lavatory on my knees. I spend two hours a day polishing frames in the stock-room. I have to deliver paintings all over London (I haven't told the Styleses about the Underground and me. It takes hours: the stacked buses are late and go nowhere I need to go. They get very angry with me and there's nothing I can say). I sweep up. They never let me do any selling. They treat me like a nasty schoolboy. They don't even *fancy* me, not any longer. They pay me exactly half the national-average wage, less than anyone I know or have ever heard about. And they say that this will soon be cut, because they are going under too.

I worry about money all the time — I feel like the buckled L of a pound sign or like a note on a thin rippling banner. I daren't open letters any more. I've sold whatever I had that I could sell. That 'expensive' green car of mine (absent, you'll have noticed, for some while now) went long ago: I hoped they might give me perhaps £100 for it, but the village idiot at the Garage of Thieves said that I'd be lucky to sell it for scrap (the brute was quite right of course: it was a worthless car, barely capable of getting you down the street). I haven't bought any new clothes since March; I go on about the bounty of my wardrobe, but indeed it is sorrily threadbare now (and most of my clothes are ridiculous — I can't wear them to work). Buying anything non-essential makes me feel furtive, criminal, a counterfeiter. Damn it, *any* exchange of money for goods fills me with inordinate fear. Inordinate? I cannot live on the money I am paid. Nobody could. I cannot get to and from work every day and eat and not quite go mad. I cannot *stay alive* on what I earn. My overdraft grows in lines of figures and print, spawning bank charges, interest payments. I can no longer read a book or even watch television without this other drama rearing up inside my mind, mangling page and screen. I cannot do anything without money leering over my shoulder. I think about money all the time. Money has robbed me of everything I had.

And there is no more where I came from. Oh, we're posh all right, and I really do hate the yobs (as they hate me — I can see that now. They will turn on me soon.

They are waiting. I am waiting. I live in perpetual fear of violence. A young man approached me abruptly in the square last week and I veered away with my arms protectively raised. The young man looked puzzled, concerned; he only wanted to know where the Underground was. Any scuffle or disturbance in the street — and there are plenty these days: the world is boiling up; everyone *is* getting nastier; everyone is drunk; everyone is desperate — makes me sweat and makes me run. I don't walk out at night if I can help it. People are waiting there to break my teeth. People are waiting there to do me harm), but we never had much money, and my father has nearly spent it all, that mad fuck (my language will be the next to go). It lasted his time. It won't last mine. Thanks. I wish now that I had studied more, and done all that. But I didn't do anything. I thought proper people didn't need to. They do now.

I expect, too, that you think my sexual life is as gleaming and ripe as Terence's is joyless and jejune. I expect you think I'm an absolute corker when it comes to the cot. Well, I used to be, I admit (everything I've said about my extraordinary good looks, for example, is fact, spot on, to the letter, gospel. I am indeed wonderfully handsome). There was a time when I was widely thought to be the cutest catch in London: queers came to Torka's from miles around, just to have a glimpse of me, to find out if all everyone said was true (and it was true, it was); any girl, any girl whatever, was mine at a nod, at a smile, at a hardly perceptible twitch of my artistic fingers. Both graceful and athletic, at once supple and firm, now submissive and obedient, now menacing and strict, I was what they called 'a miracle', with a marvellous talent for sex and play. But then all that's gone bad on me too, bad and sad, bad and sad and mad. And they treat me like shit at Torka's these days.

Why? Is it part of the same thing? (Suddenly I keep needing to ask all these questions. Why? Tell me, some-one, why won't someone *tell* me?) I know there are other bits of my life just waiting to go next; they have no other function but to snuff out when it will do me most harm. I wander into the kitchen first thing, and it looks intensely familiar and yet intensely irritating, as if all night I had wearily dreamt of forks and spoons; and the lies of the past are already queueing up to point their fingers.

And Terry. What is this with him now? No, *don't* tell me. Don't tell me he's becoming a success. No, don't tell me that.

Although I may have been inclined to draw my foster-brother in a playfully disadvantageous light, his ineptitude, stupidity and charmlessness must surely come warmly across, with or without any elaboration from me. Again, veracity has been the keynote of even my briefest descriptions of his person. He really does look like that! His nasty hair thins by the hour; his polychromatic teeth (all of which bear the variegations of cheap dental work, surfacing like invisible ink as the fillings live and the bones die) now taper darkly off into the metallic hecatomb of his jaws — the bent, self-pitying mouth, the appallingly malarial eyes. They're all there. He has got the word YOB scribbled across his mean forehead. Both gutless and aggressive, as craven and sentimental as he is sour and crude, lacking any genetic tradition, any pact with good behaviour, Terence is simply the representative of the values that have got to him first.

But the yobs are winning. And Terry, of course, is 'doing well'. He is *doing well*. Of course. He has shown that he will perform what is necessary to succeed. He has shown that he is prepared to trade his days. He is doing well.

I am going to try to tell the truth from now on. It has all become too serious for lying, and I must protect myself as best I can. I'll try. But will you listen? No, I suppose you'll trust Terence's voice now, with its dour fidelity to the actual, rather than mine, which liked to play upon the surface of things.

184

And Ursula.

'Ursula,' I said in the passage (I've been hiding from her too long), 'why won't you come to my room at night?'

She turned towards me but did not meet my eye. I could see the wonky parting on her lowered head, and she smelled of the old smell, of the outdoors.

'Can't,' she said.

'Can,' I said — '*can*. You won't wake him. You won't wake *him*.'

'I just don't think it's a very good idea, that's all.'

'What? What do you mean? Do you mean you think it's only a *fairly* good idea?'

'It just doesn't make me feel any better, doing that.'

'Now what the *hell* do you mean?'

'Oh, Gregory, please' — and her head begins to swirl with confusion, in the way that used to make me ache with tenderness, in the way that now makes me throb with hate — 'I don't feel well *ever* now, I don't ever *feel* well. Nearly everything makes me feel worse. I don't — '

'Why? Why, why, why?'

'You *know* why,' she said in sudden outrage, in defiant, goaded outrage. 'Why don't you *leave me alone*?'

'Look at me! Now you're not getting *silly*, now, are you, Ursula? Remember how angry it makes me when you start getting *silly* … '

Remember (I want to say), remember, my princess, when it happened? Listen. Your first day at the big girls' school. Mama and Papa had driven you in (to while away the time at shops and aunts', and to drive you back). You wore a dark smock, two thin straps over your white-shirted shoulders, and a smart beret. I myself stood in the drive, with good Mrs Daltrey, and waved as the car sped confidently through the gates. You waved back, without fear. You were nearly fourteen (God forgive me). All morning, as I sat perched up in my tree-house, sculpting aimlessly with my penknife at some twig, or practising my tennis against the prickly garage wall, or thinking of my own school — its welcome back, the beds laid out in rows, the Captain of Swimming, whom I had found tearfully fondling my rugger boot one day when I returned unexpectedly to the dorm — I thought of your day too, the oblongs of claret stone, this is the new girl, the self-sufficient hysteric standing like a flag at the head of the classroom (ah, the fatal corporeality of school-teachers). Once lunch was finished, and once I could hear Mrs Daltrey's complacent snores from her parlour dog-basket, I took to the webby attics (the trunks, the bed-posts and winded mattresses, the single sunlit pine plank leaning against a wall), as beneath me the house lay suspended and still, a great brick ship basking in the afternoon. I was by the window, scanning the cricket scores of a yellowing newspaper — Graveney, Barrington, Dexter — when I glanced outside at the front lawn and blinked through the sun and leopard-shade. What I saw made my blood jolt. (I so wanted that day to be a success.) You were running up the drive, a tiny blur of pain — I couldn't see your face but everything about you looked like distress, stiff and creased and weak, a machine's last attempt to work, as if all that kept you from collapse was the desperate rhythm of your stride. We met head-on in the first-floor passage; you were in my arms: *Quiet*, I said in terror. You were breathing so hard that I clamped my hand over your mouth, to keep you there, to keep you in, to put you back. You talked in tears (only the young do that): *They hate me — They said they hate me!* I thought you might snap, explode, zoom through the air. *Make it stop — make it, make it!* We went into the nearest room. It was my room. You lay on the stripped bed. I lay on top of you. You were shaking insanely. You wanted to be smothered, joined up, plugged, to stop the bits of you from flying apart for ever. You wanted me as close as I could get. Who would have borne it? I couldn't. Your pants were navy-blue and slightly furry. The insides of your thighs were goose-

186

pimpled with dread but inside you were boiling. I only remember the smell, the smell of young sweat and salt-and-pepper tears, and the other smell of fluid and blood. I just lowered my trousers. Everything was over in a moment. I hoped I didn't break anything.

'Oh, Gregory, don't do this to me, don't *do* it.'

'Then tell me why, tell me *why*?'

'You *know*. So just *stop* it.'

And I stop it — quickly. She can see I'm as frightened as she is.

(There might have been a moment when we could have helped each other. That moment has passed. We're on our own now.)

It was the last night of the month. It was midnight. The secret agents of sleep no longer glanced at me with interest or suspicion. I sat up straight in bed and clasped my hands together. My eyes were streaming (how ridiculous) — why won't my body behave? And why is sleep so hard to find, and why do dreams spring in to translate your fears in measures of forgetfulness and failure? I sit here upright in my bed, sobbing into my hands. I am six-feet-one-and-a-half. I've been an adult for some time now. Surely I'm too big to go on like this ... I crawled from the bed. I put on my dressing-gown and moved towards the stairs. Ursula (I don't care. I need someone to go mad with). I used to love the man I would become. I don't any longer. Look at him, look at him.

The flat was full of a neutral headache grey. I paused at the bottom of the stairs. The grey was boiling up, climbing, as if it wanted to spill into harsh laughter. Through the narrow hall window I saw squares of life on the backs of the houses opposite. A dirty bulb came on near by. An exhausted man in a vest, with a stubbled neck, hunched over a sink. Would he turn towards *his* window, and find me out?

I stumbled on. The grey thickened in the passage, its dust wired to the dust in my throat. I stumbled on past the cupboards. I hurried — never stop now. I threw on the light as the door swung open. And I focused.

On what?

I turned and ran back up to my room. I put on clothes. I chased my heartbeat out of the flat, down the stairwell, through the doors into the black air.

10: October

(i) I think I'm beginning to like the way the world is changing — TERRY

Of course, you know, it was all his fault in most respects. The whole thing was his fault really. None of it would ever have happened if it hadn't been for him. We can look back on these events now, and see that that's the way it was.

I wouldn't, naturally, have planned it *quite* the way it turned out (I didn't get laid yet, is a powerful for-instance). And I completely lost my bottle during those first shrill seconds. Had it occurred to him to do so, Gregory could have struck me to the floor and given me a sound thrashing there and then. I would have given no resistance: you can fuck with the upper classes only so far, as every true yob knows. I just put on my dressing-gown and lit a fag and stared at the wall. As soon as we heard the flat door being wrenched shut — Greg off for his Byronic storm out into the night (marvellous stuff) — Ursula slipped from the bed and strode past me, with no expression whatever on her face. Well, that's that, fat boy, I thought to myself, watching her anorexic ass disappear through the door, which shut unemphatically behind it. Your control over that girl has gone for good. You'll see no more of her.

They should have come for me then. They should have got me then. If I had been in their shoes, *I'd* have got me then. They couldn't have known how vulnerable I felt. Otherwise they would surely have taken the chance to give me payment for all that I've done to them.

Ursula avoided me for several days. I avoided her. Gregory avoided me. I avoided him. He avoided her, too, and she avoided him (I'm pretty certain), which was some comfort. We kept nearly bumping into each other, unavoidably. I wished we could stop avoiding each other long enough to agree to avoid each other properly.

All this avoiding that was going on posed certain logistic difficulties. I was so keen on avoiding Ursula that I didn't even dare use the bathroom in the mornings. I staggered out of the flat with moustachioed teeth and a bladder like a molten cannonball, and hit a local café for breakfast and a hairtrigger bowel-movement in the cardboard cubicle; I shaved at work, in the nasty lavatories, which are still loud with exploding old men.

So is the office now. The rationalization has begun in earnest. Wark left last week. He went *tonto* opportunely; he had been looking secretly but hard for other jobs — he never found any, he never got a glimpse of a single one; he stalked out of here without opening the ominously stamped brown envelope he saw one morning among his mail, which means he won't even get the derisory non-Union compensation, that idiot. Fish-eating Burns will leave next week; he is not the kind to give trouble. Ex-beatnik Herbert clings grimly to his desk: he hasn't been fingered yet, but he is already talking about squatters' rights, protests and letters to the press (he shouldn't do *anything* like that — the Union *hates* anything like that, according to my friend Veale). John Hain is calm, or thinks he is. So am I. My advice to the professionally inviolable Damon, however, is to resign *instanter*, while he's still alive: the boys from downstairs beat him up with growing brio; Damon doesn't need this. A heavy-set, trendily dressed, unsmiling man in his late twenties has moved into Wark's room. He is a Union man, and so keeps himself pretty much to himself.

After work I have time for — let's say — three big whiskies before going off to my evening classes in the derelict caverns behind Farringdon Street. You sit in a dirty lecture-room while some old deadbeat tells you about positive thinking and how to evade certain sorts of questions. There's a bit of speedwriting too. We are all very lonely and friendly there, and some of us tend to go on to the pub, including two unremarkable girls, whom I shall approach in turn the minute I get my bottle back.

I'm glad I get home late. I'm glad Gregory is dangling up in his room and never comes down any more and never goes out. I'm glad Ursula lies curled up with her face to the wall, playing possum, playing dead, when I sneak through to wash and pee (and vomit briskly, if I feel up to it). I think: we're all on an equal footing at last, more or less. We're quits. We're even.

And then — guess who I ran into the other day?

I was lunching in the pub for once — normally I go to an agreeable little Greek place round the corner — when I noticed a familiar figure in a familiar stance up against the bar. The long legs restlessly sharing the burden of that tiny waist, the energetic slouch of the disproportionate thorax, the corkscrew hair. Jan.

Oh, Jesus (I thought), where can I hide? But she turned at once, saw me, gasped, smiled, waved, and gestured that she would be right with me. I did a quick mental check: hair in some sort of possession of my crown, not bad shirt, shaved this morning, haven't farted for at least ten seconds. I drank deep and lit a cigarette.

'Well, well, well.'

'Aha.'

'So.'

'Well then.'

'And how are you?' Jan asked.

'Oh, you know. And you?'

'Why didn't you ever ring me?'

Because you cut my cock off, you bitch, is all. That was the only reason. 'Ring you? When?'

'After that mad night at your flat. Is your sister okay?'

'Yes, she's okay.' Couldn't quite believe all this was going on. 'Yes, it was rather a mad night, wasn't it.'

'You're telling me. That flatmate of yours — cor.'

An unrealistically tasteless remark, I thought, but I said, mildly enough: 'How do you mean, "cor"?'

'Boy, has he got problems.'

'Oh he's got problems, has he?'

'I'll say.' She sipped contentedly on her whisky and orange. Her extraordinary irises, with their violet webbing, held no activity, ironic or otherwise.

'What kind of problems?'

She laughed, lifting a hand self-reprovingly to cover her mouth. 'Well, the minute you left he started talking to me in this funny way. He is queer, isn't he?' She laughed again.

'What kind of funny way?'

She imitated him, with her customary exactitude. 'You know, sort of: "Ah now, and if this delightful sky-urchin would merely reveal her mysteries, then mayhap the — " Oh, you know. I can't remember. God it was funny. I kept laughing.'

'Then what?'

'Then ... ' And for the first time some commiseration entered her face. She looked down quickly, but only for a moment. 'Oh God. Then he asked me to do this strip. Still in that funny voice, "unveil your several treasures, my sweet", and stuff like that. Well I — I was anybody's that night — I sort of did a dance for him.'

'What, a strip?'

'Kind of.'

'How do you mean, "kind of"? Did you take your clothes off or didn't you take your clothes off?'

'Well I kind of took off my T-shirt. And my jeans.'

'Then what's all this about him having problems? It doesn't sound to me as if he had any problems at all.'

'No, but then he didn't — he couldn't get a hard-on.'

'Neither can I, sometimes.'

'No, but it didn't get that far. It was *awful*. It really was. It was *awful*.'

'In what way?' This was interesting all right, and reasonably consoling. But I felt oddly remote, even protective, too. It was a family affair.

'He started crying,' said Jan. 'Really loud. It was awful. Him crying. *Him* crying like that.'

'What about — not getting hard-ons?'

'A bit, I suppose. And about being queer and broke. And about his sister going mad. He said that if she went mad he knew he would too. And about — oh everything. He sounded really fucked up.'

I lit another cigarette. I felt, again, that sense of invigorating coldness that has strengthened me so much recently. And I said — but it was only an afterthought by now — 'So you'd have gone to bed with him anyway? If of course he could have got a proper hard-on.'

She held my eye. 'Yup. And I would have with you too. If *you* could have got one.'

'Why didn't you *stay*, damn it? Why didn't you stay?'

'I was going to! But he said I'd better leave. He said you wouldn't come back, or you might bring your sister back with you. Or something.'

'So that was that.'

'I told him to tell you to ring me. You never did.'

'He never did either.'

'You never got the message?'

'No. But I've got it now.'

So at last we know. So at last we know a lot of things we

didn't know before. (Or I didn't — did you?) Christ. It's all faintly alarming, isn't it? I meant him harm — I meant to give him imagination, to make him see the difference between himself and everything else — but I assumed there was more to avenge. It's easy enough now to see what it was that fucked him up. Her too.

I won't be scared of them *any more*. I won't ever let them make me feel I've done wrong. They are the strange ones these days, to be pitied, allowed for and put aside. They don't belong any more. What they belonged to has already disappeared; it is used up, leftovers, junk.

On the evening our lives sorted themselves out for good, on the evening when all came clear, I happened to pass Gregory in the passage. He was returning from that ridiculous 'gallery' of his, whereas I was preparing to stroll off with my book for an expensive meal in Queensway. 'Hi,' we both said. He looked bedevilled and morose as he took off his overcoat. He *is* going downhill, I thought: his clothes aren't nearly as queer as they used to be.

'How are you?' I asked aggressively as I put on my new gloves. Despite my firm stance and brazen proximity, Gregory declined to meet my eye.

'I'm okay,' he said.

'Good. And how's the gallery?'

'Okay,' he said.

'Good. Still doing well there, are you?'

'Perhaps I won't take off my overcoat,' he said uncertainly. He slung the coat over his thin sloping shoulders and began to move up the stairs.

'Ursula's in her room,' I said loudly, 'moping about something or other as usual. Go and cheer her up, why don't you?'

— And with that I slammed the door on him and sauntered towards the lift with a chuckle. Outside, through the bendy window, I could see people scurrying like leaves across the street.

I dined well. I now have so much of this curious thing that men call money — I seem to be able to do more or less as I please. Good evening! Hello again there! Yes, I don't know but what I *won't* have that vodka-and-tonic before my meal. The potted shrimps, if I may, and then I think the usual sirloin, if possible. That sounds splendid. And a carafe of — what? — red? Thank you. No, I won't see the menu again — I know it backwards now anyway! — just the coffee, please, and also let me see, why, I think perhaps a large *brandy* too??? I feel posh here. I *am* posh here, now I come to mention it. The restaurant — a traditional, familial, up-market Italian place — is full of men with puffed, unintelligent faces and muscular pot-bellies, full of women with hard mean mouths and untidy teeth, women who look as though they don't much like going to bed with the men but are bloody good at it once they do. True, the men are often fantastically hideous — yobs can be: no one minds — and seem to be all-thumbs with the platefuls of exotica they grumblingly request from the maternal waitresses ('Nah, you put lemon on it, you cunt,' I heard one gourmet tell his rather less sophisticated friend). True, also, the women glance at me quite a bit; perhaps they have me fingered for a coming yob; or perhaps they think I look rather grand and enigmatic, with my paperback, my cigarettes and my wine, my relative composure, sitting here alone in this crowded place.

Having settled the bill, and handsomely, I walked out into the street. The pubs had just closed and there was an agreeable whiff of Yahooism in the air. Over by the supermarket, I noticed, a promising scuffle was already well underway. I crossed the road, joining a small but appreciative audience, and watched two fat middle-aged men hurl a drunk about among some dustbins. The two men did this tirelessly, long after the drunk had surrendered consciousness. There seemed no reason for them to stop — but then they pantingly dusted their palms, and we all crackled away on the broken teeth and glass. We *are* getting nastier. We don't put up with things. We do as we want now. I wouldn't go out too late too often, if I were you. There are plenty of people here who would be quite happy to do you harm. You shouldn't take anything for granted: you ought to be very careful. It suits me, all this, with no one being safe any more. I think I'm beginning to like the way the world is changing.

I recrossed the road to my local late-night pornographer's. I prefer it when a decent amount of perverts are already in there, and also when the Jamaican girl isn't at the tobacco counter: she has a bad habit of veering up without warning from her chair and shooing all the perverts into the street. Tonight, luckily, the Greek owner sat in her stead, disconsolately picking his teeth with a nail-file, and there were at least six or seven perverts spaced out along the pornography shelves, like dreamers at a urinal. I joined them. I flicked through six or seven magazines, all of which were evidently still in the business of showing men what the insides of women's vaginas and anuses look like. There are hundreds of these girls in every magazine, and there are hundreds of these magazines in every shop, and there are hundreds and hundreds of shops. Where do these girls come from and how do they get hold of them and make them show us what the insides of their vaginas and anuses look like? They must have asked nearly every girl in the world to do it by now. Have they asked Jan yet, or Ursula, or Phyllis at Dino's? Pretty soon they'll run out of girls who will do it. Then they'll have to find ways of making the girls who won't do it do it. Then we'll know what the insides of every girl's vagina and anus look like. That'll be good too.

The night was electric — the night was in italics. When a sharp rain began to dot the air I thought the pavement was going to sizzle. What is everyone doing up so late? Are they too hot to sleep? The moisture brought out the sweet smell of dead fruit from a forgotten barrow. I stopped and stared upwards. I was seeing stars.

Who needs the bathroom, I thought, as I came into

the flat. Once in my room, I poured myself a potent nightcap — whisky: better than any toothbrush — removed my clothes in favour of some old pyjamas, and got quickly into bed. A cigarette, the day, the office, next month, the future, ah life, ah death. I gargled and extinguished my cigarette. I turned the light off and stared at the ceiling. But the ceiling wouldn't go to sleep. My mind was busy busy busy.

Then I heard it. A sound too close for human grief, too deep to separate itself from the humming and dripping of the night. I sat up straight. A mauve baby that has reached the end of breath, a madwoman in a vacuum, murder beneath many pillows.

'Ursula?' I said.

Everything was over in a moment. I just lowered my trousers. I only remember the smell — sweat, tears, fluid. Her thighs were cold and goose-pimpled but inside she was seething. She wanted to be joined up, plugged, glued together again. I thought she might snap before I could do anything. She was shaking insanely. She was breathing so hard that I clamped my hand over her mouth — to keep her there, to keep her in, to put her back. '*Quiet!*' I said in terror. She lay on the bed and I lay on top of her. Everything was over in a moment. I hoped I didn't break anything.

'He hates me,' she said afterwards.

I moved away a few inches. 'Him?'

'Yes.'

'Because of me?'

'Yes.'

'Is that why you ... ?'

'Yes. Someone's got to look after me.'

'Have they?'

'It was him or you.'

'Why?'

'But none of that matters now, does it?'

I turned over. I could hear fresh rain rolling across the

skylights. I wondered how long it would take before she went back to her room.

(ii) You're not at the bottom yet. There
      is a lot further you can fall — GREGORY

What happened?

What happened? I think I must have been outside for at least an hour before I realized I was outside, before I realized I was anywhere, before the fog of hot distress had a chance to clear from my eyes. I had 'stormed out' into the night. Suddenly I was in the streets, and suddenly the streets were black and empty and cold. There was no sound, no sound whatever, except for the dry sheen of cars in the distance and the blanket murmur of the air, like a gramophone record between tracks. And where was this? I stood at the top of a slope beyond a low dark railway bridge. Weak light came from the entrance to a dead Underground station across the street; next door was a little driving-instructor's shop which ambitiously kept a pink neon L fluttering feebly in its window. Over the prefab wall banking the pavement I could see a vast razed area like a cordoned-off bombsite, with deep scars in the earth, mounds of sand, steaming ditches. Great head-in-air cranes loomed above me. What happened?

Further down the road lay rows of houses clumped in shadow (they seemed to have sprung up out of their own front gardens). I could tell from the fake-brick plastering and absurdly garish window frames that I was in nigger country, the mau-mau hell between Ladbroke Grove and Kilburn. The cars irregularly spaced along the street were boogie cars, so impossibly lurid that only boogies could bear to drive about in them. But the boogies slept. I experienced no fear — of what, anyway? I'm on my own now, I thought, feeling saner than I had felt for weeks — saner than up there in that room, lying on that nailbed of nerves. Which way home? I started down the hill towards the dark bridge.

Then I saw them, two men, just beyond the viaduct. I hesitated for an instant (cross the road? No), and walked on. A third figure clambered over the building-site fence. The yellow streetlamps flickered. Is this it? Seen through the deeper shadows of the tunnel, they looked strangely becalmed in the glow. Two of them leaned against the corrugated prefab wall; the other, a young man in an old man's overcoat, faced me squarely. I entered the tunnel (never stop now), using the darkness to slow my pace. I halted. A wire tugged in my throat as the two leaning figures steadied themselves and took up position by their friend. I could outrun them, perhaps, but I could not outflank them — those mad little legs of theirs ... and run back where? Into that? And start again? I went to the edge of the shadows, ten yards from the three men. I halted. I heard water, a sudden rustic trickle. The men were lean, dirty, long-haired; they gave the sense of being outside everything, their nerves flexed tight for the streets. No one moved. There wasn't any noise anywhere now.

'What do you want?' I called from the shadows.

They did not come forward but seemed ready to change their posture for attack. Thick fingers were itching at my heart.

'Money,' said one of them quietly.

I haven't got any either! I've got an overdraft! 'Listen!' I said. 'Three pounds and some change — you can have it. Please. It's all I've got — I promise.'

'Three pounds,' said one to another. They stepped forward.

My legs disappeared. 'I'll get you *more*! I'll — ' Then two heavy hands seized me from behind.

I wheeled round, half toppling over. I felt my trousers go wet and hot. Inches from mine was a face with orange skin and no front teeth. It let out a shout of rank laughter.

'*Hey*,' it said — 'he's only *shit* himself. You can smell it. He's only *shit* himself.'

The other three converged. 'Don't hit me, please,' I said in tears. 'I'll give the money. Please don't hit me.'

'He's *crying* now. Gor, you little *shit*. Hah! Shit himself! Poof fucking *shit* himself!'

And as I stood there scouring my pockets, even through the mist of alarm and humiliation, I realized that they were beggars only, and very sorry ones, young and sick, with no more strength in their bodies than I could summon in mine.

'I'm sorry,' I said, holding out the money in cupped hands. 'Believe me there is no more.'

The fanged one laughed again. 'Keep it, shitty,' he said. 'You keep it, there's a good little shit.'

I reeled away from them, stumbling into a run. They yelled until I could hear them no longer.

'Go on, shitty. Go on, go on home and change your panties. Go on, shitty. Go on, you little *shit*.'

Two o'clock. I stood in my shirtsleeves at the kitchen table, the change and crumpled notes spread out before me. I had buried the trousers in the rubbish-bin. I had cleaned myself at the sink, with water, Squezy and the tissue roll. I turned to the blank window. There was my face, suspended among the rooftops and the beads of passage lights of the blocks higher up. It looked like me, I suppose, or like other people think I look. 'You're not at the bottom yet,' I said. 'There is a lot further you can fall.'

This month hides in unfamiliar places.

I avoided them for as long as I could — and with some success. (I couldn't face them. The shame was mine too, somehow. Why?) In the early evenings and over the weekends I stayed away from the flat. I sat in coffee-bars with au pairs and transients, with self-possessed middle-aged women and trim, well-spoken middle-aged men, coffee-bars in which everyone knew all about everyone else's failures, and nobody had anywhere they would rather be. I lingered in bookshops and antique-marts and junk shops among the ponderous hippies, the cruel-faced spivs and the trusting students with their valuable plastic bags. I sat through films in the afternoons, next to noisy kids and sleepy pensioners, beside faceless unemployables and gibbering tramps (how can they afford it? *I* can't). I try not to stay out later than nine or eight-thirty. I stick to the crowded streets, where the foreigners are still busy looting the shops. I have been keeping my eyes open. I have been looking round about me.

Correct me if I'm wrong, but it seems that approximately one in three of this city's indigenous population is quite mad — obviously, openly, candidly, brazenly mad. Their lives are entirely given over to a bitter commentary on the world, the light, the time of day it is. In every busload there will be six or seven people who just sit there growling about nothing with tears in their eyes. Every café contains, at all times, a working minimum of two gesticulating maniacs who have to be shown or chucked out into the street, where they will hover and shout and threaten until someone redoubles their efforts to make them go away again. On every street you walk along you find the same proportion of people who do nothing but fizz all the hours there are, fizz with hatred or disappointment or grief, or fizz simply because they are ugly and poor and mad. They ought to get together. They ought to organize (they would form a very powerful lobby). They ought to organize, and make everyone else fucked up and *tonto* too.

Am I like that? No, not yet. But I'm treading lightly wherever I go now, testing all the surfaces. At any moment I expect to hear them crack.

Work is impossible these days. (It always was really, as you know, but it's even more impossible now.) They bawl me out. They bawl me out when I come back late from delivering their shitty pictures all over town (perhaps I should tell them about the Underground and me. Perhaps they would be kinder then). They bawl me out when I drop things, and I drop things quite a bit these days. Last week I dropped a teapot, and the fuckpigs made me buy them a new one. This week I dropped a picture frame; it was a hideous picture frame, naturally, but so valuable that not even they expected me to buy them a new one. They just bawled me out instead. Yesterday they bawled me out in front of some friendly students I was chatting to (apparently I had misaddressed most of the private-view invitations). '*Get* down to the stock-room,' said Odette. The friendly students looked baffled. So did I. I cried for a while as I cleaned the frames.

You know what I had for lunch the other day? (Ah, thank you, good Emil, yes, the usual, please.) A Mars Bar. A fucking Mars Bar. Suck on that. Terry pays all the bills now. He doesn't seem to mind. One day I returned from work to find that the powerful Grundig had disappeared from my room. I assumed the men had come for it (I couldn't keep up the payments). I went downstairs and saw that it was in Terry's room. I didn't say anything about it.

I want to go home. I want to go back to that big warm house. I want to be among people who love me. I can't find anything to use against people who hate me.

On the evening our lives sorted themselves out for good, on the evening when all came clear, I happened to pass Terry in the passage. I had just got back from work; he was putting on a new pair of gloves, getting ready to stroll out with a book for an expensive meal in Queensway.

'How are you?' he asked aggressively.

'I'm okay,' I said, without meeting his eye.

'Good. And how's the gallery?'

'Okay.'

'Good. Still doing well there, are you?'

'Perhaps I won't take off my overcoat,' I said uncertainly as I began to move up the stairs.

'Ursula's in her room,' he shouted, 'moping about something or other as usual. Go and cheer her up, why don't you?'

All that month I had expected to want Ursula to come to me, to come to me and ask for forgiveness. I knew things could never be good again, but perhaps I could find a way to stop hating her, a way to throw off this frenzy of solitude which mantles me now. I didn't want her to come, though. I really didn't. I knew that I could not tolerate it, that it was intolerable. I'm on my own here. Let's face that.

I was sitting by my window. I was still in my overcoat (I often am these days. It means that I'm not here to stay and can bolt any time I like and, besides, I'm paranoid about putting on the fire). I was sitting by my window, staring out at the aeroplanes that wafted through the grey clouds. Then I heard the intimate footfalls.

'Gregory?'

I could not turn. 'Yes?'

'It's me.'

'I know.'

'Won't you talk to me?'

'I can't.'

'Won't you ever talk to me?'

'I don't know. I don't think so.'

'Won't you look at me?'

'I can't.'

'When we were young we said we'd never be mean to each other.'

'I know.'

'Then why are you being mean to me now?'

'Because I hate you,' I said.

'You *can't* do that. What will become of us?'

And why is it always clichés that make you cry? I leaned forward on my table and gave vent to the saltiest tears I had ever shed. So much water flooding out —

where does it all come from? I felt her presence behind me. I turned, startled.

Her hand was raised, as if she would rest it on my shoulders. Her face was full of migraine. She moved nearer with her hand.

'Don't!' I said. I was pleading. 'Don't. I'll go mad if you touch me.'

Late that night the swirl of sirens came slantwise across my sleep. I turned over (shut the doors, shut the doors. Sirens are ten-a-penny round my way, where everyone is always getting fucked up or going *tonto*. Sirens always have to be waiting near by). I had dreamt I was walking down a bombed-out street; there were children playing, and the air was nostalgic with that forgotton concord — bat patting ball, the soft-shoe shuffle of hopscotch, the flick of a skiprope, the weak protesting trebles of their cries; I reached the house I had come to find; I knocked on the door and turned to enjoy the children; now all was silent, and I saw with a sob that they were not children after all, but mad old dwarves, every one, their faces boiling as they crossed the street towards me ... The sirens yawled, screaming for blood. I opened my eyes. A blue light was shooting round my room like a spectral boomerang — *whoosh, whoosh, whoosh*. I sat up with a shiver. The sirens cried warning as I moved down the stairs. I opened the flat door.

Then all at once: the clout of cold air through the shattered glass, the men churning at the jaws of the ambulance, the snapped figure in the white nightdress.

I fell to my knees. 'Terry,' I said. 'Someone please help me.' The passage folded on to its side. I skidded down the floor. The blue light boomeranged above my head, coming closer, getting brighter, turning black.

11: November

(i) Now that wasn't so bad,
was it? — TERRY

Big deal. Do you want to know how *my* sister died? Suck on this.

Whoosh. Terence at the square table in the corner of the front room, his homework fanned out on the green baize. In the chair by the three-bar fire, my father, tall, heavy, his thin, red, damp, smalltown hair ironed flat across his crown. Rosie is late. The smoke from his wet pipe formed a dusty shelf at table-height, and when I turned in my chair to look down on him through the tobacco trance — to see how mad he was getting, tell him something quickly about the other side — I felt as if I were on an elevated plane, like a god, or a scientist observing the behaviour of controlled animals. This is going to be bad, I thought; but of course another part of me (that perverse, recipro-cating part) was thinking: this is going to be good. Where is the headache? Down there somewhere.

We heard the front door being tugged shut. I turned again as she came into the room — she came into the room, dropping things on chairs, saying hello to her father and to me, without fear. He showed no vexation at her lateness. He made no response. He sat before the fire, smoking his pipe — it must have been delicious, that sense of rightful anger deferred, letting the power trickle in through his mouth to feed the busy static. Rosie limped smiling to my table, where she sat and doodled until it was time to eat. She felt well. She was seven.

My father, as always, prepared the supper — cheap, basic, complexion-ravaging foods, invariably fried — while my sister, as usual, laid the table (she was required to wash up, too, ever since my mother went), while I, as usual, did nothing. Did nothing, except listen to that old eerie tinkle, that scraping false clarity of sound, those noises that recede just as they seem to climb, and climb again, and then recede, and then begin to climb.

He eats with fastidious relish. Silence is commanded by the sure way he loads his fork, loads it with a representative of every foodstuff on his plate — sausage stub, bean cluster, white flap of egg, tomato seeds — and lets his head drop to devour it, loading his fork once more as he chews. He starts to speak, without looking up. He does not look up. Neither do I.

You were late again, Rosie.

Had to go to Mandy's. I said I'd be late.

Don't interrupt me, please. Never interrupt me again. You were late again, Rosie. You know how *angry* that makes me feel ...

Dad, I told you.

And I told you not to interrupt me. Did I tell you not to interrupt me?

Yes, Dad.

Then don't interrupt me, please. Now let's start again. You are late. This makes me angry. I would not be angry if you were not late. But you are late. This makes me angry.

(I can barely hear him now. The room is so loud and he won't look up, won't stir or bend in any way ... I wait for Rosie's tears, although she never cries.)

You know what happens when I am angry. And I am angry because you are late. I am angry. You know what happens. But you are late.

He stands and turns. He is quite still, his back to us. He stands before the cooker, as if its dials might help control what is happening to him. He begins again —

You know all this and yet you are —

And I look up to see that Rosie is on her feet. Her face is burning — with what? With outrage, with defiant, goaded outrage, as she moves down the table towards him and starts to say,

'*Stop* it, *stop* it, why don't you *leave me alone* — '

Whoosh. He has swivelled and *crack* she is up in the air with a fluttery wriggle and down on the floor in an instant, used up in an instant, snapped, dead.

He turned again. He replaced the frying-pan on the ring. With deliberate movements he washed his hands. The air made my heart itch. I sensed I had fouled my trousers. He dried his hands and reached for his coat, hooked on the scullery door. He came towards me. I hope he can't smell it, I thought — he'll kill me if he finds out.

'I'm going now,' he said. 'I won't be back. Don't worry. I'll tell them. There's nothing you can do.' He gestured at the body. He hesitated. 'It was her or you. I don't know why. There's nothing you can do.'

I changed my pants in the cold bedroom and buried them in the kitchen dustbin. I didn't look at her. Then I went upstairs to hide. There was nothing I could do.

Now that wasn't so bad, was it? Actually — between ourselves — the episode hasn't retained much reality of a very pressing kind. Oh, it happened all right; I *was* there; it *was* real. But nowadays the memory seeks me out like a bore tapping on my shoulder, a vivid reel from an otherwise unremarkable film, an encumbrance, second-hand stuff. Goodbye, Rosie. You turned out all right in the end. Who needs you now? I don't.

As for Ursula, well, that's clearing itself up too. There was no autopsy or anything, thank God ... The judge lowers his spectacles: 'Now, Mr Service, "gentleman of the road", as you are described here. Quantities of plebeian semen were found ... ' No, with her long history of disturbance, previous suicide bids and so on, everything was formal and brisk. She got cremated with *no* sweat. Neither of her parents could get down for it, so Greg and I went as her guardians. It was sad. We both cried. We didn't guard her very well, did we?

Of course, I've decided not to blame myself at all. That chat I gave her, after the absurd scene in my bedroom, couldn't have been more indulgent and conciliatory. I merely pointed out, gently but firmly, that there was no sense in which I could assume responsibility for her, that you cannot 'take people on' any longer while still trying to function successfully in your own life, that she was on her own now, the same as me, the same as Greg, the same as everybody else. I never said I wouldn't stick by her. I never said I wouldn't give her help if she needed it.

Gregory, however, *has* decided to blame himself. Patently, and rather hurtfully also, his rift with her that night was more decisive than mine ever could have been. The first few days were rough — the three of us sharing that ambulance, Gregory staying on for forty-eight hours' sedation, the curiously unresponsive messages from Rivers Hall, Greg back up in his room, a creature of the middle-air with his pallor and his tears and his odd lightness of presence. I sort of hate to see him now. His grief is an unmanly and demeaning thing. He looks so pathetically at-a-loss, staring out of windows all day long, as if the rooftops might suddenly realign and make themselves new for him again.

He has been out of hospital for — let's see — about two-and-a-half weeks now. On the first Monday after his discharge he went back to the gallery. When I returned from the office, at about six-thirty, I found him sitting at my desk, staring dully at the sky. He hadn't switched on the lights; the sallow sodium from the streets played upwards on his unhealthy face.

'Hello, kid,' I said. 'Are you all right?'

'I've packed in my job,' he said.

'*Christ*. Do you want a drink?'

'Yes. Yes, please. I packed it in.'

'*Why?* Jesus, what'll you do?'

'I just told them. I told them they could keep it.'

'What did they say? Will they give it *back*?'

'I couldn't bear it any more. I couldn't bear them, it.'

'What did they say?'

'They said they understood. It wasn't a very good job, anyway.'

'What will you do?'

He held the glass of whisky with both hands, cupped on his chest, lowering his mouth to sip. He said,

'Don't know yet. There are lots of things I can do. I'll do them in the new year. I'll talk to Papa. When we've been home for Christmas. You are coming home for Christmas, aren't you?'

'There's nowhere else to go.'

'Terry, how did you feel ... Do you mind me asking this? How did you feel when your sister ... ?'

'Sad and frightened,' I said.

'Me too,' he said.

'But more frightened, in a way. Frightened about me, what would happen to me.'

'Mm, that's how I feel. I'm glad you felt that too.'

'And now, in a way, I've lost two sisters,' I said, rather daringly.

'Yes, you have in a way.' He looked up. 'Things must have been very hard for you, Terry,' he said.

'Not that hard.'

One night towards the end of the month — I had just completed the course at the City College and we'd had a little celebration — I came lurching and burping down Queensway, enjoying the cold air on my numbed cheeks. Hanging a left on Moscow, I followed a wayward instinct to cut across the car park behind The Intrepid Fox. Ten yards into the darkness I saw the lumpy mass of rubbish bags under the light of the rear door. I walked over. I knew he'd be there and he was, a bundle of misery and filth, a compact compost-heap, surrounded by spent cider bottles and patches of reddish vomit. I came nearer. I thought I had nothing more ambitious in mind than one of our pseudo-Socratic little dialogues, but there was something different about me that night.

'Well *hi*,' I said. 'Hi, it's me, the little shit.'

A car passed down the street, throwing a stripe of light across the fucked-up hippie's face. He was awake and his eyes were open. He had been watching me. 'The big shit,' he said.

'Things still rosy? Life still treating you right?'

'Yeah.'

'Some guys get all the breaks ... Hey, you've done something to your place, haven't you? Looks different. Had it done up or something? Been shelling out the cash again?'

'You're not funny.'

'Neither are you. You're not anything. I wouldn't swap you for a dog-turd.'

'Fuck you.'

'Fuck me? Fuck *me*? You'd better watch what you say, tramp.' I knelt, and added in a whisper, 'I could do what I liked to you, you dumb hippie. Who would protect you? Who would care what happened to you? No one would notice or mind.'

'Go and shit yourself, shit.'

I straightened up. A curled hand protruded from the bulk of his overcoat. I stood on it with my left boot, quite hard, and asked: 'What did you say?'

'I said go and shit yourself, you *shit*.'

I kicked him clumsily on the side of the head. I'd tried to keep my left foot on his hand — for extra tension — and half lost my balance in the process. This made me much angrier. With a two-step approach, like someone chipping a rugger ball, I caught him a good one right under the jaw. There was a gummy crunch as his mouth clamped shut, then the thud of the second impact as his head hit the concrete. He rolled over with a gurgle. The vented overcoat had ridden up and a part of his bare back was exposed; the thin chain of his spine tapered into his waistband. Should I kick that too, with my heavy boot, that fragile tube containing so many vital odds and ends? It *would* be nice. He rolled over again. No. Why bother? He's taken care of. I flicked a tenner from my wallet and pressed it into his stomped-on hand. A fair deal, probably. Fair for him and fair for me. As I lurched and burped away, I heard the muffled scurry of approaching feet. For a moment I felt the squeeze of fear — but when I turned I saw it was only a couple of his wrecked hippie mates, running up to help their friend and to share his money.

£1,750? They're *kidding*.

I was in the office, the next morning, dozily glancing through my newspaper — the more powerful you are here, it seems, the less there is to do. Momentarily my eyes had strayed from the crossword to the classified ads, where I noticed the following entry:

> ART GALLERY ASST. reqd. Polite, well-spoken, male (21–25 yrs) private gallery Mayfair. No qualifs. nec. Contact Odette or Jason Styles 629–3095. Sal. £1,750.

No wonder he went out of his mind. Why didn't they pay him in buttons? I swivelled in my chair for a few minutes. Of course, I thought: of *course*. I dialled the number. I spoke to a harsh-voiced woman. I made an appointment for lunchtime the following day. 'Yes: Veale,' I said. 'Stanley Veale.' I would wear my new black corduroy suit, that yellow shirt of mine, and a tie. I would clean my fingernails and brush my hair flat. I would be on time.

'Good morning.'

'Mr Veale, is it? Good morning.'

'Yes. How do you do?'

'Shall we go through into the office?' asked a large, menopausal hillock of a woman — 'My husband's in there.'

I trailed her through the gallery, her thighs swishing and her shoes clicking on the cork floor. The place had something of the quality of a film set, over-bright and exemplary, as if staged for our historic progress across its floors.

'Here we are,' she said, as we entered the deeper shadows of the office. 'This is ... Stanley Veale. This is my husband Jason Styles.'

'How do you do?' I said to the horribly fit little unit of a man who stood alertly by a grey filing-cabinet.

'Please sit down, Stanley,' he said.

As I lyingly reconstructed my *curriculum vitae* — read Fine Arts at Kent, completed some external studies at the Courtauld — I sensed a growing restlessness from my interviewers: they were politely willing to hear me out, it appeared, but anxious that this formal interlude should come to an end. And I sensed too, as I lied on, the peculiar feel of the place — the murky damp of the sofa on which I sat, the bloodlessness of the air, the close breath of the room.

'I see,' said Mr Styles, glancing at his wife. 'Let me ask you ... what is your, your ambition. How would the gallery here fit in with it?'

'Well, my ambition is to make some kind of contribution, however small, to the art world in general. I've visited this gallery before, of course, just as a casual viewer. And I find I've come back many times. I like the work you show here — it's good work, and I would like to be a part of the whole thing.'

Perfect, identikit stuff, I thought; but again they seemed disappointed, apologetic, almost embarrassed.

'Mm. You see,' said Styles, 'there isn't really a great deal to do here from your point of view. The gallery more or less runs itself. We just sit and hope, really. The

trouble with our previous assistants has always been' —
and he laughed a little — 'that they've had too *much*
ambition, too many interests. We really want someone
with no interests *at all*, really.'

Really?

'It's a quiet job,' said Mrs Styles. 'It would suit a quiet
young man.'

'Ah, I see,' I said quietly. 'Was that — is that why the
job is open now?'

'Ah no,' said Mr Styles. They both relaxed. 'The last
one was rather different. We were both very fond of him,
but he was an extremely unhappy and unstable boy.
Talented in some ways, but a bit — you know. Not suited
to the ... '

'And then he had this personal tragedy ... '

'All a bit too much for him ... '

'We had to let him go, I'm afraid.'

'I see,' I said. *Christ*: he got aimed from *here*? 'How sad.'

'Well, the salary's not much, as you know,' pursued Mr
Styles. 'To be frank, we wouldn't have replaced the
previous young man if we could have helped it, things
being as tight as they are. But then if one of us is ill, and
then one of us has to go out to the post ... ' Their eyes
had been in conference. 'We might as well say that the job
is yours if you want it. You needn't think of it as particularly long-term. Why don't you think about it and give
us a ring?'

Why don't I think about it and give you a ring? Why
don't *I* think about *that* and give *you* a *ring*?

Poor Gregory. That sad bastard. Things are certainly
changing fast for him now. Faster than yet he knows.

There has been more news from Rivers Hall. I've been
talking to Greg's mother at pricey length on the telephone.
Greg's mother is not worried about Ursula any more.
'How can you worry about the dead?' she asked me.
Ursula is dead and gone; I agreed: that's true — and so,
in a way, is my past with her, with them, with him.

Greg's mother says there are other things to worry about now. Other things. She knew Greg was going under; she knew, even before Ursula went. That's why she doesn't want him to hear about these new things yet. She has told me. I am not to tell him. I am just supposed to get him up there, and she'll tell him. I will tell you:

Greg's father has gone broke. Broke scares her; broke scares him. Broke broke his heart. His heart attacked him again. And they think it's going to win this time.

(ii) We're going home early
for Christmas — GREGORY

That's it. That's it. All the bits that were me have been reshuffled yet again. Where are they? I'll never find them now.

I've packed in my job. I just packed it in, is all. Odette and Jason were sitting in their office — I sauntered through and said, with classic insouciance, that I was no longer prepared, thank you, to squander my days on ...

No. They aimed me. They aimed me. They called me into their office and said I was no longer 'up' to the job. (Up to that? *Up* to *that*?) They gave me £80 in cash. They said they were sorry. They probably were sorry.

Perhaps you think they aimed me because I wouldn't fuck them? Well, I don't think it can be that, because I have fucked them, more or less. Remember that afternoon, when she dropped the coffee on my trousers and then tried to fuck me? Well, I dropped the coffee and I tried to fuck her — tried very hard and without much success (she *did* let me feel her horrible tits and so forth, but she wasn't keen. She said she never wanted to do anything like that with me again. Why? Who's changed?). Jason has blown me. Once. I've blown him. Twice. I did it because I thought they might aim me if I didn't. I did, and they aimed me anyway. Oh God. I suppose I can't blame them, really, what with me so silent and *tonto* the whole time.

It happened at mid-morning. I walked home with £80 in my pocket (it was lucky no one knew). I sat downstairs in Terry's room, next to Ursula's. I worry about Ursula all the time, far more than I ever did when she was alive. Something could always be done then. How close to nausea grief is. I want to be sick all the time. I would be sick all the time, if I felt up to it.

It was no one's fault. It was inevitable, just as what's happening to me is inevitable. I only wish I hadn't spoken to her like that. God damn me for speaking to her like that. How did I *dare*. I'd never been mean to her before. Does Terry know I did? I hope he doesn't tell anyone.

We talked when he came in. It was all right — he is much more relaxed now. We talked about home. Mama and Papa are believers. They don't believe in worrying about the dead. I hope they still believe that. We'll see. We're going home early for Christmas.

I feel incredibly strange out of doors now. I'm not working (no point in looking for new jobs yet, so near the holidays). I feel like an impostor, a ghost, just putting in the odd appearance as I do. Everyone is so compact and energetic. They breathe heavily and sweat in the cold. The meanest of them watch me with curious and un-friendly eyes. (They don't like me. Who does, I wonder? Even the random babblings of the foreigners — and they speak in languages I've never heard of — come to my ears in cadences of obscenity, imprecation and threat.) I used to like their stares. I don't any longer. I wish I looked a bit more like Terry. Unpleasant though his appearance certainly is, he does, in some important sense in which I do not, look like a *person*, one put together with this life in view. I don't — I know it. I used to like the way I looked, and I liked the way they looked at me. But now it's all wrong and I wish I looked like everybody else.

What went on? What became of the people who would protect me? Kane and Skimmer never telephone or come round any more. Why should they? I never had anything to give them and couldn't afford to go out. (I never cared for them anyway. They were cocksuckers, blind cocksuckers.) Torka cared for me at first, but now he and his yobs think I'm ridiculous. (I kept feeling sure that if I went there *one more time* they would beat me up, for sex or just for fun.) Odette and Jason might have looked after me for a while, perhaps. They *were* fond of me, I know. (But not that fond.) I see the tramps, standing in resentful knots behind the pubs. They don't look like tramps used to look. They are not old and small and well wrapped-up. Some of them look quite young. (Some of them look quite rich.) Perhaps they aren't all tramps. If they are, there must be an awful lot of tramps about.

I don't like staying in the streets too long (that's natural. It's a very cold November). I like to get back inside quickly. I like to doze on Ursula's bed in the afternoons (it's a small room. You can make it warm just by being in it). Her suspended future and my dead past get mixed up now in my mind. The trials that await her in death are probably no different from those she faced while she lived — new schools, the hatred of your peers, the voices in your head. The past weaves round all this; we still duck in and out of its lost but shimmering kingdoms. I don't like it when I fall asleep down there. I have dreams. I don't see what you're supposed to do about dreams. You're always asleep when they happen. Perhaps sleep is to blame, pulling the wool over your eyes in that deceitful way it has. Dreams wouldn't dare do what they do to me when I'm awake. That's why they wait until I'm asleep before they do it.

I lie on her bed until Terry comes home. We talk, and quite often he gives me some of his whisky to drink. Quite often, too, I drink some of his whisky before he comes home. He looks at the bottle and he looks at me.

I feel ashamed. I wonder what he can think of me these days.

Christmas at Rivers Court. A cartoon, Dickensian scene — the mansion lapped in snow, the windows golden with great crackling fires, everything set for the miracle: cottagers and farmworkers humming carols in the courtyard (did they ever come? If they did, someone took them hot drinks), the heavy village bell obsessively counting its notes in the distance, robust caterwauling from the servants' parlour (if there was one. Did we ever have any?), the beaming silence of the East drawing-room as we all converge on the teeming tenements of *cadeaux* grouped round the crystal Christmas tree. The family feels strong again. I can almost see my face, here and there in the whirl of merriment and memory. There he is! Did you see him? Twenty Christmases put me together and make me up: my height jerks in the time machine, my clothes change like a prismatic cockatoo, arms reach out towards me like, like ...

Oh come on — were we ever that happy and grand (and it's Hall, not Court, you lying fuck)? My parents were probably old and *tonto* long before we actually noticed they were, and my sister and I were always heading that way too ... I live more in the past these days. Christ knows why. I used to think I'd never had a good time since I was twenty. Now I wonder if I ever had a good time since I was ten.

The telephone rang suddenly, as if in fright or warning. I picked it up and said,

'Yes?'

'There you are. Terry, now listen. It's getting worse quicker. *No* one seems to know how soon. You must get Gregory up here. How soon can you?'

I sat up in bed. This was my mother's voice. And I am not Terry. I leaned forward. I wanted to hurl the telephone against the wall or crack it to pieces on the floor.

'Mother, this is *me*,' I said. 'This is *Gregory*.'

' ... Oh, *Greg*ory.'

There was a pause — the silence quite undistraught — before I heard the receiver being gently replaced.

I got up and put on clothes. I started off.

It took a hundred bad minutes to find him.

I walked all the way to the bus-stop (a helicopter thudded low overhead and a cat in an empty restaurant stood on a table to scratch the glass) before it occurred to me that I had no idea where Terry worked. I thrashed through the books of a urine-steeped telephone kiosk. What was I *looking* for? I ran back to the flat. I found a printed address on one of his staggering pay-slips. But where on earth was Holborn Viaduct? I ran back to the bus-stop. I consulted the meaningless yellow timetables on the billboard. I went through my pockets, watching for taxis. I had no money. I had no money *at all*. (What happened to that £80? Something did: coffees, boxes of matches, bus-fares.) I ran back to the flat. I looted my drawers and pockets. Eighteen pence. I ran down to Terry's room. In his money drawer were several £5 notes. I took one. I took two. I ran outside. There were no taxis (it was raining. There never are then). I ran back to the bus-stop. On the 88 I rode. I asked the coons. I changed buses twice. I found myself standing on a street that became a bridge. I asked the newspaper vendors (I bought three *Standard*s and a *News*). Holborn Viaduct was 'down there'. I descended steep steps. I stumbled through the gloom. The oyster light was full of drizzle, and when I asked men where to go they replied too quickly or too slowly or not at all and then hurried away or lingered strangely, making me walk fast and forgetful in any direction and praying that they would not call out to correct me. It got a shade darker suddenly. I began to run.

Masters House loomed up at me through a silk of rain and tears. It was a big efficient building; a uniformed man guarded its portals. I hung back. There was some sort of café in the alley where I lurked. I put my head round its door momentarily — a teddy-boy with a great glistening quiff, a frizzy-haired old tart, unfriendly eyes. I fastened my coat. Beneath some rusty scaffolding I saw a pool of frozen vomit. I walked forward.

'The third floor,' said the whiskered doorman.

I stood in a carbolic vestibule. Three big women with faces like cruel pigs stood watching me critically from their office or parlour or rest-room (cheap newspapers on a green chair, a leaning mop-handle). The doors of the lift were open. The liftman hovered. Shut the doors, shut the doors. As we moaned upwards I felt someone was watching me, watching me with sneering, lethal hate. The lift had a mirror. I didn't look.

The third-floor landing led nowhere. I walked up a half-flight of stairs. I walked down a passage. I turned a corner. Something crackled beneath my feet. I stared down and saw with a rush of horror that I was treading on human teeth. I heard a wet sob. In a gloomy nook to my left sat a young boy with a blood-stained handkerchief pressed to his mouth. A woman was with him.

'Oh you poor young boy,' I said.

His shoulders shook.

'The boys from downstairs,' said the woman. 'They just flicked them out.' She made a flicking gesture with forefinger and thumb. She winced. 'Just flicked them out.'

'You poor boy. Why? Couldn't you stop them?'

'No. You can't stop them,' she said.

'Oh God. Where's Terry? Is he here?'

'Mr Service? Through there.'

I walked on, round a curved corner. A tableful of secretaries looked up at me.

'Is Mr Service here?' I said. Mr Service. Who the hell is *he*?

'Who?'

'Mr Service?'

'Terry? Through there.'

I turned a second corner. A large open-plan area edged by cubicles disclosed itself. Heavy young men with close-cut beards moved confidently about in the middle-distance. They stopped what they were doing and turned towards me. Through where? Through where, where, where?

Then a cubicle door wafted open — and there was Terry, hunched over a telephone, his back to me, the smoke of a cigarette curling up above his head.

'Yes,' he was saying. 'Well, no, it wouldn't be me, would it? I mean, *I* go to work in the mornings. I don't know. I don't know. I've tried already — no answer. They must have *some* idea how soon. Yeah, I'll get him there, I'll get him there. It's just that I do a job, you know? I can't just — '

He swung round in his chair and saw me.

'Later,' he said, and hung up.

We stared. He seemed brisk, dressed-up, adult, like somebody I'd never met.

'Have you seen the boy out there?' I said.

'Which boy?'

'The boy out there.'

'Damon?'

'They broke his teeth.'

'I knew they would,' said Terry, 'one of these days.'

' ... I spoke to Mama.'

'I know.'

'She ... '

'What did she tell you?'

'She didn't tell me anything.'

He straightened his jacket. 'Things are not good,' he said.

'I know,' I said.

'Do you?' he asked, puzzled.

'I don't know. Do I?'

'Things are not good,' he said. 'We're going home early for Christmas.'

12: December

One cloud shadows the life of the British Passenger-Railman: in the ointment of his daily labour there is but this single fly. The passenger. The passenger is forever causing him trouble. The passenger is forever getting in his hair. The passenger is forever interfering with his job. The passenger just seems to fuck him up all the way along the line.

'Wait here,' I told Gregory and the porter, my tone sharpened by the latter's show of insolence when I tried to enlist an unattended trolley. I joined the long queue which was slowly offering itself up to the one operative ticket-counter. In due course I bawled our destination through the plastic grill. 'How much?' I asked. After a relatively brief period of mutinous incomprehension, the brute told me — a startling sum. 'Why do you advertise?' I said. 'No one uses you unless they have to.

'Come on,' I told the porter and Gregory. Light music flitted among the high stone stanchions. Tramps were selling bales of newspapers. It was Saturday and the station was empty and unswept, bearing the litter of last night's delinquencies like the remains of a prehistoric rout. It was eight in the morning: the air had started to defrost; the trains lay stretched out exhausted, slumped panting on their buffers, wheezing steam.

'Here you are,' I told the porter when he had installed us in our carriage. 'Sit there,' I told Gregory. Gregory hesitated, while the porter fixed his stunned gaze on the mere twenty pence in his palm: 'Is that *okay*?' I asked them both.

I turned to Gregory as the train pulled out. 'Now do you want to eat? There's a restaurant car, where you can get a plate of shit for five quid, or do you just want coffee? Do you want to eat something? You can if you like.'

'I don't *think* so,' he said.

I looked up from my work as the train back-pedalled into some suburban whistle-stop. Greg was staring boyishly out of the window. I noticed with a sigh that his cheeks were fretted by dried-up tears.

'How long will you stay?' he asked in a normal voice.

'Depends. I can't just stay on indefinitely. I've got a job to do.'

We rode on.

' ... And how long will *you* stay?' I asked him.

'Depends,' he said.

It was all over by the time we got there — I had known it would be. We arrived at the house by taxi. I pay because I'm the eldest now ... this family is costing me a fortune. As I rewarded the driver I watched Gregory climb out of the car. He stood with his back to the house, buttoning up his coat, snarling gently at the wind.

His mother received us at the door. Gregory dropped his eyes and nodded a few times when he was told the news, as if it were the least he could have expected. She asked whether we should like to see the body: Greg and I shrugged and said yes. We moved along the hall to the stairs. The past tried to flood back. How I hate this place, I thought, with its worn carpets, its oddly shaped corridors good for hiding in, and its dangerously antique round-pin plugs. I would tear it apart with my bare hands if I could. I always felt bad here. It wasn't their fault, of course. They tried.

He was staked out on the master-suite bed. Mrs Riding pulled back the sheet. Her husband's face, I now saw, was caught in a rictus of angry surprise, gat-toothed — the posh keep their teeth, you know, however old or fucked up they get — eyes open, brow clenched, like a proud man being told he is the victim of a humbling joke. I looked at that starry, messianic face. What was he? I knew what he was. A good man — or a nice man, anyway; a fool; a fool who was kind to me when he didn't have to be; someone who was allowed to do pretty well what he wanted pretty well all the time. Gregory cried a bit more here, but with restraint — introspective tears, almost.

I was glad I managed to get three glasses of sherry before lunch, which was taken with frugal and teetotal haste in the kitchen. My foster-mother was brisk and laconic throughout — the next few days, at least, would be fairly well mapped out for her — and she repaired unfussily to the study once the cheese was cleared away. I joined her for a few minutes, as agreed. No surprises: she would live with her cousin in Shropshire; there were debts; the house was rotting and near-worthless; the lease on the London flat had eight years to run — I told her what I could get her for it and she told me to go ahead and get it; she said she would manage; I said I would do what I could for them both.

I rejoined Gregory and we wandered out into the drive. We stood shivering together for a few minutes. I offered him an expensive cigarette, which he shyly accepted.

'What will you do?' I asked.

'Oh, there'll be lots to do here,' he said.

'There's nothing for me to do here, is there?'

'Not really.'

'I might as well get back straightaway, before it gets dark. That's okay, isn't it?'

'Oh yes.' Gregory gazed up the drive. 'I think I'll go for a walk too, while it's light.' He turned to me with a half-smile.

'Goodbye then,' I said.

'Goodbye, Terry.'

'When are you coming back?' I called as he started off.

He looked over his shoulder. 'I'm not coming back,' he said.

Nor am I, I thought, as an hour later I took my seat in

the restaurant car of the 5.15. Life is finished there. It's just a damp house where I grew up. Let them stay for as long as they can. I hope they'll be all right.

Now I've got the flat to myself for a bit — I'll sell it in time — I think I'll do some proper entertaining this winter. Have you heard? Terence Service is entertaining these days. He didn't used to be, but he is now. There are people I can ask round. Friends from the Night School. All Veale's boys at the office — some rationalization that was: there are twice as many Sellers as there ever were before; no one seems to mind, though, and we all get lots of money. There are even a couple of girls I can ring up now and take out and go to bed with. I fucked Jan, for instance. It was okay — with myself in sparkling form, both athletic and pitiless — but nothing special.

The train bombed on, through fields wedged by advancing shadows. The countryside gives me the horrors these days: I long for the reassurance of underground stations, streets, tramps and pubs. I waved for a drink. I lit a cigarette. I uncrossed my legs to accommodate the great hydraulic erection which trains always give me whether I need them or not. I smiled.

The machine pounds along on slick silvery rails. I squint down the unravelling track, on the look-out for London. I sip my drink. I'm going to be all right.

(ii) I'm going to stay out here, where
     nothing is frightening — GREGORY

I'm cold. This old rag keeps nothing out. (It looks nasty, too.) I fasten it up all the time, but that only reminds me how poorly protected I am.

I'm walking east, behind the house, towards the D-Pond (the D-Pond isn't in our land any more. A yid owns it now, but you're still allowed to go there). The grass on the lawns is rank and knotted, smelling faintly of dirt and cheap scent. In the overhung pathways by the abandoned rose-garden the air seems dark suddenly and I want to run back to the house — but when I re-emerge, and climb over the stile into the sloping field, I sense that the day still has some life in it. The sky is clear and colourful. The shepherds are delighted by what they see.

I'm not going back. To what, anyway? I'm not going back to spend my life peeing in kitchens. Ursula has gone. (Papa has gone.) And now Terry has gone too. I hope he comes into his own at last. This was the part he was meant for, the stage at which his life would begin to be good (he hated all the other bits). Not me, though. I can help mother — there are still some things left to run (God, I hope she can afford me). This will just have to do for the time being. I'm not going back. I'm going to stay out here, where nothing is frightening.

I'm cold. Dew is falling. In the distance, to my left beyond the Indian file of silver birches, the railway line runs on its banked mound. Something's coming. I pause as a smart blue train streams by. I look down to see that my hand is waving childishly. How absurd. Why? Always wave to trains, my nanny or my mother or my grandmother said. I remember now. Someone nice might see you and wave back.

I'm entering the woods that gird the water (I used to play there as a boy). The D-Pond glistens whitely, two hundred yards away, through the lattice of bark and darkness. It really is dark. I pause again. Can I get there and back before nightfall? The woods are drenched, dripping with dreams and death. A wind blows. The trees attempt to shake their shoulders dry. Why won't the wind let the leaves alone? The lake is trying to warn me — danger in the streets of the trees. The wood is fizzing. A log rolls over on to its back. One bird sings.

I stand behind the row of birches. I'm cold — I want to shiver and sob. I look up. Something's coming. Oh, go *away*. Against the hell of sunset the branches bend and break. The wind will never cease to craze the frightening leaves.